VERONICA'S BOMBASTIC SCHEME

THE SPUNKY GIRL'S GUIDE TO DATING

SARA JO CLUFF

CHAPTER ONE

Jane the Virgin was basically the greatest TV show of all time. I mean, it spoke to my soul. I remembered watching it for the first time and thinking, did the writers of this show write this script just for ME? And even after watching the series for the twentieth time, I still wondered that.

Yeah, okay, so I wasn't an adult that was accidentally artificially inseminated and now pregnant with some hot rich guy's kid. I was a Mexican teen trying to navigate through my adolescence without combusting into flames thanks to my embarrassing family.

I understood Jane's overbearing and overprotective abuela. In my life, that role belonged to my abuela *and* my mom, and they played it well. Oscar-worthy performances.

I also understood the virgin-until-marriage-or-else-my-mother-will-murder-me-and-the-guy part. And it didn't bother me. I liked the idea of waiting until I found the guy I wanted to spend the rest of my life with. There was something downright romantic about it.

Which was why my relationship goals were Jane and

Michael. Most perfect TV couple. Ever. Well, aside from the whole Michael dying thing, coming back to life, losing his memories, and Jane ending up with Rafael. That I could do without. No offense to Rafael, but I was most definitely team Michael.

What I didn't like was my mom reminding me to "save myself" every time I left the house with her infamous phrase, "Keep all your pretty petals intact." There was a reason I never let my best friends, Daphne and Taylor, come over to my place. We hung out at their homes with their non-invasive-question-asking families. Especially now that both Daphne and Taylor had found their soulmates. I didn't even want to imagine the inappropriate questions my mother would throw their way.

The door to my room swung open, and my nine-year-old sister Luciana strutted inside. "Ma and Pop have some big announcement."

"Luci! What have I told you about knocking first?" I pressed pause on the remote, the TV screen freezing on Michael and Jane gazing at each other in the most adoring way. I sighed, wishing and hoping to have that one day.

"Maybe you should lock your door." Luciana jutted her hip to the side and rested her hand on it. "Oh, wait, you can't." She flipped her long hair behind her, all sass.

If my parents thought dealing with me as a teenager was heart-attack-inducing, they were in for a rude awakening when Luci hit puberty.

I brushed flaming hot Cheetos crumbs from my lap. "You're the one who has been planning your quinceañera since you could talk."

My parents had a rule. Once we turned fifteen, they took the locks off our bedroom doors. Because, according to my mom, we'd suddenly have the urge to do "Lord knows what" behind closed doors. Like some magical switch flipped.

Luciana lifted her chin. "I have five years and two months to figure out how to change Ma's and Pop's minds."

"Good luck with that."

"Thank you. Now, get your butt out of bed and come downstairs." Luciana turned on her heels and disappeared down the hall.

I grunted as I snatched a few more Cheetos from the bag. What did my parents want to tell us? I chewed on my bottom lip, worried it would be something traumatic. Like they were separating again. Or they were moving us back to México.

Although, maybe separating would be a good thing. I still hadn't forgiven Dad for abandoning us and then thinking he could waltz back into our lives unscathed.

A loud bang sounded on my door frame. I jumped, sending flaming hot Cheetos into the air and raining down around me on the bed.

My fourteen-year-old brother, Javier, stood in the doorway, smirking. He wore a loose-fitting white tank with his personal artwork printed on it, ripped red skinny jeans, and red Nikes. "Let's go, loser. The parents don't have all day." He had his hair in two Mohawks, both dyed red, so they looked like long devil horns. The rest of his head was in a buzz cut.

"Thanks, Satan." Glaring at him, I shimmied off the bed, ignoring the mess of Cheetos. I'd have to clean it up later. "Do you always have to be so loud?"

He folded his arms and leaned against the doorway. "Yeah."

I approached him, noticing that he'd bulked up a little. "Have you been working out?"

He flexed. "Someone in this family needs to sexy represent." He glanced at my oversized tee. "Since no one else is doing it, I took matters into my own hands."

I rolled my eyes as I shoved past him and out the door. "Yes, because muscles are the only sexy trait out there."

"Exactly." Javier chuckled as he followed behind me.

As I descended the stairs, I took in the abundance of Día de Muertos and Halloween decorations smothering the downstairs. Mom and Dad had gone all out this year. Orange marigolds and sugar skulls covered the banister. Cobwebs and fake spiders hung from the chandelier in the entryway. Dad had replaced the normal bulbs with dim ones that flickered, adding an eerie vibe.

We found our parents sitting on the love seat in the front room. Mom had her black curly hair pinned back at the sides. She wore a knee-length floral dress she usually wore to work at Dad's accounting firm. She'd recently gotten a job there as a bookkeeper. She mostly worked remotely, only going into the office once a week.

Dad had his arm draped around Mom. He'd taken off his tie, but still wore his dress shirt and slacks. The gel in his hair had worn off, making his thick hair a little wild.

Luciana sat in the middle of the couch. She patted the spots on either side of her, smiling at Javier and me.

An unnatural amount of worry flushed through my body. Why did I have this horrible feeling something bad was about to happen? Daphne always told me to look on the bright side of life, but she didn't have my family or body issues. And she had a guy who loved her exactly the way she was. Quirky and all.

Once Javier and I had settled onto the couch, we all looked expectantly at our parents. They stared back, mischievous smiles on their faces like the time they randomly sprung a last-minute family trip to visit relatives in México.

"Tell us already." Javier scrolled through his phone. "I have followers needing to hear from Hottie Javy." He adjusted his phone, angling it so my sister and I were in the frame. Javier cranked up our family perfected Rodriguez smolder right before he snapped the picture, so both us girls rolled our eyes.

When Luciana and I both sighed our annoyance at the same time, we shared a look before we busted out laughing.

Mom clapped her hands, demanding our attention. "We need you kids focused here. We have a big announcement."

"If you tell me you're pregnant," Javier said with a disgusted look on his face, "I'm filing for emancipation."

"Could you please do that anyway?" I crossed my legs, noting how difficult it was becoming now that I gained weight. I needed to go on a diet.

Ugh. Diet. I hated that word.

"Are we going to Disney World?" Luciana clasped her hands together in a plea, scooting her butt to the edge of the couch. "*Please* tell me we're going to Disney World. I'm sick of Disneyland."

Both Javier and I gasped and slapped Luciana upside the head.

"How dare you, Luci," Javier said at the same time I said, "I never want to hear those words come out of your mouth again."

Luciana shrunk back into the couch, rubbing her head and frowning.

"Children!" At mom's booming voice, we all perked up, turning our attention to her. Even Dad maneuvered so he could see her better.

Mom turned on a sweet smile. "Your father and I are ..." She turned to Dad, who grinned wildly.

"Getting re-married!" they said in not even close to unison.

Mom slapped Dad's knee. "We rehearsed this, Matías. So many times."

Dad rubbed his knee with a grimace. "Trust me, I know."

"Wait, you're not married?" Luciana's eyes went wide. "You've been living in sin this whole time!" She jumped up from the couch, pointing a shaking finger at them. "You lying hippos!"

Mom's head jerked back. "Excuse me?"

Dad chuckled and patted his round belly. "Well, I have put on a few pounds."

I leaned forward, gently touching Luciana's arm. "Did you mean hypocrites?"

Luciana looked over her shoulder at me. "Oh, yeah, that's the one." She turned back to our parents. "You lying hypocrites!"

Mom pursed her lips and then tsked. "We never got divorced."

"So how can you get remarried?" Javier held up his phone. He was live streaming the whole encounter. Well, his reaction to the encounter since the camera faced him. I could see a massive number of hearts float across the screen as his followers "liked" his video.

What was wrong with people?

"Well, we took a break," Mom said, "and now we want to get back together."

Dad wrapped his arm around her and pulled her close, kissing her soundly on the temple. "We want to renew our commitment to each other."

"So, you want to renew your vows?" I asked.

Mom snapped her fingers. "Renew our vows." She looked at Dad. "That's the phrase I was trying to remember."

Dad nodded. "Makes much more sense." He grinned. "We're going to renew our vows!"

As Luciana went on to ask a million questions about renewing vows, and Javier got up from the couch, asking his followers what he should wear to the event, I quickly snuck out and ran up the stairs to my room, shutting the door softly behind me.

Renewing their vows?

This was so not good.

My phone buzzed on my bed. I snagged it, and when I saw a message from Daphne, my mood lifted.

> Daphne: V! Go and listen to Meghan Trainor's album Takin' It Back. NOW!
>
> Daphne: Also, I love you so much!

I went to pull up the album when another text came in. This time, though, it was from my horrible excuse of an ex, DeShawn, and my mood plummeted again. He'd sent a meme of a whale eating a cheeseburger.

Why wouldn't he leave me alone? Guys were the worst.

I glanced at the frame on my nightstand, which contained my number one rule to live by. A rule that kept getting verified over and over again: Never trust guys.

CHAPTER TWO

I immediately video called Daphne as I flopped down on my bed, flaming hot Cheetos crunching against my back.

As it rang, my face stared back at me, the roundness seeming more extreme by laying down. I really was a whale. I pulled back my hair, tugging so my skin stretched with it. Maybe DeShawn had been right about the Ariana Grande look. It definitely slimmed the face.

I let go of my hair and then straightened my bangs. I needed to focus on the more important problem.

Renewing their vows? Why would Mom want to do that?

Daphne finally answered, her bright face taking up the entire screen. "Hey, beautiful!"

"You don't have to stand so close to the phone," I said, holding back a smile.

Daphne wiggled her TLC-needing eyebrows. "But don't you want to soak in all this glory?" She paused for like a millisecond. "Oh! Have you listened to the album?"

"Daph, you sent me the text two minutes ago."

A thoughtful expression flitted across her green eyes. "Good point."

A light clinking of plates sounded behind her, followed by some shuffling. Chatter hummed in the air, like she was out in public.

"Where are you?" I asked.

Daphne quickly shook her head. "Nowhere. Just chilling. By myself. All alone. No one's here. So, what's hanging?"

She wasn't alone. Dork.

"If this is a bad time—" I started.

Daphne lifted a finger and pointed it at the screen until all I could see was a big blur of skin. "Now, you listen here, you beautiful, sexy thang. I always have time for my V. Always."

"Move your hand, Daph."

Suddenly her face came back into view. "Talk to me, sugar."

Tears trickled down my cheeks. I reached up, wiping them away, only to smear orange Cheetos dust across my skin.

"Daph ..." I pressed a hand to my mouth. Why was I getting so worked up over this? It shouldn't have been a big deal. My parents were officially back together. That should have been a good thing. Right?

"Code red breakdown!" Daphne turned her head, talking to someone. "Get over here."

Daphne finally pulled the screen back to reveal our friend, Taylor.

They both had their hair done cute, perfect make-up, and Daphne had ditched her ever-present Mickey ears.

I frowned. "You're on a double date, aren't you?"

"What? No," Taylor said as Daphne frantically shook

her head and said, "Double date? Us? Who would we even go out with?"

"Rude," Huntley said in the background. Taylor's boyfriend. What was he doing in town? He was currently going to college up north.

Taylor turned toward him with wide eyes. "You seriously have so much to learn."

"Yeah, he does," Weston said. Daphne's boyfriend. "You never speak when they're having girl talk. Wait. Whoops." He cleared his throat. "I'm not here."

I snatched one of the Cheetos next to my head and ate it.

Taylor scrunched her slim nose. "Why are there Cheetos everywhere?"

Daphne's eyes lit up. "You should make a Cheeto angel on your bed!"

"That would be awesome!" Weston's voice rang out in the back.

I wiped away some more tears. "Daph, call me back when your date is done."

She shook her head. "We can help you right now!"

"Daphton, party of four," a hostess said. "Your table is ready."

Daphne smiled sheepishly. "I don't want to abandon you, V."

I sat up. "You're not. I'm assuming Huntley is only in town for the weekend?"

Taylor nodded. "Just for tonight actually. He's driving back with Ryker tomorrow for the football game."

"The four of you should have fun." I hiccupped. "This is me overreacting over something stupid." I needed more Cheetos.

Taylor grinned, looking beautiful with her red lipstick.

"Be at my house at eleven tonight. You and Daphne can sleep over and we can talk all about it."

"Eleven?" Huntley sounded disappointed.

My parents didn't like me sleeping over at peoples' homes. When Dad left, Mom felt so bad, she allowed me to sleep over at Daphne or Taylor's homes a few times. It took a lot of guilt-inducing begging. Now that Dad was back, Mom had reinstated her strict no-sleepover rule.

Thankfully, now Dad was the one who felt so bad that I could usually break him down. It helped that he knew and liked the Thomases and that their family was as religious as mine.

"I'll be there at midnight." I raised my volume. "A whole extra hour to get your kissing on!"

Snickering sounded in the background, probably other patrons at the restaurant.

"See you then!" Daphne said.

"Love you!" Taylor and Daphne said in unison. They both leaned toward the screen, making kissy faces.

I snorted a laugh. "Love you, too."

I tossed my phone back on my bed and grabbed a handful of Cheetos.

Even though it had been a brief conversation, and they were having a night of fun *without* me, my friends could always cheer me up.

I understood why they didn't tell me. They wouldn't want to hurt my feelings, and I hated being the fifth wheel.

I seriously needed to find my Michael. Or even another friend to bring along.

The door to my room flew open.

"Does *anyone* knock in this house?" I sat up, seeing my mom standing in the doorway.

She took in the Cheetos scattered on my bed. "I wanted

to see how you're doing but it looks like I already have the answer."

Mom knew I hated having Dad back.

I started picking up the Cheetos. "Why, Ma?"

She joined me at the bed, scooping up Cheetos with her palm. "We love each other, Veronica. You should be happy we're back together."

I set the Cheetos in the bag, then held it out for Mom to dump more in. "How can you trust him? He's going to walk out on us again. I know it."

Mom sat down on my bed, brushing the Cheetos dust off her hands, her red acrylic nails clinking together. "Mija, you need to get past your fears. Dad isn't leaving again."

I plopped down next to her, shaking the bed, and held the bag close to my chest. "You don't know that. He did it once. It's just like cheaters. Do it once, and they'll do it again."

And there had been another woman. If they never got officially divorced, then he did cheat on her. Break or not.

"He broke your vows and commitment to this family." I turned to face her. "He left us hanging. Did you already forget you worked three different jobs to make ends meet? And that I had to take care of Luci and Javy so you could?"

She ran a hand down my long hair. "I know the sacrifices you made, V, and I'll always appreciate it."

"But don't forget about *your* sacrifices."

I thought back to all the nights my mom came home well after midnight, dark rings under her eyes and complete exhaustion consuming her. For over a year, she was basically a zombie. Honestly, it was almost like we had lost both of our parents.

"Life throws us challenges." Mom took my hands in

hers. Her skin was super soft, like always. "We work through them and come out better on the other side."

"And the next time life throws Dad a young hot intern? What then, Ma?"

Anger flashed in her deep brown eyes, but not about Dad's affair. She was mad at *me*. She let go of my hands and stood, straightening her dress. "I'm done having these conversations with you, Veronica. Your father made a mistake and apologized. You need to forgive him and move on like the rest of us have."

She stormed out of the room, slamming the door behind her.

I flinched.

Maybe she could move on that easily, but I couldn't. You don't abandon your family. You don't leave them with nothing, letting them scrape by while you have the time of your life.

The only small comfort I had was that Mom now worked with Dad so she knew everyone at the company, including the interns.

I laid back down on the bed and pulled up the Meghan Trainor album Daphne suggested. I pressed play, closed my eyes, and let all the songs sink in. It was so bizarre how each track hit home. How did Daphne know I needed this? The girl had magical powers.

By the time track six "Bad For Me" ended, tears flowed freely down my cheeks, soaking the sides of my pillows.

Was Dad bad for me? For the family?

Mom may have forgiven him, but I never could.

He'd completely broken my trust.

CHAPTER THREE

Taking a huge gamble, I packed up a bag for the sleepover and hopped into my Prius, not letting anyone in the family know I was leaving. When I was a few blocks away, I pulled over and texted Dad.

> Me: I'm sleeping over at Taylor's. Don't worry, her parents are home. I'll let you tell Mom. You owe me.

I quickly stuffed my phone in my bag so I wouldn't see the answer.

There was a high possibility that once Mom found out, she'd drive over to Taylor's house and demand I go home.

Which was why I wandered around the city for over an hour before I finally parked in front of Taylor's house. It wasn't even ten. Taylor and Daphne wouldn't be here for another couple of hours.

Taylor's family had decorated their yard with a *Nightmare Before Christmas* theme. Blow-ups of all the characters scattered the lawn and Jack Skellington yard lights lined the pathway to the door. My mood lightened at the sight.

I turned on some Post Malone, and then reached into the bag on the floor and grabbed the fifty-two-ounce strawberry lemonade I'd gotten at the store. Maybe I could chug my worries away.

I took a long swig before I reached into the bag again and snatched the bag of Takis. I reclined my chair and settled into place with the lemonade in one hand and the bag of chips resting on my leg. I popped a chip into my mouth, and the spiciness hugged my tongue in the best possible way.

I really wanted to think about anything else than my parents upcoming vow renewal, but my mind kept wandering there. Luciana was, of course, over the moon about it. When we'd asked her what she wanted for her birthday or Christmas during the time Dad was gone, she always responded with, "I want Pops to come home."

Javier didn't care one way or the other, as long as it created drama for him to stream to his social media accounts.

Mom wanted me to be excited about it, but I couldn't. It was only a matter of time before I'd come home to find Dad gone again. The man always abandoned ship when things got even the slightest bit hairy. I mean, he'd shove his family toward the sharks if it meant he'd get to the shore safely and live a carefree life.

I guess maybe that was why Mom didn't trust any of her children to make the right choices. She'd given all her trust to Dad. And he so didn't deserve it.

Reluctantly, I fished my phone from my bag and checked my messages.

> Dad: Don't worry, my angel girl. I'll make
> sure Mom doesn't break down the door of
> the Thomas household. Be safe. Love you.

A smile spread on my face, but I quickly erased it. I couldn't like anything he said if I intended to stay angry at him.

Suddenly, the passenger door flew open and Samson, Taylor's older brother, plopped down into the driver's seat. He rested one of his long legs outside of the car since there really wasn't room for both legs up front. The guy was tall, yet the shortest of all of Taylor's six brothers.

Ever since I'd told him to get rid of the stubble on his chin, he'd been clean-shaven. Much better look for him. The oldest Thomas brother, Neo, could pull off the beard. The rest of them? Nope.

My cheeks warmed as I remembered I hadn't touched up my make-up after crying or made sure my hair was perfect before coming over. I flipped open the mirror on the visor and straightened my bangs that were getting too long. Then I ran a finger under each eye, wiping away any remnants of smeared mascara.

"Ryker and I are having a bet as to how long you're going to sit out here before you come to the door." Samson reached over and grabbed a few chips from the bag resting on my leg. The overhead light lit up his face. An eyelash rested in the indented crescent-shaped scar next to his right eye.

Without much thought, I reached up and wiped it away. He grinned wildly for no reason at all as he settled back into his seat. The guy was always happy.

"I was waiting for Taylor and Daphne to come back." I snatched a couple of chips and threw them in my mouth.

Sometimes it was the food, but sometimes it was the chewing motion that calmed me. Maybe I needed to invest in some gum.

Samson licked the spices from his fingers. "V, you know Taylor doesn't have to be here for you to come inside. You're family." His grin somehow grew. "Remember the first time I ate one of these?" He snatched another chip from the bag. "How old were we?"

I thought back to the moment. "I think I was around five, which puts you at seven." I laughed as I remembered Samson casually taking one from me and popping it in his mouth. His eyes went completely wide, and he immediately spit it out.

Samson joined in my laughter. "I think I drank a whole carton of milk trying to get the burn out of my mouth." He ate the chip in his hand. "I've come a long way since then."

I reached over and patted his shoulder. "I'm so proud of you. All grown up and wearing your big boy pants."

Samson pushed my hand off his shoulder but laughed the entire time. "Anyway, Ryker and I are playing a riveting game of Rummikub, and the guy is completely crushing me. You need to come in and save me."

I took a quick drink of strawberry lemonade and then offered the bottle to Samson, who happily took it.

"Who says I'll be good at it?" I asked.

Samson gulped some down and then handed me back the bottle. "This game is all about strategy and numbers, two things Tay says you're brilliant at."

His words startled me. Taylor said that about me? Yeah, I tutored her and Daphne in math because they could never quite catch on like I did, but I wasn't brilliant at it. My straight A's were from hard freaking work. And my desperate need to get a scholarship.

He tilted his head to the side. "Have you changed something recently? Like your hair?" His eyes roamed my body like he was trying to pinpoint something.

I held the lemonade and bag of chips close to my chest. "No."

The last thing I needed was another guy telling me I was too fat. I had enough of that from DeShawn and his brainless friends.

His grin came back, lighting up his eyes. "Well, whatever you're doing, it's working. Don't tell Daphne, but I've always thought you were the hottest of Tay's friends." He got out of the car, not skipping a beat. He rested his hand on top of the car and leaned down so he could peer at me. "You coming in? I need your brain, your chips, and well." He shrugged. "You. Way better company than Ryker."

He turned and slowly walked toward the house, his hands in his pockets.

My cheeks were about as hot as my mouth from the chips.

Samson had always said what was on his mind since the day I met him. He never held anything back, and never lied.

So, he really thought I was hot? Like this? Whale and all?

I quickly plucked the thought from my head. Samson was also incredibly nice. Maybe Taylor had mentioned something about my insecurities to him and he was trying to make me feel better.

After a few deep breaths, I grabbed my stuff and shuffled toward the house. I hated that I wore such a baggy shirt and sweats, but they were the only clothes that fit right now. I was too embarrassed to go shopping for bigger sizes.

Samson and Ryker sat at the kitchen table. Snacks lined

the edges of the table while tiles from the game neatly lined the center.

Spencer, Ryker's gecko, perched on Ryker's shoulder, sound asleep. Ryker tucked his hair behind his ear, curling perfectly against his earlobe. He'd created a short wall out of cardboard to block anyone from seeing his tiles. Since he was so tall, his face, shoulders and most of his torso were visible. Ryker wore sheer determination as he stared into the box, analyzing his tiles.

Samson smirked at me and waved his hand toward Ryker, his face saying, "see what I'm dealing with?"

A smile spread across my face, and it felt good. This was exactly why I preferred hanging out at my friend's houses. Their families didn't drive me crazy.

Samson motioned to the seat across from him. Ryker sat at the head of the table. Samson sat on the side, on the complete opposite end of Ryker. They had a huge table to accommodate their family of nine.

I sat across from Samson, my eyebrows furrowed in confusion. "Why are we all the way down here?"

"We can't have me seeing Ryker's tiles, now can we?" Samson asked with a mock seriousness.

Even if we sat right next to Ryker, with his cardboard wall, we still couldn't see anything.

"Well, obviously," I said as I sat down. I placed my drink and chips on the table.

Ryker suddenly appeared at my side, setting down a tile holder, some tiles, a piece of paper, and a pen. "This should be everything you need."

"Oh, hey, Ryker." I smiled up at him. "Nice to see you, too."

Ryker blinked at me, and then returned to his seat. Spencer hadn't stirred the entire time.

After he stretched out his neck, Ryker spoke, his focus on his tiles. "It's about time I had some competition in here."

"Hey!" Samson said.

Ryker didn't tear his gaze away from his box. "You already admitted you were dumb."

Samson picked up a chip and threw it at Ryker, hitting him on the head. It bounced onto Spencer and then out of sight.

"I never said I was dumb," Samson said, leaning back in his chair. "I said this isn't my favorite game."

Ryker shrugged, Spencer lifting with the motion (but still sleeping). "Same thing. Veronica, have you played this before?"

"Nope," I said.

He finally looked me in the eye. "I'm assuming you'll catch on fast, so I'll start and explain things as we go. Think you can handle that?"

I quickly stood, bent forward, and threw my long hair over my head before twirling it into a loose bun. I snatched the hair tie from my wrist and secured the bun in place. Then I stretched out my neck like Ryker had done, before turning on the Rodriguez smolder. "Bring it."

CHAPTER FOUR

Playing Rummikub had been way more fun than I thought it would be. Probably because I beat Ryker a few times, causing him to slouch in defeat and mutter things under his breath.

Since I knew their family had an Alexa, I asked her to play Meghan Trainor's album, starting after track six. I didn't need to cry again in front of Samson and Ryker.

After Ryker lost for the third time in a row, he quickly stood. "Let's take a break. I need to recharge." He hurried into the kitchen and grabbed a Dr Pepper from the fridge.

"Mama Wanna Mambo" came on, and Samson grinned wildly. He stood and came to my side, holding out his large hand.

I stared at it. "What are you doing?"

He reached down and took my hand in his. "Let's dance."

My eyebrows shot up. "Dance?"

He tugged on my hand. "Come on. It will be fun."

With a light chuckle, I stood and let him escort me into the front room. He moved the coffee table out of the way.

"Wow," I said, folding my arms. "You mean business."

Samson winked at me. "Always do." He casually placed his hands on mine and unfolded my arms. Such a simple gesture, but I found myself heating up.

Then Samson started dancing and my mind was blown. He set his hand high on my back, and took my hand in his, leading me through the steps. His hips swayed like he was a professional salsa dancer.

"Uh, where did you learn to dance like this?" I asked, not able to contain my awe. Thank goodness my family loved to dance, so I could keep up with him.

Samson spun me out, and then pulled me back in so my back was to his chest. He interlocked our fingers and set our hands on my stomach, our feet moving to the rhythm of the beat.

He grinned down at me. "I've been taking some classes at school."

I had to strain my neck to look up at him behind me, but his smile and smooth rhythm made it worth it. My Rodriguez smolder surfaced without much thought on my part, and Samson pulled me a little closer as his infamous happy grin turned into something that felt like it was just for me. For a moment, I found it difficult to breathe.

He spun me out again, bringing me back so I faced him this time, with hardly any distance between us. All my stiff muscles loosened, and I was so glad Samson asked me to dance. It was a great form of therapy.

Both of us were grinning madly by the time the song ended and he dipped me back.

A deep voice rumbled near the front door before it broke out in a chuckle. That boom of a laugh belonged to Taylor's oldest brother Neo. He'd been living at home ever since he lost his well-paying job and girlfriend. Separate incidents that unfortunately happened quite close together.

Samson helped me right myself and we turned to see Taylor, Daphne, and Neo rounding the corner into the kitchen, talking about Sour Patch Kids.

"Mountain Man, I'm telling you the watermelon ones are the *only* way to go." Daphne shook her head in frustration at Neo. She used to refer to Taylor's brother by the number of the order they were born in, but ever since Daphne gave them wrestling names for the Wrestle-Mania Taylor's family had during the summer, Daphne had been using those.

Daphne had her hair in double Dutch braids, something she'd been doing more often with her mom's boyfriend Cody around all the time. He'd basically raised his little sisters, so he knew all about hair and make-up. The guy had style.

Taylor's hair was in two buns on top her head. She wore her black leather jacket and a red dress that looked absolutely stunning on her.

Neo opened the fridge and pulled out a can of Coke. "The originals are the best. This applies to everything." He held up his can. "Regular Coke. Original Starbursts and Skittles. Enough with these weird flavors, man."

Daphne scoffed. "Watermelon is not a weird flavor."

"Do they actually taste like watermelon?" Samson asked, moving toward the kitchen casually like nothing had happened between us.

Daphne quirked her head to the side. "No flavor tastes like the real thing, Terminator." She reached into her bag and fished out her cherry syrup flavoring she brought with her everywhere. "Like this. Does it taste like real cherries? I don't know. I don't eat cherries." She wiggled the bottle at

Neo. "But I do know it would make that Coke taste a million times better." She paused. "Wait, is that Meghan Trainor playing? How do you like the album, Veronica?"

"It's amazing," I said. "Just what I needed."

Daphne did a little dance that involved a little too much butt shaking. "Knew it."

Ryker suddenly stood up, his chair scooting back. He must have sat back down while Samson and I were dancing. "Let's hurry and get this cleaned up. I'm tired."

Taylor and Neo both looked at Samson with "what's wrong with him?" faces.

Samson grinned and motioned to me. "Our girl here whipped his trash. It was freaking awesome."

My cheeks flared, something they'd been doing too much of lately. I'd always been so confident and ready to take on the world. Both my dad and DeShawn had stripped that from me. Which was why I needed to distance myself from guys until I found my Michael.

"Sounds about right," Taylor said with a smirk. "Wish I could have been here to see it."

I quickly went to work helping Ryker clean things up.

"What's the rush?" Samson asked as I threw tiles into the box with so much force some clinked against other tiles and flew back out of the box. He looked at me, and okay, his eyes said something *had* happened between us.

"I need to talk with Taylor and Daphne about something super important." And I probably needed a little distance from him so my heart could find a regular rhythm.

Samson reached across the table and gently set his hand on my arm. "We got this. Go do your girl thing."

My skin heated at his touch. I jerked my arm away and hustled toward my friends. Why was Samson getting me so flustered? He was just Taylor's brother. He was almost like a brother to me. A hot brother.

Ugh. Something was seriously wrong with me.

I rushed over to Taylor and Daphne, took them each by an arm, and dragged them up the stairs to Taylor's room.

Taylor had barely closed the door when I started talking and paced in front of her bed. "They're renewing their vows, which makes it totally official. They're back together. Probably not for good because my dad will somehow screw things up again." I balled my hands into fists, my artificial nails digging into my skin. "This is the absolute worst. I mean, I don't know exactly what I wanted to have happen, but it isn't *this*. We were finally finding a rhythm of things before he moseyed back into our lives. We were all reaching a happy, content place. We don't need him. Yet here he is. Making Mom act like they're newlyweds or something. It's disgusting."

Taylor and Daphne had both perched themselves on the edge of Taylor's bed, watching me pace.

Taylor removed her leather jacket and set it on the bed behind her. "Maybe we should think this through."

I rounded on her, making her jerk back. "I just talked it through! We have to stop it from happening."

That was it. I somehow had to break them up again and get Dad out of our lives for good.

Daphne took my hand into hers. "Have you ever thought about forgiving him? He has apologized. Like a million times."

I ripped my hand away from her. "Whose side are you on?"

Daphne sighed and slid the Captain America shield pendant dangling from the necklace she wore back and forth on the chain. "The side where everyone is happy. V, I know your dad made a mistake—"

"A mistake?" I choked back a hysterical laugh. "He cheated on my mom, abandoned our family, left us to fend for ourselves with absolutely nothing, and completely destroyed my mom. You didn't have to watch her be miserable for months. It was devastating."

"Exactly," Taylor said. "If your mom is willing to forgive him after what he did to her, don't you think maybe you should do the same?"

I threw up my arms. "You two were supposed to back me up here! Not be the sound of reason."

Taylor's phone started ringing. She looked at her screen and furrowed her eyebrows together. "It's your mom, V. Why is she calling me?"

Daphne tsked. "And at this hour."

I quickly checked my phone to see if she'd tried to reach me, but she hadn't. "I don't know." Was Mom so mad I was sleeping over that she went straight to the source instead of me?

Taylor answered before I could stop her, putting it on speaker phone. "Hello?"

"Taylor," my mom said, her tone full of excitement. "Veronica's mom here. I have a favor to ask. Well, it's more of a proposition."

Taylor looked about as confused as I felt.

"Do you know what time it is?" Daphne asked, leaning toward the phone. "It's well past your bedtime, young lady."

Mom laughed, so warm and full of life, and I couldn't help but smile.

"I'm lucky if I get to bed by two every night," Mom said.

It was true. My parents were night owls and always in motion.

Taylor leaned forward and rested her chin on her palm. "So, what's the favor?"

"Oh! Yes." Mom paused for a few beats. "I'm not sure if Veronica told you or not, but Matías and I are renewing our vows."

"Yeah, she told me," Taylor said. "Congratulations!"

I glared at her, but Taylor rolled her eyes.

"After seeing what you did for your father's birthday party," Mom went on, "I was wanting to hire you to be our party planner."

Taylor shrieked. "Are you serious? I'd love to!" When she saw my anger, she quickly cleared her throat. "I mean, if I'm available that day. When were you thinking?"

"We don't have a set date," Mom said. "We were thinking about a month from now. After Halloween. Will that be enough time?"

Taylor swallowed, her face full of hope and confusion. "Um, I'll have to check my calendar. School keeps me pretty busy, and I usually see my boyfriend on the weekends."

"Oh, Veronica told me about him." Mom's smile was obvious in her tone. "He sounds like quite the catch."

"He is," Taylor said with a sultry tone.

"I hope you're being safe," Mom said.

I closed my eyes and sighed. Here we go.

Taylor's cheeks turned red. "Uh, we haven't. I mean, we're not. Um."

"Good," Mom said. "It's important to save yourself until you're one hundred percent certain they are the one. And if you can hold out until marriage, even better."

Daphne had her hand over her mouth, covering up her laugh. She fell back on the bed, kicking her feet in hysteria.

"That goes for you, too, Daphne," Mom said in her scolding parent tone.

Daphne froze on the bed.

"Ma!" I yelled.

"You *are* there," Mom said. "Are you staying the night?"

Dad said he'd told her. "Uh, yeah."

There was a long pause, and my stomach sank. Daphne opened her mouth, but I held up a hand and mouthed, "*No!*"

Anything we said could and *would* be used against us. The ball was best left in her court if I didn't want to make a total scene in front of my friends.

"Did you remember to pack your retainer?" Mom finally asked, and I let out a breath of relief. "After how much we spent on those pretty teeth of yours, we need to keep them in pristine condition."

We? I couldn't believe she was acting like Dad helped pay for it. It was all Mom.

"Yeah, Ma, I got it."

"Good. Taylor, please think it over and get back to me as soon as you can. We'd love to have you be a part of this and know you'll do the perfect job."

Taylor pressed her lips together, obviously holding back a smile. She would do an awesome job, and I knew she was saving up for college. Her parents did well for themselves, but Taylor was their seventh child going to college. That added up quick.

"You ladies keep all your pretty—" Mom started.

I quickly rushed over and ended the call.

"Keep all our pretty what?" Daphne asked.

I shook my head. "Nothing."

Taylor must have not registered what my mom had said.

Or started to say. Her eyes held so much hope. She was probably already planning the event in her head.

I needed to clear my mind. "I'm going out to The Hideout so I can sort through my feelings without saying things I'll regret. Neither of you deserve my anger right now. You two stay here."

"Are you sure—" Daphne started.

"Stay. Here."

Daphne nodded. "Got it. Staying put. Oh!" She suddenly jumped up from the bed and threw her arms around me. "Take one of these before you go."

Taylor joined in on the hug, and my anger slightly melted. I knew they were trying to help, but, for once, I wanted someone to understand what I was going through.

CHAPTER FIVE

Taylor's dad had built her a treehouse—aka The Hideout—in their backyard. As the youngest in the family and all her six siblings being boys, she needed an escape from the craziness the house offered growing up.

The treehouse was totally Taylor. Red and black leather, twinkle lights, and a shag carpet. I sat down on the makeshift bed and crossed my feet at my ankles. I stared at them, frowning. They'd become cankles.

I wasn't sure exactly when I started to turn to food for comfort, but I believe it was about the time my dad came back. Another reason he needed to go. I was sick of trying to slip into my clothes only to notice I'd grown too big for them. Daphne had made me some cute rompers that fit well, but even they were becoming too tight. The olive green one I currently wore used to cinch at the middle. Now it bulged. It wouldn't be much longer until Daphne would need to make me new ones.

Closing my eyes, I sighed. I hated that I'd gotten here. I missed the old me. The skinny, confident version that never cared what anyone thought.

My phone vibrated in my pocket. I took a deep breath before I pulled it out and looked at the screen to see a text from my dad.

Dad: Sleep well, my sweet girl.

I probably should have responded, but I couldn't bring myself to. Especially when I saw I had another text from DeShawn. My fat thumb hovered over the text as I debated whether to open it. Whatever it held wouldn't be good.

But this stupid, irrational part of me wanted to know.

It was an image of Dr. Phil. The caption said, "You're fat. Don't sugarcoat it cause you'll eat that too."

My fist tightened around the phone, wanting to smash it. I glanced at the wall of The Hideout. I could destroy my phone right here and now. End this torment.

But that wouldn't stop him. He'd find another way.

Someone knocked on the door to The Hideout.

"I told you to stay put!" I wasn't ready to talk with Taylor and Daphne. They didn't understand.

"I don't ever remember you saying that to me," Samson's amused voice said.

I flinched in embarrassment, even though he couldn't see me. "Sorry. Thought you were someone else."

"Can I come in?"

I debated for a moment. I really wanted to be alone but hanging with Samson tonight had really cheered me up. He always seemed to make me forget my worries. Although, he also made my hormones super confused.

"I'm taking your silence as a yes and coming in." The door popped open on the floor and Samson's head peaked in. He grinned when he saw me, melting some of the tension eating away at me.

After he climbed in, he took a seat on the beanbag chair, his longs legs spread in front of him. "Taylor and Daphne driving you crazy?"

I wrapped the bottom of my tee around my fist. "It's not them. I just ..."

What could I say? I didn't want to bring Samson into my drama.

"What's going on, V?" So much sincerity resided in his brown eyes. "You've seemed ... off lately."

"It's complicated." I so didn't want to tell him about DeShawn's texts. It was humiliating.

"Try me."

"You won't understand."

Samson lightly smiled. "We won't know that until you tell me. If I don't understand, then I'll leave you here to wallow by yourself."

I rolled my eyes, but a smile tugged at my lips. I wasn't bringing DeShawn into the picture, but I could bring up my dad. Samson knew some of it.

"My parents are renewing their vows." My gaze was unfocused on the ground.

"Wow." Samson let out a small whistle. "That's a shocker."

I looked at him. "Right?"

Samson rubbed the back of his long neck. "Your mom has to be the most forgiving person I've ever met."

"It wasn't that long ago when she was working three jobs to make ends meet. She was always tired, running pretty much on empty." I tightened the bun on my head more out of frustration than anything else. It felt good to strangle something, and better my hair than a person.

Samson looked shocked. "Was it really that bad? Tay told me some stuff, but not much."

I leaned back against the wall. "Condensed version: Dad suddenly took off one day. We didn't hear from him for weeks. When he finally called Mom, he said he needed a break from it all." I scoffed. "Like we were living such a crappy life. Everything had been fine." I tapped my nails along the bed. "Turns out he had a thing for a new intern at his firm. They had an affair, and he left us high and dry. Like I said, Mom worked all hours of the day to make sure we still had everything we had when Dad was there. She tried so hard to make it normal, but her never being home and me raising my brother and sister is so not normal."

"What made him want to come back?" Samson asked, leaning forward like he'd been soaking up all my words.

I unwrapped my fist so it wasn't in the confines of my shirt. "I don't know. He showed up on the doorstep one day and begged Mom to take him back." I swallowed back my tears. "I think she was so exhausted and excited to have him help with the family again."

"That's understandable on her part." He came over and sat next to me on the bed. "And completely understandable on your part for being wary."

I turned my head along the wall so I could see him. "Really? Taylor and Daphne think I'm being too emotional about it."

"They've never been stabbed in the back by someone they love," Samson said in a quiet voice.

It took me a few seconds to process what he said. "You have?"

Samson sighed and leaned his head against the wall like I was doing. "Did Taylor ever tell you about Kylie? Or my old friends?"

Oh, Kylie. That beautiful girl he dated in high school. I knew he was smitten with some girl my eighth-grade year. They were sophomores and off my radar until I got to high school and I had to witness them floating around campus, practically attached at the hip. It had been nauseating.

I'd been surprised when Taylor said they'd broke up. I asked what happened, but Taylor didn't want to talk about it and Samson never brought her up again. "The hot blonde? Yeah, I remember."

I'd never liked her for some reason. She rubbed me the wrong way.

He gazed straight ahead as he spoke. "We started dating sophomore year. We clicked so well."

"How long did you date?" I asked like I didn't know the answer.

"Two years."

Two years too long.

"We talked about our future all the time." Samson closed his eyes, squeezing tight, like it was painful to talk about. I reached over and took his hand. His muscles loosened at my touch.

"I thought we were going to get married," Samson went on, his voice low. "Everyone in my family thought that, too. They all accepted her into the fold."

I thought about his parents, brothers, and Taylor. "That's not an easy bunch to win over."

Samson cracked a smile. "Especially Ryker. But Kylie was so nice to him. He's always struggled with friends, so it meant so much that she treated him with such respect."

"So, what happened?"

"Found out the beginning of senior year that she was cheating on me and had been for a year." He clenched his jaw. "I couldn't believe I never saw the signs. I was completely oblivious." He looked at me. "Worst part? It was with my best friend, and all my friends knew about it. Not one of them said a thing to me. They let it happen."

My jaw dropped in shock. What kind of friends would do that to someone? I'd murder Daphne or Taylor if they ever did something that stupid.

I placed my free hand on his arm. "Are you serious? How could they do that to you? And how could Taylor keep that a secret? She can't keep anything a secret."

Samson placed his hand over mine. "I made her promise. I was so embarrassed and traumatized. The one person I loved most in the world had completely betrayed me."

An unexpected anger rose in me. "I seriously want to punch Kylie in the face."

Samson smirked. "And I want to see you punch Kylie in the face."

"And all your friends." I sighed. "What is wrong with people? If you don't want to be with someone, end it. What's the point of dragging it on?"

"Wish I knew." Samson squeezed my hand. "What are you going to do about your parents?"

A memory flitted into my brain. A story my abuela used to tell me about a curse upon her family but I couldn't remember all the details.

"I think I need to talk to my abuela. She always knows the right things to say."

"Sounds like a good plan to me." Samson let go of my hand and wrapped his arm around me. I leaned into him, welcoming the warmth. "I really believe everything always works out in the end, even if it's a complete mess getting there. You're strong, Veronica. One of the strongest people I know. You'll make it through this."

I really, truly hoped he was right.

I pulled back a little so I could look at him. "Everything

with Kylie and your friends, is that why you started hanging out with Taylor more?"

When he'd come back to visit for the summer, he'd never gone to see any of his old friends. He'd spent so much time with us. I hadn't really thought about it until now.

"That's one reason. I also quit wrestling, which left me with a lot of free time on my hands that I'd never had before." Samson grinned. "Main reason, though, is that I like hanging out with you."

I thought back to all the fun we'd had and how nice it was having him around to talk to, especially with Daphne and Taylor focused on Weston and Huntley.

"I think you hanging out with us should become a permanent thing." I needed a sixth member of the group so I wasn't always the fifth wheel.

He nodded. "I like that plan."

Turning my head, I leaned against his shoulder.

"Ready to go back to Tay and Daph?" Samson asked. His voice was a little lighter than normal, like he had a difficult time breathing. Maybe I was squeezing the life out of him.

"Can we hang out like this a little while longer?"

Samson held me tight. "We can stay here as long as you'd like." He chuckled. "I obviously have nowhere to go since all my friends suck."

I tapped his chest with hand. "They were never your friends, Samson. Friends don't do that to each other."

He let out a long sigh. "I think that part hurts worse than Kylie cheating on me. Knowing that I've never really had true friends."

"I know I'm just your little sister's friend, but I've always considered you a friend. You're a good person, and a lot of fun to be around."

He'd been coming home for the weekends way more often than he ever had while he was away at college, and I was grateful for it.

He gently kissed the top of my head. "Thanks, V. That means a lot."

We stayed in The Hideout for a while, embracing in silence. It was the calmest I'd felt in the longest time. Maybe I needed to spend more alone time with Samson.

For some odd reason, my face went ablaze at the thought.

CHAPTER SIX

My abuela lived in a cute Spanish-style house in Placentia. She had the best-looking lawn on the block thanks to her love of gardening. Rose bushes lined the walkway to the front porch, the red flowers adding the perfect aroma.

While most of the houses on the block had been decorated for Halloween, Abuela only had a wreath hanging on the door that said, "Who needs Halloween. I'm a witch all year."

I hadn't let her know I was coming, but she was almost always at home. She had a the-door-is-always-open policy, so I let myself in.

"Abuelita!" I slid off my sandals and placed them in the wicker basket next to the front door.

"Is that my Veronica?" Her rich, warm voice reminded me of my mom. "I'm in the kitchen!"

She was *always* in the kitchen making something for someone, whether it was a family member or a neighbor. Aside from her family, cooking and baking were the things that made her most happy in the world.

When I stepped into the kitchen, I froze. Tamales, empanadas, enchiladas, beans of every variety, and so much more smothered the table and counters.

It smelled like absolute heaven.

"I'm so glad you're here." My abuela stood near the stove next to a huge pot. She had a red apron tied around her plump frame.

I went to her side and gave her a huge hug. When we ended our embrace, I pulled out my phone and turned the camera to selfie mode. I held it high above our heads, trying to get the best angle. "Smile, Abuela."

Instead of smiling, she kissed my cheek as I snapped the picture. I scrolled through until I found a glittery filter, applied it, and uploaded the picture to my social media account.

Abuela turned her focus back to the pot on the stove. "You must try these esquites and tell me what you think. I can't tell if it needs more chili powder or not." She heaped a huge helping onto a wooden spoon. She held her hand underneath the spoon as she reached out to me, her deep brown eyes lighting up.

With a smile, I opened my mouth and took a bite. The flavors exploded in my mouth, taking me to my happy place. It was my dream to be as great a chef as she was one day.

I wiped at the corner of my mouth and finished off the food in my mouth. "If you have to ask, then the answer is yes."

My abuela winked and then kissed my cheek. "You've been paying attention to what I'm teaching you."

"Of course, I have." I picked up the chili powder and sprinkled some into the pot. "Someone needs to carry on your legacy."

"And you, my Veronica, are the perfect one to do it."

She mixed the esquites with her spoon. "I'm trying to decide what to make for your parents vow renewals."

My good mood plummeted. "You're happy about it?"

She shrugged. "If my daughter is happy, then I'm happy."

"The whole time my dad was gone you brought up all different ways Mom could kill him and get away with it."

"Always keep your options open, mija." She moved toward a plate of empanadas. "You need to try one of these."

I quickly took a bite, wanting to get my mind off vow renewals. I couldn't help but groan at the amazing flavor.

"That good?"

I nodded. "You added poblano peppers this time." My favorite.

"I wanted a little bit more kick."

"It's perfect."

Abuela's smile grew wide. "I'm glad you came over." Her smile faded as her eyes switched to all-knowing. "Why are you here, mija?"

I sat down at the table. "Can't a girl want to see her abuela?"

She turned off the stove and joined me at the table. "Spill it."

I flipped on the worry in my eyes, hoping I could sell this. "Do you remember our family curse?"

Her eyes grew dark. "I know it way too well. Why?"

Reaching forward, I quickly grabbed an empanada, wanting to give my hands something to do aside from fidget. "It's just." I sighed. "It's probably not a big deal, but I saw three crows perched on our roof this morning."

My abuela sucked in a sharp breath and clutched her hands close to her chest.

"I don't remember the whole story," I went on. "I

remember something about three crows. It probably doesn't mean anything, right?"

Abuela closed her eyes and muttered something that sounded like a prayer under her breath. When she opened her eyes, they were surprisingly dark.

"It began with your tatarabuela oh so many years ago." She sat tall in her chair, her presence commanding attention. "Renata's parents had arranged a very promising marriage to the son of a wealthy businessman in México. Cristobal was smart, handsome, and very respectful. Renata instantly fell in love. Cristobal, however, was secretly seeing another woman. When Renata's three brothers found out, they confronted Cristobal and demanded he cut ties with the other woman. Cristobal promised he would, but a few days before the wedding, the brothers caught Cristobal in bed with the other woman." Abuela's eyes went wide, waiting for a reaction.

So, I gasped and clenched my long hair in my hands. "No."

"Sí." She clasped her hands and rested them on the table. "Cristobal didn't want Renata to find out, so in a desperate rage, he killed all three brothers."

My gasp was real this time. I hadn't remembered that part of the story.

"The next three nights, the ghosts of the brothers terrorized the home, trying to persuade Renata to call off the wedding. On the first night, they unleashed dozens of grasshoppers throughout the home, knowing that Renata always believed they were a bad omen. On the second night, bees were released in the home, a sign that even though they can produce sweetness, they can sting you in an instant." She paused, drawing a deep breath.

"And on the third night?" I leaned forward, really

soaking in all abuela's words. She knew how to tell a story well.

"The night before the wedding," Abuela said in a serious tone, "a snake slithered into Renata's bed, a symbol of who she'd be sleeping with if she married Cristobal."

I shivered. Snakes were the worst. "Please tell me they didn't get married."

Abuela shook her head. "With her three brothers missing, the grasshoppers, bees, and snake, Renata fled, going into hiding until her parents agreed she didn't have to marry Cristobal." She folded her arms. "When Renata finally came home, she found three crows perched on the roof. They stayed by her side until the day she died, watching over and protecting her and her family."

"I mean, it's kind of a happy ending, right?"

Abuela tsked. "Except for the fact that Cristobal was outraged. He had his aunt, a local witch, cast a curse upon our family that no one would ever have a happy marriage. Renata eventually married, but it was a loveless marriage."

"Okay, but you and Abuelo, you had a happy marriage, right?"

Abuela looked over at their wedding photo hanging on the wall. "We did. Until he died five years into it. He's haunted me since then, never wanting me to move on." She motioned to the photo. "After he died, he came to me in my sleep and begged me to put that picture of us in every room of the house, so I did."

She'd never told me any of that before. "That explains the one in the guest bathroom. I've never wanted to ask. What about your parents?"

"Their marriage was plagued with problems. We had a house burn down, a house flood, they filed for bankruptcy, plus Mom had a few miscarriages and a still born. All I remember growing up was a ton of fighting."

How was I just finding out about all of this? "Why keep all of this a secret?"

She reached forward and patted my hand. "Your mother made me promise to never tell you. She didn't want it to affect your relationships. I tried to shield her and her siblings as well when they were kids. I rarely talked about it."

I arched an eyebrow. "Why are you telling me now?"

Abuela smirked. "She's staying with Matías despite my protests. Besides, you're old enough to know now. Maybe not tell your brother and sister, okay?"

I nodded as I sat back in the chair and drummed my long nails along my arm. All I needed were some grasshoppers, bees, and a snake to let my mom know who she was truly marrying.

I'd definitely need help, which would mean confiding my plan in Daphne and Taylor.

I left my abuela's house with an armful of storage containers filled to the brim with food. I'd shut them in the trunk when my phone suddenly went berserk, chiming like crazy.

I had an onslaught of messages on my phone and my social media accounts from DeShawn and all his friends. The messages were all gifs of ginormous pigs either eating or rolling around in the mud.

With a roar, I chucked my phone as far as I could. It smashed against the asphalt, the crunching sound music to my ears.

CHAPTER SEVEN

Since my phone was in pieces in my bag, I couldn't call or text Daphne and Taylor to find out where they were. I drove over to Daphne's house, grateful when I saw her Civic in the driveway. Another newer Civic sat next to it, which meant Cody—her mom's boyfriend—was there.

I grabbed some of the storage containers of food before heading up the walkway.

Daphne was an avid horror book and movie lover, so their Halloween decorations were beyond disturbing. Headstones littered the lawn with piles of dirt to look like fresh graves. Decaying hands that looked alarmingly real stuck out from the dirt.

It looked like Daphne took a photo of herself covered in fake blood and her fists raised, and then taped a huge copy inside the front window so it looked like she was begging for someone to rescue her.

With a shiver, I rang the doorbell, only to hear a piercing scream come from within their house. Of course,

Daphne would create a temporary doorbell sound that would make you want to turn around and run.

Daphne's mom, Laura, answered the door with a strained smile. "I heard the news about your parents. Are you okay?" She'd grown out her blonde hair, so it went well past her shoulders. She wore pink skinny jeans and a white blouse with the front tucked in.

"Not really."

Laura went to hug me but finally noticed all the containers in my hands. "I'm so sorry, Veronica. I wish I knew what to say."

"Knowing you care is enough." I lifted the clear containers and peered in the sides so I could see which ones I grabbed. "I come bearing empanadas and tamales."

"Did you make them?" Laura asked, taking them from me.

"My abuela did."

"You'll have to thank her for us. We love her food." She smiled softly. "Veronica, things always work out how they're supposed to, even if it's not what we want."

I wiped away a single tear that had escaped. "If I could know whether or not he'd stay this time, it would be much easier."

"Only time will tell." She motioned for me to come into the house.

Cody sat on the couch. He was definitely a good-looking guy. He was only in his mid-twenties, closer to Daphne's age than Laura's. But their relationship seemed to be going well, which I guess was all that mattered. He waved at me. "Hey, Veronica! It's good to see you."

"Same." I looked at the TV. It was paused on some period piece. "What are you watching?"

"The new *Persuasion*." Laura smiled. "Probably the best adaptation I've seen of that book."

"So much better than the other ones," Cody agreed. All three of his sisters had been named after Jane Austen characters. His first name would have been Edmund if his mother had gotten her way, but his dad intervened, and it ended up being his middle name.

Laura showed Cody the containers. "She brought empanadas and tamales."

His eyes lit up. "You made my day, Veronica." He paused. "Have you thought about going to culinary school? I think you'd make a brilliant chef."

I nodded. "Oh, yeah. The Institute of Culinary Education is high on my list of schools."

"I remember you talking about that when you were younger," Laura said. "Where's it located again?"

"Pasadena. But I'm mainly looking at UCLA, along with Daphne and Taylor."

Daphne, Taylor, and I wanted to get business degrees, and do it together at the same place. We had a dream of one day owning a business where Taylor could plan grand events, Daphne could create the wardrobes and unique party favors, and I could do the catering. Basically, a one-stop shop for a wedding. We'd settled on UCLA because it was close to home, plus Ryker and Huntley were already going there. Weston was applying for UCLA as well.

"I'm sure you'll all get in," Cody said with a hopeful smile.

Laura motioned to the hall. "Daphne's in her room. She's on the phone with her grandparents."

Her grandparents were traveling the world while Laura and Daphne stayed in their home. Total dream vacation.

Laura had taken over as owner of their antique shop, but I think she'd been looking to sell it.

When I got to Daphne's slightly opened door, I was about to knock, but heard what she was saying.

"So, you would or wouldn't take him back if he cheated on you?" Daphne asked.

"I wouldn't cheat on her," her grandpa said on speakerphone. They were probably video chatting.

"Gramps!" Daphne let out a frustrated huff. "That's not the point. *If* you did, would Grams take you back? That's the question."

"But I wouldn't—" her grandpa started.

Grandma Fletcher cut in. "It really depends on the situation, sweetie. Who's the hussy? How long did the affair last? How long had we been together?"

I held back a laugh when she said 'hussy.' It was so something someone from Daphne's family would say.

"Um, married for sixteen years, have three kids together, he also abandoned the family being absolutely no help during the time he was gone, and the affair probably lasted about six months. I'm not positive on that, though. Oh, and the hussy was a young intern at his work. Totally cliché, I know. At least spice things up a bit if you're going to do something incredibly stupid."

"Nope," Grandma Fletcher said. "I would definitely not take him back."

"I wouldn't take myself back," Grandpa Fletcher said.

I pushed the door open. "Thank you! This is what I keep telling everyone, but no one will listen."

Daphne—in her Cheer Bear onesie—screamed and jumped at the same time. She fell out of her hammock chair and onto the floor. "Holy Wonder Woman, Batman! Don't sneak up on someone like that."

I chuckled, reached down, and helped Daphne to her feet. We sat next to each other on her bed, and she maneuvered the phone so I could see her grandparents.

Even with their white hair and wrinkles, her grandma and grandpa had a youthfulness to their features that made it seem like they'd live forever.

"Oh, my sweet Veronica." Grandma Fletcher shook her head sympathetically. "I'm so sorry, dear. I wish I could magically fix everything for you."

"Thank you," I said, holding back the tears that wanted to come. Daphne's family had always been so nice to me.

Grandpa Fletcher leaned toward the screen. "I will say this, Veronica. While I don't condone cheating, real true love can make the heart forgive almost anything."

I chewed on my bottom lip. If they were so deeply in love, why would Dad do that to Mom? The thought shouldn't have crossed his mind.

Grandma and Grandpa Fletcher yawned at the same time.

"Guess that's they cue to let you two go," Daphne said with a smile. "Love you both! Have fun in Croatia!"

"Love you, too!" they said in an adorable unison. "Bye Daphne! Bye Veronica!"

"Bye!" Daphne and I said.

After Daphne ended the call, she turned toward me and lowered the hood of her onesie. "I think I'm wearing the wrong onesie. Should I switch to Grumpy Bear?"

"I have a plan." The more I thought about it, the more I realized it could work. If Daphne's grandparents believed true love could get through anything, then my parents would see all the signs of the family curse and still go through with the wedding. If they weren't soulmates, then they'd break up.

Daphne smiled, but then it faded. "Is this a good plan or bad plan?"

"Good."

Her smile came back. "Okay. What's the plan?"

I told her all about Renata and the family curse. Daphne gasped at all the right moments, which would have made my abuela really happy.

"So, we need to test my parent's love for each other," I finished. "Dad and Mom need to prove that nothing could ever come between them again."

Daphne held up a hand. "Hear me out. What if instead of doing creepy things like grasshoppers, bees, and a snake —" She shuddered. "—we dangle a hot, young intern in front of your dad and see if he takes the bait."

"Says the girl who eats horror books for breakfast."

She rolled her eyes. "I like *fake* creepy things because I know they aren't real. Live insects? Nope. Clowns? No, thank you. Real blood and guts? I'm out."

"You seriously make no sense." I took the hairband from my wrist and wrapped my hair in a high, loose bun. "It's crunch time, Daph. I need to pull out the big punches."

Daphne punched at the air, a determined scowl on her face. "Got it." She lowered her hands. "Can I at least talk you out of the snake?"

"Maybe we won't get there. Maybe the first two signs will be enough for Mom."

"Let's hope." She tapped her lips. "Does your family have any curses that involve ghosts? We could have so much fun with that. And it wouldn't involve anything living."

"Not that I know about." I stood. "Call Taylor and tell her to meet us at my house."

Daphne shot up, her eyes wide. "Wait, you're letting us

go over to your house?" She placed a hand to her forehead. "I'm not sure how to process this."

I gently pushed her arm. "You need to see the layout of the house if we want this to work. Besides, maybe if you finally see how crazy my family is, you'll understand where I'm coming from."

Daphne blinked. "My mom is dating a guy closer to my age than hers and Taylor has a brother that carries a gecko on his shoulder everywhere he goes. I think we understand." She motioned to her onesie. "I also wear these a lot, so ..."

I rolled my eyes. "Whatever. Let's go."

Daphne unzipped her onesie, letting it fall to the floor. She wore a Cherry Coke shirt and red shorts underneath. "Wait, why am I calling Taylor? Why can't you do that?" She perused her wall of Mickey ears until she found the one with cherries for ears and slid them on over her wavy hair.

"My phone broke. Maybe we can stop on the way and get one of those prepaid phones or something."

"That sucks. Didn't your dad just get you that phone?"

He did. The latest version, too. So, all the images sent to me were the best quality ever. I needed a flip phone with no smart screen.

And probably a new number to get DeShawn off my back.

CHAPTER EIGHT

We stood on my porch as some nerves flitted into my stomach. I couldn't believe I was finally letting Daphne and Taylor into my family's crazy circle. It was a lot for anyone to take in. I suddenly wished I had something to munch on.

I glanced over at Daphne, only to see her hand over her eyes. "Why are you doing that?"

Daphne shrugged. "I've never been over here. I want a grand reveal."

With a sigh, I took her hand and led her into my house. Taylor was right behind us, clearly not as interested as Daphne was to see the inside of my house.

Honestly, our house looked like any other house in Southern California. Dad had renovated the kitchen to the farmhouse style, everything bright and cheery. He kept doing grand gestures, trying to win over the whole family, but really, we needed to know he wasn't going to abandon us again. Brand new stuff didn't make up for the torture we went through with him gone.

I let go of Daphne's hand. "We're in the family room."

With a squeal, Daphne dropped her hand so she could see. The huge smile on her face evaporated as she took in my home. Her shoulders slouched in disappointment. "This is it?"

"What were you expecting?" I asked.

Daphne threw up her hands. "I don't know. Like maybe you were hoarders, or you'd gone for a carnival theme with creepy clowns everywhere."

"Who would go for a carnival theme in their house?" Taylor asked through her laugh.

Daphne held up a finger. "Hoarders." Another finger. "Someone who grew up as a carny." Third finger. "Serial killers."

I sighed, pushing her arm down. "You know none of those apply to my family."

"Technically, I wasn't sure about the hoarders thing until now." Daphne plopped onto the couch. "This is such a disappointment. Why haven't you let us come to your house before? It's like totally normal." She glanced at the jars of fake potions on the coffee table. "The Halloween decorations are nice, though. I'll give you that."

"It's not the house itself," I said, moving toward the stairs. "It's the people living in it." I cupped my hand over my mouth, looking toward my parents' bedroom upstairs. "Ma! Can you come here a sec?"

"Coming!" Mom yelled from her room.

After grabbing a bag of Takis, I joined Taylor and Daphne on the couch. I'd decided not to tell Taylor my plan, so I'd sworn Daphne to secrecy. If Taylor knew about my plan, she'd try to talk me out of it. Ever since she started dating Huntley, she'd been acting older than her age. She wanted Huntley to think she was mature, but sometimes it was annoying. Yeah, he was in college, but he was only a year older than us.

Daphne, though, would happily ride my crazy train. She'd be the conductor if I asked her to.

I held out the bag to Daphne, who stuck out her tongue. "Get those out of my face."

I knew she'd turn them down. I just loved her grumpy face. Daphne couldn't handle anything too spicy.

Taylor happily took some, like I knew she would.

Both my mom and dad came down the stairs, and I frowned. I didn't know he'd be here as well. Didn't the man have a life?

"What do we owe this pleasure?" my dad asked as he took a spot on the loveseat. He wore his favorite 49ers jersey and joggers.

Mom sat down next to him, a twinkle in her eyes. "If I'd known we were having guests, I would have prepared some snacks or something."

Daphne punched me on the arm. "Girl, why didn't you tell them we were coming? Oh, wait, you don't have a phone."

I glared at her, making her shrink back. "Girl, don't hit me."

"What happened to your phone?" Dad asked.

With a sheepish smile, I took the broken pieces out of my bag and set them on the coffee table. "I may have run over it with my car." Or maybe I chucked it because my ex was making my life miserable.

Disappointment settled in Mom's eyes. "You need to be more careful, mjia. Those cost a lot of money."

"I know," I said. "You don't have to get me a new one. I'll be fine without one for a while." Mostly because I didn't want to deal with texts and easy access to social media and all the crap it offered. I turned a smile to my parents. "Taylor has decided to accept your proposal."

"I have?" Taylor asked. When she caught my forceful gaze, she cleared her throat. "I have! I'm so excited and honored to do this for you, Mr. and Mrs. Rodriguez."

Mom clapped her hands in glee. "Oh, this makes me so happy! We know you'll do a wonderful job, Taylor. We know you'll truly capture the essence of our love."

I forced the smile to stay on my face. I'd have time to truly capture the essence of their love later when I brought out the big guns. Well, bugs in this case. Mom was a huge believer in signs, so there would be no way for her to ignore them.

Taylor shot me a glare. "If I'd known we were going to discuss details, I would have brought my notebook."

Dad quickly stood and shuffled into his office, coming back with a pad of paper and pen for Taylor.

She greedily took them like she couldn't begin making notes soon enough. "Have you thought of a theme?"

Dad gazed adoringly at Mom, and I stuffed a bunch of Takis into my mouth.

"What about 'endless love?'" Dad said, making Mom grin.

"Aww! So cute." Taylor jotted on the paper in a fury. "What else?"

As they dived into the details, I took Daphne by the hand and dragged her up the stairs to my room.

Daphne clasped her hands together and glanced around my room, her eyes lit up in excitement. "It's so pretty!"

The walls were a sky blue, one of my favorite colors. Daphne skipped over to a framed picture that my abuela had made for me. It was a silhouette of my face, made from burgundy flowers. Burgundy was my other favorite color.

"I wanna kiss this." Daphne leaned in close to the frame. "This is *ah*-mazing, and how come you've never mentioned this before?"

Because it was my abuela's way of saying I was a beautiful, pure flower and needed to stay that way until marriage. It wasn't that I was against saving myself, I wasn't into the daily reminder.

But it was beautiful. Abuela did a wonderful job on it, like everything she did.

I didn't get to answer because Daphne had already moved onto the silk burgundy bedspread, her body sprawled out on it. "I want to marry your room. Is that weird?"

I sat down on the bed and tucked one of the sky-blue pillows under my chin as I held it close. "Yes."

She kicked her legs up behind her and crossed her feet at her ankles. "I should have known your room would be perfectly clean." Her eyes went wide as she took in my vanity. My abuelo (my dad's dad) had hand-crafted it from redwood. He'd owned his own wood working business but was on the verge of passing it on to my uncle, Felípé.

Daphne scrambled off the bed and over to the vanity where she took a seat on the burgundy cushioned stool. She pressed her palms against the top. "Did your grandpa make this?"

"Yep. Gave it to me for my quinceañera." It was one of my prized possessions. I almost worried about Daphne sitting there, but I realized she wasn't actually pressing her palms against the wood. They hovered over it, like she knew it was sacred territory.

Daphne glanced over all my make-up lined up on the shelves circling around the mirror. "I've never seen so much make-up in my life."

I motioned to my face. "How do you think I get this flawless look?"

Daphne shrugged. "I thought you were naturally flawless."

I choked back a laugh. It took me at least an hour to get ready in the morning. Daphne and Taylor had never seen me without make-up. Even when I slept over at their houses, I kept the make-up on. They didn't need to see the acne-scarred skin underneath all the layers. No one did.

"Oh. My. Gosh." Luciana stood in the doorway, her hands on her hips. "You *do* have friends. I thought you'd made them up."

Daphne waved at my sister. "Hey, Luciana!"

Luciana tilted her head to the side. "Cherry Coke shirt. Wearing Mickey ears like it's totally normal. Let me guess, you must be Daphne."

"Luci!" I practically hissed her name. "Don't be so rude. And you've met Daphne before."

Luciana swept her hair behind her. "Oh. Sorry. I forgot."

"You know," Daphne said with a parental scolding look, "sassy doesn't always equal classy." She mimed pulling on some reins. "Might want to rein that in."

Luciana rolled her eyes. "You're so weird. No wonder you're friends with V." She spun on her heels and marched out of the room.

Daphne tried to whistle but did a terrible job. "You weren't kidding when you said she has a mouth on her."

"I honestly don't know where she gets it from."

"Says the lady who's about to unleash a plague upon her household."

"Speaking of that." I squished next to Daphne on the

vanity stool and kept my voice low. "Where are we going to get grasshoppers?"

Daphne grinned mischievously. "I only know one person who would know where to go."

"Why are you smiling like that?" I asked, my eyebrows arching up. I caught a glimpse of myself in the mirror. I pushed aside my bangs and smiled on the inside when I noted that my eyebrows were still perfectly drawn on.

Daphne's grin grew. "Because it's fun."

I bumped her arm with mine. "You thinking Ryker?"

"Yep. He got us the crickets we let loose in Simone's car."

I stared at myself in the mirror, noticing my double-chin. "Do you think we can ask him without him mentioning it to Taylor?"

"Mentioning what to Taylor?"

I spun in the stool to see Taylor standing in the door-way, the pad of paper clutched to her chest.

"You're already done?" I asked, hoping my voice was steady.

"Yes, and don't avoid my question." Taylor stepped into the room, scanning it with her bold eyes. "Love what you've done with the place."

Daphne hopped up and hustled over to the flower picture, holding out her hands in an elegant display. "And look at this flower interpretation of Veronica." Her eyes lit up as she looked at me. "Do you think your abuela will make one for me? She could even do like Mickey Ears made from flowers." She clasped her hands together. "How amazing would that be?"

Taylor cleared her throat. "What are you keeping from me, V? No way you'd agree to me helping your parents out of the goodness of your heart. What do you not want to mention to me?"

I sighed. I really hoped she'd forget about that, but Taylor never forgot anything.

Daphne came forward and took Taylor's hands in her. "Okay, so Veronica still has some reservations about the whole thing, but she didn't want to steal your thunder. We know how much this means to you and want you to be able to fully focus on the job without any worries wiggling around in your head."

I smiled at Daphne, so grateful for her quick thinking.

Taylor turned to me. "I appreciate that, V, but if this isn't what you want, I feel weird doing it."

I took one of Taylor's hands from Daphne and held it in mine, so we were standing in a circle. "Am I happy about this? No. But I obviously can't talk my parents out of it so I'm going to roll with it for now."

Taylor let go of our hands and threw her arms around me. "Way to take the high road, V. I know everything will work out the way it's supposed to."

I held in a smirk.

Oh, it would turn out in true Rodriguez fashion.

Drama, drama, drama.

CHAPTER NINE

After Daphne and Taylor went home, I closed my door and changed into my pajamas—basically a different pair of sweats and an oversized tee.

I turned on some Meghan Trainor and laid down on my bed. Since I was out a phone, I opened my laptop. Against my better judgment, I scrolled through my TikTok as I sang along to the songs. Javier appeared on my screen, flexing for his audience and talking about what products he uses in his hair. With an eyeroll, I went to his main page and scrolled through it.

I hadn't looked at it in the longest time. My scrutiny quickly changed when I took it all in. Yeah, he did some posts that focused on his image, but it he also had a bunch with his artwork.

Javier was an amazing artist. It had started out as weird scribbles but progressed as he got older. I hadn't realized how proficient he'd become. He was all about the abstract art. He had one series all about mood that was downright captivating. Full of various colors, lines, swirls, dots, shapes, it was like his hand had danced across the canvas. Or tablet in his case. He'd mainly switched over to digital art.

He also had dance videos. I sat up on my bed as I watched some of them. When had Javier learned to salsa?

Someone quietly knocked on my door.

"Yeah?" I asked, setting down my phone.

"Can I come in?" Javier asked.

"You're asking permission?" I asked with mock shock.

Javier opened the door and peered in. "Just didn't want to walk in and see you changing or something." He dramatically shivered, and then smiled.

"What's up?"

He shut the door and came and sat next to me on the bed. "I saw you liked about a hundred of my posts."

I looked at the screen on my laptop. "I highly doubt it was that much."

"Why the sudden interest?" Javier's tone sounded almost hopeful. Had he been wanting me to take an interest in his posts?

I pulled up one of his salsa videos. "Uh, when did you learn to dance like that?"

Javier actually blushed. I wasn't sure if I'd ever seen him do that. "I follow some people who teach the steps. I've been slowly learning them over the years."

Then I scrolled to my favorite piece of art I'd come across. It had sky-blue and burgundy all swirled together in intricate patterns that took my breath away. "Javy, you're really good at this."

He softly smiled. "That's the Veronica mood."

My jaw dropped, and I took in the painting again. "For real?"

"I picked your two favorite colors and then drew how I see you."

My heart swelled and I tried not to tear up. The descriptive and vivid lines of the image screamed confidence.

"I'm so flattered," I said in a quiet voice.

"I mean it," Javier said. "You're one of the strongest people I know. I've always admired that about you." He smirked. "When were you going to tell me you could sing that well?"

My head jerked back in confusion. "What are you talking about?"

"I heard you singing in here earlier. Your voice was as good as Meghan Trainor's."

I laughed but then stopped when I saw he was serious. "That's a little extreme."

He pointed to the Veronica painting still on my screen. "I call it as I see it. Or hear it." His eyes lit up. "You should make a TikTok! I can help you."

"Of what?"

"You singing along to 'Made You Look.' It would be awesome."

I quickly shook my head. "I don't have a phone right now."

Surprise flitted across his eyes. "Why? Did Mom and Dad take it away or something?"

"No, it broke."

He shrugged. "No problem. We'll use my phone."

I glanced at my baggy clothes. "Besides, I have nothing to wear."

His eyes got super wide and then he bolted out of my room.

"Uh, okay ..."

Javier rushed back less than a minute later holding a T-shirt. It had *The Veronica* painting on it. "I made this for you."

I jumped up from my bed and took it in my hands. "Why are you giving it to me now?"

"Uh, because I just had it made?"

I held it up to my chest. "Looks like it fits."

He took in my room. "Change into it. I'll go get my equipment." He ran out of the room, shuffled back, smiled, and closed the door so I could have privacy.

I switched shirts and went to the mirror. It was a lot less baggy than my other shirt. It fit pretty well. I hadn't looked at the size and I was glad I hadn't. I didn't need to know the truth.

"You dressed?" Javier called from the other side of my door.

"Yeah."

"Cool. Open the door for me, please."

When I opened the door, I was surprised to see all the stuff in Javier's arms. He had a few different stands, a ring light, and a bunch of cords.

I tried to help him set up, but he ended up swatting my hand away after a couple of unsuccessful attempts on my part.

While he finished up, I touched up my makeup. My hair was in a messy bun, so I took it down and ran a brush through it.

Javier appeared at my side, his face all business. "Let's start with you singing into the mirror." He pointed at the brush I still held. "Use that as a microphone. I'll have the phone angled to get your reflection, then I pan out, and you turn toward the phone and finish the clip."

"It's like you do this for a living."

He slowly blinked. "I do."

"Wait, do you make money from your videos?"

He rubbed his forehead. "I swear, no one in the family pays attention to anyone but themselves. Haven't you seen the packages come for me?"

I tried to think, but nothing came to mind.

"Well, they're from companies that want me to advertise their products. They send me all sorts of free stuff. I also sell my artwork online." He pointed at my shirt. "Like that."

My cheeks heated in embarrassment. "I've been the worst sister in the entire world."

Javier twisted his hand back and forth. "Not *the worst*. You had a lot on your plate when Dad was gone. Now that he's back, all your focus is on hating him."

I sat down on my vanity stool. "We can remedy this, right? So I don't feel like complete and utter crap for the rest of my life?"

Javier motioned to the ring light. "We're about to do that."

I looked behind him to make sure the door was closed. "Hey, Javy? Are you okay with Dad coming back?"

He pulled his phone out of his pocket. "No. Not at all."

His answer surprised me.

"You've never seemed upset or anything," I said.

He always seemed to relish the idea of not having parents around and doing whatever he wanted. He'd never once spoken badly of Dad when he was gone. It almost sounded like he'd idolized him. But maybe that had all been a front.

He attached his phone to the stand. "I figured since no one pays that close of attention to me, they wouldn't care what I had to say."

I frowned. "That's horribly sad."

He smiled at me. "Don't feel bad, sis. We've gone through a lot the past couple of years."

I debated for a moment and then found myself blurting, "Have you heard of our family curse?"

"I remember abuela talking about it once, but I can't remember any details."

I dove into the story, and then told him my plan. I wasn't sure how Javier would react. Maybe he'd try to talk me out of it. Maybe he'd tell me I was crazy.

A mischievous smile broke out on his face. "Can I help?"

I sighed in relief. "Yes, of course you can."

Javier pulled up TikTok on his phone. "Ready to give this a try?"

I stretched out my neck and then fixed my hair. "Am I lip singing?"

"No way. You *have to* sing. Seriously, V, people will eat this up."

I took a deep breath before I cranked up the Rodriguez smolder. "Let's do it."

CHAPTER TEN

I wasn't sure what to expect after we posted my video, but it got a fair number of views and comments. Overall, his followers were pretty nice. They complimented my voice and my shirt. Javier deleted the few mean comments so fast it was like they hadn't even happened.

With Javier now on board with the plan, I was eager to get started. I'd thought about texting Ryker during the week, but I didn't have his number. I didn't know how to ask Taylor or Samson without it being weird. Ryker would be coming home for the weekend again, so I just needed to survive the school week until he got here.

When Dad had finished going over the vow renewal plans with Taylor the night before, he went to the store and got me a brand-new phone. He'd set an old photo of him and me as the background. I was around five and sitting on his shoulders at a 49ers game. I wore a jersey and had black lines painted under my eyes. I yelled in outrage, along with my dad, probably at a terrible call on the field. I hadn't remembered liking football that much. When had I stopped watching games with him?

I found it interesting that out of all the photos of us, he'd chosen that one. Was it to show me we were once friends? Or to show how feisty I used to be? Maybe both. A part of me wanted to change the background photo to something else, but I couldn't force myself to do it after he'd spent so much money on a new phone.

I immediately went to blocking DeShawn's number, along with all his friends. I even made all my social media accounts inactive so they couldn't send me messages that way. Then I set up a brand-new private account using the picture of my abuela and me as my profile pic. I followed Daphne, Taylor, and Samson so they knew about the new account.

Daphne texted me seconds later.

> Daphne: Is this you, or a spam account?

I smiled as I responded.

> It's me. Just wanted a fresh start. Trying to shed the negativity in my life.

> Daphne: Smart. See you at school!

$\mathcal{N}$ot long after I got to school, Dad sent a text:

> Dad: Have a good day at school, sweetie.

I debated for a moment, trying to decide whether to

respond. I finally tucked the phone in my pocket without sending him a reply.

Ever since DeShawn decided to make my life a living hell, I'd gone out of my way to avoid him and his friends at school. I knew all the lower-trafficked routes to my classes. Some took me well out of my way to where I was going, but I preferred it over being heckled.

I hid behind the side of the math building, waiting for the area to clear. DeShawn and his friend Christian stood near an oak tree talking to some beautiful, and totally skinny, juniors. The girls shamelessly flirted with them, touching their arms at any and every opportunity. DeShawn and Christian would flex their muscles, making the girls giggle.

I rolled my eyes, wondering what I saw in DeShawn in the first place. I should have listened to my gut back in third grade when it told me he was a loser and not worth my time. I mean, the guy wasn't anywhere near the caliber of Michael from *Jane the Virgin*.

Maybe I'd been in desperate need of attention with my dad gone. Daddy issues and all that. It was the only reasonable explanation as to why I would date him.

Suddenly, someone came up behind me and grabbed my arm, squeezing unnecessarily tight. "I've wondered where you've been hiding." His deep and rich tone added a layer of ickiness to it.

I spun around to see DeShawn's friend Jaylen looming over me. He was a lineman on the football team and his large frame screamed it.

Anger ignited in me at him being so close, but I couldn't get my body to shove him away. It was like I was frozen in horror. What was wrong with me?

Jaylen dragged me out from the cover of the math building. "Found her!"

My arm burned where he held me. I tried to pry myself from his grip, but the guy was way too strong. I stumbled along his gigantic steps until we were near the others.

DeShawn and Christian ripped their attention from the hot juniors to see what Jaylen was talking about. When they saw me, they both mooed in unsettling unison. DeShawn laughed and side fist bumped Christian, the two of them so completely proud of themselves for being scumbags.

The girls huddled right behind them, trying not to laugh and watching everything like it was a soap opera.

Jaylen tossed me by the arm over to DeShawn, his dry hand rubbing my skin raw before he released me. When I got to DeShawn, he quickly pushed me toward Christian, who, in turn, shoved me toward Jaylen as he oinked.

Before I could get to Jaylen, I clumsily came to a stop in the middle of them, my stomach churning from all the movement and complete embarrassment. I placed a shaking hand against my stomach, willing it to calm down.

The three guys walked in circles around me, mooing and oinking like idiots. I tried to say something, but nausea overtook me making it difficult to speak.

"Where have I seen that image before?" the blonde girl suddenly asked, looking at the shirt Javier had given me.

"Right?" The brunette tilted her head, like that would help her think better. "It's like so familiar."

These guys were obviously bullying someone, and the two of them were focused on my shirt?

"It's going to drive me crazy," blondie said.

Jaylen tried to reach out and slap me, but I jerked away at the last minute. All three guys laughed and began a game of who could slap Veronica with me jumping around like a buffoon. I stupidly looked toward the girls for help.

The brunette snapped her fingers as she smiled. "Hottie Javy! From TikTok." Her smile faltered as she looked at me, head still tilted to the side. I worried her small brain might fall out. "Why do *you* have his shirt? You follow him?"

The blonde laughed. "You're way too old for him. That's so gross."

The brunette joined in on the laughter and I did my best to stay calm. They were only a year younger than me, so they were too old for him as well. Also, he was my brother. So, yeah, it was gross.

But that didn't even matter. I had these oafs heckling me and two pea-brained morons watching on, doing nothing to stop it. The contents of my stomach desperately wanted to release.

The guys paused for a moment, giving me a chance to shove my way between DeShawn and Christian. I only got two steps before I vomited all over the cement.

"Oh! Nasty!" DeShawn said through fits of laughter.

"Gross!" the girls said in whiny union.

"Stand back, Jay!" Christian said. "With how much she eats, you know there's a lot more to come."

I wanted to turn around and glare at him, but more kept on pouring out, as if proving his theory. My hand sought out the stucco wall, leaning into it for support. My knees trembled, wanting to give way. No way I was going to fall into a pile of my own vomit, especially in front of these guys.

My fingers pressed into the wall so hard, two of my fake nails snapped and flew into the air.

"She's exploding!" Christian said, so much laughter and taunting in his tone.

"It's like that one movie," DeShawn said. "You know, where that girl blows up into a balloon?"

"The Harry Potter movie?" blondie asked. "With the aunt?"

"Nah," DeShawn said. "The girl was young and blue and like chewed gum and stuff."

"Oh!" Jaylen clapped his large hands together, the sound incredibly loud. "Violet. She turned purple. Charlie and the Chocolate Factory."

"She turned blue, Jay," DeShawn said.

As they continued to argue about whether she was blue or purple, I gathered enough strength to stagger out of there and find the nearest bathroom.

I quickly locked myself in the stall and fell to my knees, but there was nothing left to come out at that point. Tears fell freely as I hovered over the toilet, wishing and praying all the torment would end.

CHAPTER ELEVEN

After school, I drove straight to my abuela's home. I was not in the mood to see any men, like my dad, and their misogynistic views. Everything that happened with the guys left me horrified. On what planet was that behavior acceptable?

My abuela greeted me at the door, like she'd been expecting me, though I hadn't told her I was coming. She had a scary sixth sense about everyone in her family.

She immediately wrapped me up in her arms. "I love you, mija."

"Love you, too, Abuelita." I swallowed back the lump forming in my throat. I'd shed enough tears for today.

She slowly pulled back and rested her warm hands on my cheeks. "Come. I have homemade gansitos for you."

My stomach rumbled at the thought. I hadn't eaten anything since I'd vacated what I had for breakfast. I was starving, but also still sick to my stomach.

I sat down at the kitchen table and crossed my ankles. I glanced at my broken fingernails, the edges jagged, and held back the tears. I still couldn't believe I'd let those snakes get to me like that.

My arm stung from where Jaylen had grabbed it. A small red ring had been left behind, so I tugged the baggy sleeve of my shirt down so it couldn't be seen.

Abuela opened the freezer and took out a plate of gansitos. She'd randomly frozen a batch a few years back and when she pulled them out at a party, everyone realized how much they loved them frozen, so we'd eaten them that way since.

Dark chocolate coated the crème-filled sponge cake with homemade strawberry jelly layered on top. My abuela made everything from scratch, which was why it tasted like heaven.

Abuela set the entire plate in front of me. I quickly snatched one up and took a large bite. I let the cake thaw out in my mouth, the flavors slowly releasing and taking me to my happy place.

"Is this about your parents?" Abuela poured me a glass of fresh strawberry lemonade and placed the cup on the table in front of me. Then she took the seat next to me, her focus solely on me.

I shook my head. I mean, I still wasn't happy about the vow renewal, but my current trigger was stupid DeShawn and his disgusting friends. Maybe they needed some insects let loose in their homes as well.

I finished off the bite in my mouth before I spoke, and my abuela waited patiently the entire time, her brown eyes soft and loving. I wasn't sure how much to tell her because I knew whatever I said, she'd turn around and tell my mom.

"My ex is being stupid," I finally said, staring at my broken nails.

Abuela followed my gaze and gasped. She took my hand

in hers. "Did you break these clawing at him?"

I stifled a laugh. "No."

"It's okay to claw him if he deserves it. Men need to be put in their place now and then."

As tempting as that was, I didn't want to resort to physical violence. Psychological torture was the better way to go.

I sounded like Daphne. She loved all the horror stuff.

"How do you get boys to leave you alone?" I quickly added the next part. "Without hurting them physically, Abuelita."

She frowned. "Well, that's not as fun." She squeezed my hand and then let go. "You need to put your foot down. Let him know his behavior is unacceptable."

"I think that will fuel him." When I tried to be firm, he threatened me. When I cowered, he laughed at me. No matter what I did, he tortured me and would continue to do so.

"Have you tried being kind?" Abuela folded her arms, tapping her fingers along them. "What's that saying? 'Kill them with kindness?'"

I rolled my eyes and picked up another gansito. "He doesn't deserve my kindness."

Abuela's eyes softened. "Oh, mija. Everyone deserves kindness. Even the bullies."

I wasn't sure how much I believed that. Did bullies deserve kindness? Did murderers deserve kindness? Child abusers? Homewreckers?

Probably not killers and child abusers. But all other humans deserved kindness and love. I hadn't tried that approach and my abuela was rarely wrong.

I stood and picked up the plate of remaining gansitos. "Maybe I'll try it. Mind if I take these?"

Abuela stood and kissed my forehead. "Of course,

Veronica. Remember that you are strong."

With a smile, I left my abuela's house and headed toward school.

Since it was fall, football was in season, which meant after school practices for DeShawn and his teammates.

I took a seat on the bleachers, setting the plate in my lap.

The team was doing drills on the field, practicing plays by the look of it. I hadn't totally gotten into football, even when I was with DeShawn. It was hard to keep up with everything going on and figure out what they were doing. And why they were doing it. The games were long and there was so much stop and go that I easily got bored.

Jaylen looked up at the bleachers and waved like he hadn't tormented me just hours ago. I really wanted to flip him off, but I chose the path of kindness and waved back even though my arm burned at the sight of him.

Christian and DeShawn followed Jaylen's gaze until they saw me as well. They both cupped their hands over their mouths and mooed.

Keep it cool, Veronica. They're stupid boys thinking they're funny.

By how a lot of the guys on the team laughed as well, they thought they were funny, too. So freaking hilarious.

When the gansitos on the plate started hopping around, I realized how hard I gripped the plate and trembled. I loosened my muscles, trying to let the anger go.

My phone rang, so I set the plate on the bench next to

me and pulled my phone out of my pocket. It was Javier.

"Hey, Javy."

"V, I've been trying to contact you for hours!" He sounded a mixture of panicked and angry.

I glanced at my screen and saw I had missed calls and texts from him. I had my phone on silent until I got to the school. I hadn't bothered to look at anything on my phone because I wasn't in the mood.

"What's going on?" I asked.

Javier swore and then apologized. "Some stupid girl posted a video of you throwing up and tagged me in it."

Shock rippled through me. "What?" Had blondie and brunette filmed me?

"Don't worry," Javier said. "I reached out to my followers, and we all reported her. The post has been taken down and her account has been temporarily disabled."

Guess it paid to have a huge following.

"Why did she tag you in it?" I asked.

"Because you were wearing my design on your shirt." He paused. "Are you okay? What happened, V?"

I chewed at my bottom lip and then stopped myself. "DeShawn and his friends were being stupid. I got sick to my stomach and threw up. I guess the girls recorded it."

"Did they do something to you?" An overprotective edge laced his voice that made me smile softly, knowing how much he cared.

I really didn't want to tell Javier what happened. I was embarrassed that I hadn't stood up for myself. I'd been such a coward. Besides, aside from the arm burn, the only thing really bruised was my ego.

"Just teasing me," I finally said. "Nothing big."

He let out a breath of relief. "Good. If they ever do something, you'll let me know, right?"

No way. He didn't need to be pulled into all my drama. "Of course, Javy."

"Guess I'll see you at home, then?"

"Yeah, I should be there soon."

He paused and then his voice came out awkwardly. "Uh, I love you. You know that, right?"

I smiled. "Yes. And I love you, too. See you soon."

"Bye, V." He ended the call.

I looked at the field to see that practice was over. I clumsily stepped off the bleachers and made my way to DeShawn and the others.

DeShawn held his helmet against his side, a smirk on his face that made me want to smash the gansitos all over it. "Veronica, I don't want you back. This is pathetic."

Christian, Jaylen, and a few other players laughed.

I stood tall, holding my chin high. "I came with a peace offering. My abuela's homemade gansitos."

Christian oinked. "Of course, it would be food."

A couple of the guys laughed, but Jaylen and another guy quickly grabbed a gansito and shoved them in their mouths. Out of instinct, I flinched back when Jaylen got close, but he was too focused on the food to notice.

Jaylen moaned as his eyes crossed. "De, you gotta try these, man!" He mumbled with his mouth stuffed. "They're so good!"

DeShawn shook his head, looking me up and down in disgust. "If they make me fat like Veronica, then no thank you."

I held out the plate, taking deep breaths to stay calm. It took me a moment before I could speak. "Can we call a truce? I'm done with all this, DeShawn."

He stared at me as the seconds went by agonizingly slow. He finally reached out and took a gansito. He was about to put it in his mouth when he slapped it against my face, smearing it in.

I gasped in shock and stumbled back.

"Get off our field, pig," DeShawn said. "Go back to your pen where you belong."

An animalistic rage roared inside me. All the anger I'd been holding in about my dad, DeShawn, and his pathetic friends came spewing up, wanting to be released.

I shoved the entire plate into DeShawn's face, working it back and forth as he screamed like a little girl.

Jaylen wrapped his arms around my waist and yanked me away from DeShawn. The plate stayed against DeShawn's face for a moment before it slipped off and fell to the ground.

I flailed and kicked, trying to get out of his grip, hating that he had his hands on me once again. I had to do *something* this time. They couldn't get away with it.

"Look at the little piggy squirm!" Christian leaned incredibly close to me, oinking over and over again.

Without much thought, I clawed at his face like my abuela had suggested. Only, it was Christian, not DeShawn. When blood trickled down his cheeks, it hit me how hard I clawed him. It probably didn't help that my fake nails were all jagged from snapping them off earlier.

"Whoa!" Jaylen suddenly let me go and I dropped to the ground.

Christian's eyes widened in terror. "What did you do?" He pressed a hand against his cheek and when his skin came back bloody, he swayed like he might pass out.

"She's crazy!" One of the other guys yelled. "She's straight up crazy!"

It was then I noticed we'd caught the attention of all the coaches, and I instantly knew how much trouble I was in.

CHAPTER TWELVE

The principal suspended me for a week. My main worry would be that it would hurt my chance to get a scholarship. My grades were perfect, and my record had been spotless until this encounter, so I hoped this would be only a tiny blemish among my well-polished career.

Absolutely nothing happened to the star football players. Heaven forbid they miss a game. I mean, the team wasn't that good. They had a losing record.

But whatever. I digressed.

My abuela explained to my parents that the clawing had been entirely her idea. Yeah, she'd suggested it, but I'd gone through with it. I was *so* mad and *so* done with being teased for my weight. Had I overreacted? Definitely. Did I regret it? Not really.

To cheer me up, my mom and abuela took me to my favorite nail salon to get my nails fixed. When my mom's sister Dulce and her daughter Bianca found out, they wanted to come as well. Dulce's other daughter Celeste wanted to be there, but she couldn't miss work. Instead, she sent my aunt and cousin with a jumbo-sized bag of Hot Tamales to give to me which I happily accepted.

When we pulled up to the salon, I looked down at my phone and saw a text from Dad.

> Dad: One of my favorite memories from you as a kid was when I'd catch you singing in the bathroom mirror, and you'd offer me a brush and ask me to join you.

Okay, that was totally random. Why had he felt the need to share that with me? Had he been thinking about me, and it popped in his mind? I really didn't understand the man.

Dulce wrapped me in a tight hug when we met outside the salon. She was much taller than my mom and my abuela, taking after my abuelo. Her daughter Celeste had inherited the height as well.

Dulce kissed the top of my head and then whispered, "I say those boys got what they deserved." Then she raised her voice. "Which is why we must control our tempers." She smiled at Bianca, who was a year younger than me.

Bianca rolled her big brown eyes as she adjusted the straps on her light blue overalls. "We all know you're totally okay with what she did. But don't worry, I won't claw at some horrible excuse of a guy and get suspended." She hugged me, which was a lot easier since she was my height. "They'd never know it was me."

When Dulce gasped, the rest of us laughed. I had a feeling this family bonding time was going to be the best form of therapy.

Mom held the door open, and we all walked in.

Anna May, the owner of the salon, greeted us. She had her strawberry-blonde hair clipped back, putting focus on her blue eyes. "So good to see you, Veronica. I know I've met your mom, but who are these other lovely ladies?"

After I introduced everyone, Anna May took us to some chairs. She gasped when she saw my nails. "Veronica, what did you do?" Her southern drawl was thick and boisterous for such a small frame.

Betty, one of the nail techs, came hustling out from the back, her high heels clinking against the tile in a fury. She handed me a glass with her famous strawberry lemonade, sat down, and then set her chin in the palm of her hand. "Tell us everything, honey. Don't leave a single detail out."

I handed her my phone. "First, can you take a before picture of us?"

Betty snapped a picture of us in our chairs, and then handed back the phone. I scrolled through the filters, trying to find the best one. I settled on a glowing effect and uploaded it to my private account.

As Anna May went to work fixing my nails, I told them everything that happened with DeShawn and his goons. Well, not *everything*. For some reason, I couldn't mention how they kept saying I was fat. It was easier to say they kept calling me ugly. I wasn't ashamed about that. Not really. Although, the more I thought about it, being fat did make me ugly. I really was a disgusting pig.

"You better not listen to a word they say," Anna May said as soon as I finished with the story. "You're pretty as a peach." She motioned to my family members. "I see exactly where you get it from."

Abuela grinned. "No wonder you love coming here, Veronica. These ladies are sharp."

Anna May winked at her. "Just pointing out the obvious."

"Well," Betty said, working on my mom's nails, "I say those boys got what they deserved. They have absolutely no manners. They should be the ones suspended."

"That's what I said!" Dulce tsked. "The principal got it all wrong. Our Veronica here is a wonderful young lady."

Mom sighed. "A wonderful young lady that made a mistake. Violence is never the answer."

I sat back in the cushy seat. "I know, Ma. I messed up. But they're as much to blame as I am. They didn't even get a slap on the wrist."

Anna May sighed. "I hate seeing what they've done to you."

I shared a confused look with my mom before I spoke. "What do you mean?" For a moment, I worried she was going to point out all my extra weight.

Anna May motioned to my baggy shirt and shorts. "You used to have so much pizazz with your entire appearance. You carried yourself with so much confidence."

Feeling confident in my skin was difficult when everything I owned highlighted all the folds and cellulite.

"And so much courage," Betty put in.

My family let out a chorus of, "Mm, hmm."

"I've looked up to you since I was little," Bianca said.

"You have?" Did I really have people watching me like that?

Bianca grabbed a section of her long brown hair and picked at the split ends. "You're like a superhero to me."

Dulce chuckled. "It's true. I used to catch her talking to herself in the mirror, pretending she was you. It was so adorable." She smiled at me. "And it warmed my heart knowing *you* were her role model."

"Aww, thank you Bianca," I said. "And Tita."

"Victoria's Secret" by Jax came on the overhead speaker.

"I *love* this song," Bianca said.

The lyrics were everything I was feeling. Thank goodness more artists sang body positivity songs. The world needed them. *I* needed them. If only I would apply the confidence they suggested to my life.

My phone buzzed in my pocket, and I tensed. Had DeShawn found another way to get through to me?

"What's wrong, Veronica?" Abuela asked.

"What?" I cleared my throat. "Oh, nothing. My phone buzzed but I can't get to it."

Abuela motioned for me to twist my body, so I did as told. She reached back and retrieved my phone from my pocket. I prayed the whole time it wasn't anything bad.

Although, this small part of me hoped it was so I'd have a reason to confide in my family about all the nasty messages I'd been receiving.

Abuela arched an eyebrow. "Who's Samson?"

I let out a breath of relief. Nothing bad. "He's Taylor's brother. And my friend."

Abuela narrowed her eyes at me. "Just a friend?"

"Yes, Abuelita." I couldn't hide the annoyance in my tone. I really didn't want a lecture on top of everything. "He's just a friend."

"Huh." Abuela squinted at the screen. "Yet he starts the conversation with, 'hey, beautiful!' Do all your *friends* call you beautiful?"

I wanted to reach over and take my phone, but Anna May had both my hands occupied.

"Yes, actually," I said. "Daphne and Taylor say that kind of stuff to me all the time."

Mom nodded. "It's true. I've heard them."

Abuela harrumphed. "Well, it's best not to have friends who are boys, Veronica. Nothing good can come from that."

"Ma!" My mom said. "Veronica said he's just a friend, which means he's *just* a friend." She looked at me. "There is some truth to that, though, V. Lines can get blurry. Better to not have the temptation there."

"What temptation, Ma?" I asked. "The temptation to have fun? The temptation to talk?"

Mom scolded me with her eyes. "The temptation to do things boys and girls shouldn't do until they're married."

"Don't worry, Mom," I said, not holding back the sarcasm in my tone. "Last time I checked, Samson and I weren't having casual sex like most friends do."

Dulce and Bianca broke out in a loud laugh.

"Veronica!" Mom blew out a deep breath. "Let's not drop the 's' word like that in public, okay? And make fun of me all you want, but I've heard of the term 'friends with benefits.' I'm hip like that."

Betty leaned toward Anna May, her voice low. "I wish Veronica brought these ladies with her all the time. This is fun."

Anny May chuckled. "Agree."

"Oh!" Abuela wiggled her eyebrows. "He sent a shirtless photo."

"What?" I leaned toward her. "Let me see." Samson sent me a shirtless picture? Why would he do that? My cheeks warmed, which was insane because I'd seen him without his shirt before. It was a common occurrence in the Thomas household with six boys around, especially when they were playing basketball or swimming in their pool.

Abuela showed me the screen with no shirtless photo.

No photo at all. "Friends, huh? Then why were you so excited to see him without his shirt?"

Silence hung in the air before Mom broke out in her deep laugh on the other side of me, and soon we were all laughing. Leave it to my abuela to pull a stunt like that.

Yet, thinking of Samson without a shirt made me blush for a reason I couldn't explain.

CHAPTER THIRTEEN

After dinner that night, I locked myself in my room. Which meant moving the dresser in front of the door since I didn't have a lock. I needed some time to myself without anyone barging in and ruining my peaceful moment.

I had *Jane the Virgin* on the TV, a bag of flaming hot Cheetos, a giant Snickers bar, and a strawberry lemonade I'd made myself using real strawberries and lemons we grew in our backyard. Jane and Michael would take me to my happy place like they always did.

I was only ten minutes into the episode when I saw a text come in on my phone.

Samson: You okay, V?

Crap. I'd never responded to him earlier when I was at the nail salon. I scrolled up to see what he had sent.

> Samson: Hey, beautiful! Tay told me you got suspended thanks to not-worth-it (my new nickname for the ex).

> Samson: Guy is a total loser and way off base.

I swallowed, heat rising in my cheeks. Had Taylor told him DeShawn had called me fat? She couldn't have, because *I* didn't even tell her that. I told her and Daphne the same version I'd told my mom and my abuela: that they all called me ugly.

> Samson: You're gorgeous, V. Never let anyone tell you otherwise.

I have no idea what came over me, but I found myself video calling Samson. I needed to see his face. Thank goodness I hadn't taken off my make-up yet.

He immediately accepted the call, his hot face filling up my screen, and I was suddenly grateful Dad sprung for the high-quality phone.

"Hey!" Samson sat on the bed in his dorm room. "How's our suspendee?"

I shrugged. "Been better. I honestly never thought I'd get suspended."

"Especially when nothing happened to not-worth-it." Samson shook his head. "Did he really smash a gansito in your face? And a homemade one at that?"

"Yep. But I got him back with about five."

Samson tsked. "Such a waste of delicious gansitos."

For some reason, the way he said 'gansitos' made me smile. It was adorably not quite right.

"My abuela will make more."

"When she does, offer them to someone who'd actually appreciate it." He pointed to his chest. "Like me."

"If you weren't so far away, I would." It had never really bothered me, Samson being away at college. I didn't think about it too much. But I really wanted to drive over and see him in person.

Granted, USC was only about an hour away, depending on LA traffic, but my parents would never let me drive up there on my own.

Samson frowned. "Don't remind me. Wish I could be there to give you a hug." His eyes lit up. "But I'm coming home again this weekend. It's BYU's big rivalry game. Most of the fam is watching it together. You should come watch it with us!"

I wasn't into football. DeShawn had turned me off to it. But I found myself saying, "I'd love to."

Samson grinned his infamous all-is-well-in-the-world smile, and it was suddenly super-hot in my room. Had someone cranked up the heater?

"What are you doing right now?" Samson asked, a genuine curiosity in his eyes.

"Watching *Jane the Virgin*." I wiggled a flaming hot Cheeto in front of the camera. "And eating these." I popped it in my mouth.

"Now I want Cheetos." Samson leaned back against his headboard. "I've never seen *Jane the Virgin*. Is it any good?"

My jaw dropped in total shock. It took me a moment to compose myself. "Samson, how have you not seen the greatest TV show with the greatest characters and most perfect couple of all time?"

His eyebrows shot up. "Of all time? Wow."

"It really hits home for me." I looked over at the flower

face on my wall. "Really close to home." I turned my attention back to the screen. "You *have* to watch it."

He pursed his lips. "I think I'm going to pass. But thanks for the suggestion."

"What? Why?"

His expression screamed, "*Are you seriously asking me that?*" He sighed. "V, you claimed The Wizards of Waverly Place was 'a masterpiece' and Selena Gomez was 'a goddess.' How can I trust you after that?"

I bit back a laugh. "First of all, how do you even remember that? Second, I stand by my opinion of Selena Gomez being a goddess."

He nodded his head in agreement at that.

"And third, I was like nine or something. My tastes have evolved."

He blew out a long breath like he was contemplating whether to believe me or not. When I clasped my hands together in a plea and batted my eyelashes, he caved.

He leaned out of view and then came back with his laptop. "Where can I watch it?"

I listed off all the streaming sites he could use until we found one he had.

"Want to watch it together?" His tone held a lot of hope.

I pressed 'back' on my remote and scrolled to the first episode of season one. "Hit play on the count of three?"

"Press play on three, or right after three?" he asked.

"On three."

He grinned. "Only way to do it. One. Two."

I pressed play.

Even though I'd seen the show a million times, it was fun watching it with someone who was seeing it for the first time.

When the episode ended, I eagerly waited for his review.

"I have to say," Samson said, "that was hilarious and about a million times better than Wizards of Waverly Place. Is it weird that the narrator is my favorite character so far?"

I shook my head, laughing. "Nope. I love him, too. He adds the perfect layer to the show."

"The icing on top." Samson reached forward and closed his laptop, and then sat back on his bed. "The whole flower thing, though. That's ... uh ... intense."

I practically snorted my laugh. "You have no idea." I changed the view on my phone so I could show him the flower face on my wall. "My abuela made that for me."

"Is that *you*?" Samson asked in awe.

"Yep." I changed the view back to me. "My constant reminder to keep my flower fully intact and blooming."

Samson smiled. "That is the greatest thing ever."

"It's the most horrifying thing ever." I took a sip of my strawberry lemonade. "My mom and abuela are constantly reminding me."

"They're looking out for you."

"They're being overprotective."

"But it's out of love. That means something, right?"

I sighed. It did. It all came from a good place. They viewed being intimate with someone as something special and only shared between the two people in love.

I thought about my dad, and his affair hit a lot harder than it ever had.

"Whoa," Samson said, pulling my attention back to him. "What just happened?"

A tear slid down my cheek. "Thinking about my dad. He obviously doesn't view it the same way my mom does. If it was so special, why would he do it with someone else?"

"That's a good question." Samson rubbed the crescent-shaped scar at the side of his eye. "At the end of the day, he's still human. Humans make mistakes no matter how good our intentions are. Maybe it was a moment of weakness or a mid-life crisis. Maybe there's more behind it than you know. But that doesn't change how you should view it. It is special, V. Don't let him make you think otherwise."

I wiped away more tears that escaped. "I know. It makes it sting that much more."

Samson pulled the phone closer to his cute face. "Man, I want to hug you right now."

"And I want you to hug me. Why are you in college again?"

He shrugged. "Something about an education and having a better life. I don't know. But I'm giving you a big hug the next time I see you."

"I'm looking forward to it."

And I really, really was.

CHAPTER FOURTEEN

Taylor had gone into full party-planner mode, handing out tasks to everyone. She assigned me the privilege to help my abuela with the food. I was so excited to keep my hands and mind busy with learning more about something I love.

Since I was suspended for the week, I spent most of it over at my abuela's home. The thing I loved about my abuela was that she made her food from scratch. She grew her own fruits and vegetables. If she'd had the land and money, she would have her own livestock as well.

I smiled at the thought of having my own little farm one day. Although, I couldn't do the whole waking up before dawn to get to work. I'd need farmhands.

I'd barely stepped into my abuela's kitchen when she placed a piece of paper on the table in front of me.

"Here's the menu." Abuela tied a blue apron around her waist. "I'm thinking we can do a practice run of all the dishes so we get them to perfection. Then, in the days leading up to the event, we can prepare the real thing." She glanced at the list. "We're going to need help at that time, though. There will be so much to do."

"Aside from the decorations, everything else should be good to go at that point, so we should have lots of people who can help us."

Abuela moved toward the stove. She had her hair pinned back with a barrette with a red flower I'd gotten her for her birthday. "We can't have *anyone*. We need people that know what they're doing."

"Daphne's mom, Laura, and her boyfriend, Cody, offered to help. They are both good in the kitchen and chill under pressure. Same goes with Taylor's oldest brother, Neo."

"Perfect." Abuela turned on the oven, paused, muttered something under her breath, and turned it back off. She hustled over to the fridge and brought out a bunch of bags filled with fruits and vegetables. "First things first, we're going to make sure you perfect the art of cutting."

I rolled my eyes. "I know how to cut fruits and veggies, Abuelita."

She placed a hand on her hip. "Efficiently?"

I shrugged. "I get the job done."

With a shake of her head and a sigh, she scurried over to her knife set hanging on a magnet on the wall. They were all professional grade and way out of my price range. But if I ever wanted to be a professional chef, I'd have to make the investment.

"Come, mija." She retrieved a tomato from a bag and placed it on the cutting board. "Watch and learn."

My abuela made everything look so easy, but it took me a few attempts to catch on. By the end of the day, I was cutting almost as well as she did.

"Prep is sometimes the most time-consuming part of

cooking." Abuela set her knives in the sink. "Perfecting that makes the rest of the process much smoother."

My phone buzzed in my pants pocket. I couldn't help but smile when I saw a text from Samson.

> Samson: We're watching another episode tonight, right? Maybe two. Or three. Or the rest of season one. Up to you.

Abuela came to my side and clucked her tongue. "Just a friend, huh?"

I gently pushed her arm. "Yes, Abuelita. He's been trying to help fill all my extra time due to the suspension."

She swept out her arms. "That's why you're here. You don't need a stinking boy."

I scrolled through my phone until I found a picture of Samson and Ryker. They were in their backyard, laughing about something. It was so perfect and carefree that I'd snapped a picture when no one was paying attention. I showed the picture to my abuela and pointed at Samson. "This is him."

She narrowed her eyes at the picture, then took my phone from me. She soaked in the screen, her face passive. She finally handed me back my phone. "I guess I can see why you want to see him without his shirt."

"Abuela!" But the biggest smile was on my face.

She smiled softly before she broke out in warm laughter.

The second I walked in the door when I got home, I headed for my bedroom. I made it halfway up the stairs before I heard my mom.

"Veronica! It's dinner time."

I groaned. Another stupid thing we'd been doing since Dad came back in the picture was eating dinner as a family every night.

I leaned over the railing and called out. "I ate at Abuela's! I'll be in my room."

I turned to head up the stairs when my mom hustled out of the kitchen, her hips swishing back and forth as she walked. She tried to wrap her hand around the rail but there were too many marigolds and sugar skulls in the way. She settled with glaring up at me. "Do I have to remind you that you're suspended? You're lucky I didn't ground you on top of it. We're eating as a family. I made tacos."

It took everything in me to squish down the anger. I took a few beats to compose myself. "Are there poblano peppers?"

She tilted her head, wearing her expression that said, "I can't believe you asked me that question."

She always grilled them for me. They were a must for my tacos, along with an unhealthy amount of sour cream and cheese.

"Fine." I stormed down the stairs, making my annoyance known.

Although, the second I really took a whiff of the delicious aromas, my stomach growled, eager to eat. All the spices, fresh Pico, cheese, and beef were most likely what heaven smelled like.

Dad and Luciana finished setting the table. Javier sat down, doing a live stream about the perfect hair products.

Dad smiled when he saw me. "I remember how you and Javy used to love to help me set the table. We'd pick a song and sing and dance as we did."

Luciana frowned. "How come we don't do that anymore? It sounds fun."

Dad shrugged. "Guess they got too grown and cool for their old man."

"I'll never get too cool for you," Luciana said as she set the silverware next to a plate.

Another random memory from Dad. Honestly, we did have a lot of fun with him as kids. But he was the one who'd changed. Not us.

Mom leaned down next to Javier and looked into the camera. "Sorry, ladies, but it's time for Hottie Javy to have dinner." She kissed him on the temple, making him flinch. She glanced at the screen again, squinting her eyes. "Who is *hot4javy* and why do they want to watch you eat?"

Javier waved to his followers. "I'll be back after dinner." He set down his phone and wiped at his temple. "Could you be more embarrassing, Ma?"

She kissed him on the temple again. "Of course."

I shook my head as I sat down across from Javier. "Someone wants to watch you eat?"

He sat back, leaning his arm on the back of the chair. "It's sexy."

I tilted my head to the side, my tone hitching up. "Is it?"

The doorbell rang.

"I'll get it!" Luciana yelled while sprinting for the door. Seconds later the door swung open, and her loud voice carried through the front room. "Who are you?"

I instantly knew the chuckle and for some reason, I found myself blushing.

"I'm Samson."

"Okay ..." Luciana sounded bored.

"Is Veronica here?" Samson asked, the smile in his tone obvious.

Mom and Dad both looked at me wearing curious expressions. He'd never come to our house before. Taylor must have told him where I lived. I'd kept it a secret for so long, but now the truth was out there in the world whether I wanted it to be or not.

"Yeah, but we're eating dinner," Luciana said. "Come back in like an hour or something."

I bolted from the chair and ran to the front door, getting there right as Luciana slammed the door in Samson's face.

"Luci!" My hand slid onto the door when it was about to close, crushing my fingers between the door and doorframe. I clenched my jaw, biting back the swear words that wanted to fly.

Samson pushed the door open and stepped inside, his free hand wrapping around mine. The other hand held a large bouquet of white orchids. "You okay? That looked painful."

I swallowed, unable to find my voice. What was wrong with me?

"Oh, sure, come on in." Luciana dramatically sighed and walked away.

Samson's skin was so warm. Concern rested in his gorgeous eyes. No, not gorgeous. They were ... yeah, okay, they were gorgeous.

This was so wrong.

"What are you doing here?" I'd texted with him earlier about watching Jane the Virgin together through a video call.

Samson, still holding my hand, bent down and quietly said, "I couldn't wait any longer for that hug."

A smile crept onto my face until it fully took over.

Dad suddenly appeared at my side, clearing his throat as he stood up tall. It didn't help in the slightest since Samson had a good six inches on him. Samson dropped my hand and smiled at my dad.

"Taylor's brother, right?" Dad asked, eying the bouquet.

Samson nodded. "Yes, sir." He reached his hand out and by the grimace on Samson's face, Dad must have gripped hard.

"Aren't you in college?" Dad asked, his intense gaze taking Samson in.

Samson smiled, not missing a beat. "Yes. My professor canceled tomorrow's class, so I thought I'd make it a long weekend at home."

Mom joined us, smiling warmly at Samson. "What lovey flowers!"

Samson held them out for me. "Thought you could use some cheering up."

"Why did you choose orchids?" They were my favorite. I clutched them close to my chest like a shield and breathed them in.

Samson grinned. "Let's see. When your crush brought you roses for your quinceañera, you went off about how he didn't know you at all. You ended up smashing all of them on the ground with your unbelievably high heels."

"'*Orchids are my favorite,*'" Mom said in a terrible impersonation of me. "'*If he truly loved me, then he would know that!*'"

"I did *not* sound like that," I said, though I knew she was right.

Dad chuckled. "Oh, yes you did."

"Would you like to join us for dinner?" Mom asked Samson. "We're having tacos."

Dad shot Mom a surprised look.

"I'd love to," Samson said. "It smells amazing."

Mom linked her arm with Samson's and escorted him into the kitchen. I watched after them in shock.

Samson was about to have dinner with my family.

This was so not good.

CHAPTER FIFTEEN

Mom hurried to set another plate at the table, right next to me. While she did that, I grabbed a vase from the hutch, added some water, and set the flowers inside. The entire time I tried to get my heart to calm, but it wouldn't cooperate. All I could think about was my family permanently scarring Samson for life.

After Dad blessed the food, everyone dug in, reaching over each other to grab what they wanted. Granted, it was an everyday occurrence, but it suddenly made us look like greedy savages.

Javier reached for the bowl of shredded beef, but Luciana snatched it first, sticking her tongue out in the process.

"Don't be such a brat, Luci." Javier sat back in his chair, almost in a pout.

"Baby." Luciana took her sweet precious time setting her meat on her tortillas.

Javier snorted a laugh. "Says the girl that still sleeps with her precious *widdle* teddy bear."

Luciana eyes went wide in embarrassment. "I can say

little now! And I don't sleep with Skittles anymore!" She flushed. "I mean my teddy bear that I never gave a name."

Samson quietly chuckled next to me.

I needed to focus on something else, so I didn't die in complete humiliation. I spread out three corn tortillas on my plate. Poblano peppers were always my base layer. They sat between my mom and Samson. I motioned to them. "Can someone pass the peppers?"

Samson picked up the serving bowl and grinned as he handed it to me, our fingers brushing each other. "Save some for me. Those look yummy."

Why did every touch send me in a frenzy? It was Samson. I'd known him for years. We'd touched many times.

Why did that now sound so wrong?

Swallowing, I plopped a ton of peppers on my plate and handed the bowl back to Samson, not daring to look in his eyes.

"Javier," Samson said as he set peppers on his tortillas, "where did you get that shirt? It's amazing."

Javier grinned. "Made it. I'm an artist." He motioned to the red and orange abstract art on his shirt. "This is 'killing it' from my mood collection."

Samson set the bowl down. "Do you sell those?"

"I have an online store." Javier pulled out his phone but then put it back in his pocket when Mom glared at him. "I can give you the link after dinner."

"I'd love that," Samson said with a huge smile.

Javier lit up like his whole world had been made. "Oh, and call me Javy. All my friends and family do."

Dad wore a very confused expression. "You have an online store?"

Javier's smile faded. "I have now for about a year."

A year? This family had some serious issues. Communication had to be one of our biggest flaws.

Mom reached over and patted his hand. "He's been doing quite well. He'll be all saved up for college in no time."

At least Mom knew about it. I shot a glance at Dad, who looked impressed. Javier's smile came back.

"So, Samson," Dad said in a booming voice. "What are you studying in school?"

Samson's smile stayed, and I was so grateful he was so ... Samson. An optimistic guy with thick skin.

"Engineering." Samson rolled up his taco, making sure everything stayed inside. "I used to intern at my dad's business, which is where I fell in love with it."

Mom's eyes lit up. "Oh, that's great! Where are you going to school?"

"USC," Samson said.

I held my breath. My dad *hated* USC. With UCLA being his alma mater, he was a diehard fan.

Dad chewed on the food in his mouth, his jaw tight, as he stared at Samson.

Mom leaned over and patted Samson's arm. "Good for you." Her sharp gaze went to Dad. "USC is a wonderful university."

Samson's confused gaze found mine.

"Our Veronica is going to UCLA," Dad said with pride in his eyes.

I stuffed a bite of taco in my mouth. Secretly, I wanted to apply for USC in addition to UCLA. But no one knew that yet. Not even Daphne and Taylor.

For starters, it was a little closer to home, and Samson was there. The biggest, reason, though, was that it was only a half hour away from the Institute of Culinary Education. I could possibly do both at once since the culinary school was only a twelve-month program.

"Dad hates USC," Luciana suddenly said. "He says they're vacant and strippers and Cheat Carroll is the worst coach in history."

Samson still looked incredibly confused, and I didn't blame him.

"What are you talking about, Luci?" I asked.

Javier sighed. "She's mixing up her words again. They had to vacate their wins and were stripped of the national championship. The Cheat Carroll thing is spot-on, though."

Understanding passed over Samson's eyes, and his resident smile came back. "Oh, I don't follow USC football. I'm a BYU fan."

Dad continued to chew his food, not saying anything. For a few minutes, an awkward silence sat in the air, no one wanting to say anything.

Dad wiped at his mouth with a napkin. "I'm assuming BYU has a good engineering program as well. Why not go there?"

Samson finished off the bite of food in his mouth before he spoke. "I wanted to be closer to home." His eyes flitted toward me for a brief second, but maybe I imagined it. "And I don't think my depression could handle Utah winters. I need the sun."

Samson had depression? Mister always happy? Maybe it was from Kylie. Maybe it was because he was human and none of us were perfect.

Dad's eyes still held some reservations. I needed to get Samson on Dad's good side.

"Hey, Dad," I said with a smile. "Did you know Samson took state in wrestling in high school?"

Dad finally looked impressed. He loved wrestling.

Then Dad had to go and make it awkward by saying, "How come you're not wrestling in college? I mean, if you were that good."

Samson kept the smile on his face. "Don't get me wrong, I love wrestling. But I really wanted to focus on my studies instead."

Dad bounced back, clearly happy with that answer.

Mom smiled at Samson. "Are you dating anyone? I bet there are a ton of pretty girls at US ... your university."

"No, I'm not seeing anyone," Samson said as he assembled another taco.

Relief rushed through me. Why was I relieved? Samson's dating life had no impact on me.

"Good." Dad's gruff voice surprised all of us. "Just like you said, you should focus on your studies. No need for unnecessary distractions."

Samson grinned. "You sound like my parents."

Dad's demeanor softened. "They sound like smart people."

"They are," I said. "Everyone in the Thomas family is very nice and respectful."

"I keep saying the same thing to Veronica," Mom said. "No need for boys. She's way too young to be in a serious relationship. Besides, boys put too much pressure on girls. We don't want Veronica to make any mistakes."

"Ma!" If I could have disappeared, I would have.

Samson softly smiled. "No worries. My family is the same as yours because of our religion. We believe in saving ourselves until marriage."

Both Mom and Dad perked up at that, sharing an impressed gaze.

"Well, that's rare," Mom said. "And very honorable."

"Save what until marriage?" Luciana asked with a confused look on her face.

Javier patted her on the head. "You'll understand when you're older. Remember, you're still *widdle*."

Luciana pushed him away from her. "I'm not a baby! I'm almost ten!"

I sighed. Why were we even having this conversation? It definitely wasn't dinner talk, and it most certainly wasn't first-time-meeting-the-family talk.

Samson set his hand on the back of my chair. "Speaking of marriage, I hear you're renewing your vows, Mr. and Mrs. Rodriguez."

Mom gazed lovingly at my dad. "We are. Time to put the past in the past and focus on the future."

"Exactly." Dad looked at me a moment when he said that. Then he moved his focus to Samson. "I think Taylor is going to do a wonderful job with the celebration."

"She's so excited about it." Samson's fingers lightly rubbed my back, and it took everything in me to stay composed. "That was very nice of you to give her this opportunity. I know she won't let you down."

"We have every faith in her," Mom said as she teared up. She waved a hand in front of her face. "Excuse me. I don't know what's come over me. Guess I'm getting overly emotional and sentimental in my old age."

"You've always been overly emotional," Javier said.

She narrowed her eyes at him. "Watch your tongue, young man."

"Love makes us irrational," Dad said, looking across the table at my mom. "But it's so worth it."

"Yes, it is." Mom genuinely looked happy, and I so didn't get it.

Dad had completely broken their vows. He'd shattered

her heart. How was it possible for her to mend it so quickly? How did you get over that?

"Dinner was delicious," Samson said. "Thanks for letting me join you."

"You're welcome any time." Mom grabbed her plate and stood. "Hope you saved room for dessert. We have a fresh batch of sopapillas."

Samson rubbed his stomach. "I always have room for dessert." He stood and pushed in his chair. "Why don't Veronica and I clean up? The rest of you can take it easy."

Javier immediately jumped up and pulled his phone out of his pocket. "Sounds good to me. I have followers needing to see me." He left the kitchen without as much as a glance in our direction.

"You don't have to do that," Mom said.

"I insist," Samson said with a smile. "You cooked it all. At least I can do this."

I didn't really enjoy the thought of cleaning everything up, but I did enjoy the thought of being alone with Samson for a bit.

I couldn't believe he wasn't itching to get out of here.

We each grabbed some plates and took them into the kitchen. Seconds after they had left our hands, Samson had me in a bear hug, holding me close.

I sank into him, welcoming the warmth and smell of his aftershave.

I'd hugged Samson many times over the years, but never like this. Never in a way that made me feel like everything was going to be okay. Never in a way that got my heart racing and wanting to run my nails along his back. Which I quickly realized I was actually doing. But Samson didn't seem to mind.

He softly kissed the top of my head. "Glad we finally got to do this."

"Same." I pulled back and looked up at him, practically straining my neck from being so close. Samson was almost a foot taller than me. "Thank you for the flowers. They're exactly what I needed."

"Thought they could help cheer you up." Samson smiled, but it was different from his normal smile that said he was happy to be here. A want nestled on his lips that took be by surprise. I found myself pushing up on my tiptoes so I could be closer to him.

"Excuse me." Dad suddenly appeared next to us, awkwardly squishing his way between Samson and me. "Gotta get some water from the tap."

Samson and I stood in awkward silence as Dad filled a glass with water. When he finished, he stepped back, glancing between the two of us. "Yeah, that's better. Good amount of space. Let's keep it that way."

As Dad walked away, I clutched the counter, trying my hardest to not keel over in humiliation.

My family really would be the death of me.

CHAPTER SIXTEEN

After we finished cleaning and had some dessert, I invited Samson up to my room so we could watch *Jane the Virgin*.

Samson carried the vase of flowers for me so we could put them in my room.

As we ascended the stairs, Mom's booming voice came from the front room. "Keep the door open!"

I cringed. "We will, Ma."

Samson held in a laugh.

"And keep all your pretty—" Mom started.

I took Samson by the hand and yanked him up the rest of the stairs.

Mom's voice faded into the background. "—petals intact."

My face was on fire by the time we stepped into my room. Why had I invited him up? I should have known Mom would do that.

But Samson casually walked into my room and set the vase of flowers on the nightstand. With a smirk, he picked up the frame next to the vase. *Never trust guys.*

He held it up before setting back in place. "I have one of these in my room as well."

I rolled my eyes, making him laugh.

He soaked in the whole room. "I've always wondered what your room looked like."

"You have?" I couldn't squash the shock in my tone.

"Rooms say a lot about a person." He stopped in front of the infamous flower depiction of me. "This is really amazing." He looked over his shoulder at me. "Your family is extremely talented."

I pointed to my vanity. "My abuelo made that."

Samson went over to examine it, stuffing his hands in his pockets like he didn't dare touch it. "Mom's side or dad's?"

"Dad's." I sat down on the edge of my bed. "He owns a woodworking business. He's about to retire, so my uncle Felípé is going to take over the business."

Samson took a seat next to me. "Does your dad work there?"

I shook my head. "No, he never got into woodworking. Neither did my other uncle, Rubén. Dad opted for being a CPA while Rubén went the lawyer route." I thought of his huge estate in Anaheim Hills. "And did *very* well for himself."

Samson tapped his arm against mine. "So being a genius runs in your family."

"I'm not a genius," I said.

"And you're humble as well." Samson looked at my TV hanging on the wall. "Is it *Jane the Virgin* time yet?"

Samson kicked off his shoes and got cozy on my bed. I immediately thought of the night Jane and Michael met for the first time. Michael stayed up late watching telenovelas with Jane, wanting to know more about them because she was interested in them. Was Samson really interested in the show? Or interested in it because *I* was? Either way, it was ridiculously sweet.

As my face heated, I snatched the remote and sat near Samson as I turned on the show, trying to keep my heart from beating right out of my chest.

Samson Thomas was sitting on my bed. I'd never had a guy on my bed for any reason.

Once I got the show going, I turned and looked at the spot next to him. Did I sit next to him? Near him? On the very edge of the bed? Maybe on the floor in front of the bed.

Samson held up his arm. "Come here."

When he turned on his Samson-smile, I melted. I crawled over and laid next to him, resting my head on the side of his chest. His arm settled around me and his warmth cradled every part of me.

As we watched the show, we kept laughing at the same moments, looking at each other during the 'you've got to be kidding me' moments, and tensing during the steamy moments.

My feelings for Samson were all over the place. I really liked him. He'd been such a great friend over the years. But there was something stronger between us that I couldn't deny. I wasn't ready for another relationship. I needed to figure my heart and head out before I dived into something serious.

Everything with DeShawn had made me completely lose my way and myself. Samson wasn't just some guy. There was potential for something astronomical between us, and I didn't want to blow it by diving into a relationship while I was a hot mess of horrible self-esteem.

Then there was the doubt that Samson could ever look

at me like *that*. The girls at USC were probably gorgeous and so mature.

Samson ran his fingers up and down my bare arm and I held in a shiver. He wouldn't do that if he didn't like me, right? Samson didn't strike me as the type of guy who toyed with girls. He was classy.

I found myself taking my acrylic nail and drawing swirls on his chest. He pulled me a little closer and my heart surged. This wasn't a friendly cuddle. Friends didn't do this, right? I'd never done this with a guy I didn't like.

Was Samson trying to comfort me? Trying to make me feel better after everything I'd been through?

He placed his hand over mine that was on his chest and looked at my fresh nails. "Went with the Halloween theme." He brushed his thumb over my ring fingernail. There was a black spiderweb drawn onto an orange background. "It looks good."

"Thanks." Wow. Totally breathless. "I love my nail lady."

He let go of my hand and wrapped his arm around me, so both arms held me close. Yeah, friends *so didn't* do this.

I thought about pushing away since I wasn't looking for a relationship but being in Samson's arms felt so good. And so natural.

A light knock sounded on the door, and I turned to see Javier standing in the doorway holding a bowl of popcorn in one hand. His other hand covered his eyes.

"I've been instructed to join you." Javier's hand stayed put. "Are you fully dressed? Can I come in?"

I rolled my eyes as I sat up and straightened out my shirt. "Yes, Javy."

He lowered his hand and smiled sheepishly. "I'll have

you know, Dad wanted to be the one to come in here, but I intervened."

"Thanks for that," I said. Dad being in here would be traumatic.

Javy came to the side of the bed and motioned between Samson and me. "I've also been instructed to break you two up. So, scooch."

With a sigh, I moved over on the bed to give Javier room. Once he was settled, he showed me the bowl of popcorn. "There are hot tamales in here, too."

I was about to reach in and grab some, when Samson took my hand and held up my nails for Javier to see.

"Ever thought about putting your artwork on nails?" Samson asked. "You could do preprinted stickers that press on or something."

Javier nodded. "I like the way you think. I also like that you also took another opportunity to hold my sister's hand."

Samson's face was deadpan. "I have no idea what you're talk about."

When Javier looked away, Samson winked at me.

I grabbed a huge handful of popcorn and hot tamales and stuffed them into my mouth.

Minutes later, Mom walked by and peeked her head into the room, smiling when she saw Javier sitting between Samson and me.

She nodded her head toward the flower depiction of me on the wall. "Look at all those pretty petals. Still intact and stronger than ever."

I sunk down on the bed, wanting to disappear under the covers.

She tapped the doorway. "So glad we can keep it that way." She pushed away from the door. "You kids have fun." She disappeared down the hall.

Javier broke out in a loud laugh, and soon Samson joined him. At least some people in the room were enjoying themselves.

To me, it was another reason why Samson wouldn't want to date me. My parents were overly protective and unbearably embarrassing.

CHAPTER SEVENTEEN

With my mom and dad ramping up their parent game, I was itching for Ryker to get back in town. I'd tried looking online for places to get grasshoppers, bees, and snakes but the places I found were either outrageously priced or sending out the creepy vibe.

With it taking so long, I almost felt like the universe was trying to intervene and tell me I shouldn't go through with my plan. Well, screw you, universe.

Taylor had said Ryker would be home tonight, so I had to get through the day.

Unfortunately, as part of my punishment from the principal, the day started off with me having to apologize to DeShawn and Christian.

We were meeting in front of the school before first period started. Christian and DeShawn demanded that their parents be there "for their safety" so I demanded my parents be there so they didn't treat me unfairly.

When we got to the school and I saw all of them huddled there, none of them happy, I was so thankful my parents came along, including my dad. Unlike breaking apart my hug with Samson, his dad game would be appreciated today. My dad may have been a flake, but he was very protective of his children. It was one of his redeeming qualities.

My mom wanted me to wear a nice dress, but I didn't have any that fit. So, I had to roll up in a baggy tee and sweats, making the whole thing more humiliating. Maybe it was time to suck up my pride and have Daphne make me new clothes. It beat going to the store, trying things on, and seeing my actual size. Daphne could take my measurements and not reveal the numbers to me.

But then she'd know the numbers. Did I want Daphne to know what size I was?

Mom smoothed out my long hair, sweeping a lot to the front so it covered up some of my tee. At least my hair and make-up were perfect.

Mom and Dad were both dressed for work. Mom wore a dark green dress and Dad had one of his nice suits on, so they were more than presentable.

My heart hammered in my chest as we approached DeShawn, Christian, and their parents. Principal O'Shaughnessy had his hands clasped in front of him as he stood tall with his shoulders squared. He wore a black and gold tie, same colors as our school.

"Miss Rodriguez," Principal O'Shaughnessy said. "Mr. and Mrs. Rodriguez. Thank you for coming today. I believe Miss Rodriguez has something she'd like to say to Mr. Mack and Mr. Wilson."

DeShawn smirked at me, probably knowing how much I hated this whole thing. It was another win for him to add to his tally.

Christian, to give him credit, looked terrified. He clung to his mom like he was a five-year-old about to enter a classroom for the first time. He had white bandages on his cheeks, probably overselling how bad the scratches were. Or maybe I had done more damage than I thought. My stomach clenched, hoping the latter wasn't true. I didn't want to be labeled a violent person. I typically wasn't.

I chewed at my bottom lip, then stopped myself. That was a bad habit that was difficult to break.

All I wanted was to get the whole thing over with. "I'm sorry DeShawn and Christian. Especially to you, Christian. You got caught up in something that didn't even involve you."

"I'm going to have scars," Christian said in a shaky voice. "I can't go into the NFL looking like this."

I took a deep breath and stopped myself before I reminded him there was no way on this earth he had NFL talent. I'd be surprised if a college team even wanted him.

Christian's mom rubbed his arm, consoling her son. She looked at me with such hatred, and she didn't even know me. "How could you do this?" She looked at my parents. "Why would you teach her this is acceptable behavior?"

"We didn't," Mom said sharply. "We never resort to violence in our family."

Mr. Wilson scoffed. "Your daughter tried to claw my son's eyes out. I'd say that's violent."

"I wasn't trying to claw his eyes out!" I snapped. Then I flushed. I needed to keep calm. They guys had already taken so much from me.

Mrs. Mack motioned to Christian. "Then what do you call that, Veronica? He has gouges in his cheeks that required stitches!"

I pulled back in surprise. "Stitches? There's no way I scratched him *that* hard."

Mr. Mack glanced at DeShawn. "You dodged a bullet

with that one, son. You could have ended up on a Dateline special."

"Okay." My dad stepped forward. "That's enough. My daughter made a mistake and apologized for it. You're all overreacting."

"Overreacting?" Mrs. Wilson placed a hand on her chest. "She's permanently damaged my son. He'll never recover from this."

"That's ridiculous," Mom said. "If it's so bad, let us see."

"You want us to remove the bandages and interrupt the healing process?" Mr. Wilson practically spat the words.

"I thought it couldn't be healed," Mom spat right back.

Dad placed a hand on Mom's shoulder and spoke softly. "Kemena."

"Why are we even standing here listening to this?" Mr. Wilson said. "They're probably not even here legally. Can't we kick them back over the border?"

Heat flared to life inside of me. He couldn't be serious.

Mom and Dad went rigid next to me. We'd heard this stuff before, but it had been a while.

The entire Mack family had taken a considerable step away from the Wilsons.

"That was uncalled for," Mr. Mack said.

"Was it?" Mr. Wilson asked. "Do you know for a fact that they aren't illegals?" He motioned to my outfit. "They can't even afford to get their daughter proper clothes."

Not sure what that had to do with anything, but I really hated that he had pointed it out.

"We were born here!" Mom shook with anger. "Were you, *Mr. Wilson*? Where's your proof, huh?"

Principal O'Shaughnessy finally spoke. "I assure you, the Rodriguez family are American citizens. While we don't tolerate violence at our school, we also don't tolerate hate and racism. I think this meeting is over. Miss Rodriguez has apologized, which is what we came here for. I think we all need to move on from this incident."

"I agree," Mrs. Mack said. She couldn't look in the direction of the Wilson family. Christian and his mom hadn't even so much as flinched at the dad's comment, like they wondered the same thing as him.

Mom took a step toward the Wilson family, her head held high. "I'm very proud of my daughter and the woman she's becoming. She gets better grades than both these boys combined. You claim she's violent, but you're over here raising your son to be a racist and a bully."

"A bully?" Mrs. Wilson asked. "What do you mean?"

Mom pointed back at me. "DeShawn and Christian have been bullying my daughter. They've been sending her horrible messages, calling her ugly and taunting her. Is this the type of man you're all trying to raise?"

"My son would never do that," Mrs. Mack said, looking completely offended. "He knows better."

DeShawn nodded as he put an arm around his mom. "Of course, I wouldn't. That's ridiculous."

"Mom?" I stepped toward her. "How do you know that?" I'd been trying to keep the whole thing a secret.

She placed a hand on my arm. "When I noticed all your social media profiles had been shut down, I was curious why." She sighed. "This morning, I checked on our home computer which has all your passwords saved. I went on and reactivated the accounts and saw all the messages."

"Why didn't you say anything?" I asked.

"I was going to after all of this. I wanted to face one problem at a time." Mom placed a hand on my cheek. "I know how stubborn you are and like to fix things yourself, but you can't do everything alone, Veronica."

Mr. Mack waved a hand. "This is nonsense. Do you have proof? Where are these so-called messages?"

DeShawn froze at that. He knew that I'd have damning evidence.

"Is this true, Miss Rodriguez?" Principal O'Shaughnessy asked. "Have they been bullying you?"

DeShawn and Christian glared at me, threatening me with their eyes. But I was so tired of everything.

"Yes, they have," I said.

DeShawn swore, causing his mom to whack him on the arm.

"Do you have the messages on your phone?" Principal O'Shaughnessy asked.

I suddenly wished I hadn't ruined my phone. I shook my head. "I got a new phone and didn't transfer the messages over. I never wanted to see them again."

"But we have some on her social media accounts," Mom quickly said. "We can print them and bring them to you."

"Is this true?" Mrs. Mack asked DeShawn.

"It's not like that," DeShawn said. "We were joking around. It was all in good fun."

My jaw dropped. Good fun? He called bombarding me with degrading messages 'fun?'

"Well," Mom said. "When we show you the proof, you can see for yourself all the *fun* they were having."

Principal O'Shaughnessy set a hand on his hip under his blazer, looking completely distraught. "I wish you would have said something earlier, Veronica. Please bring me copies of the messages and we can decide from there how to take action."

DeShawn scoffed. "You can't be serious. We've done nothing wrong!"

"It was all harmless," Christian said, though his shaking voice didn't make it easy to believe him.

"Locking herself in her room every night and eating away her feelings is not harmless!" Mom motioned to me. "Look at what you've done to her!"

"Ma!" Did she really need to point out the fact that I was fat now because of them?

Both DeShawn and Christian chuckled, but quickly stopped when their moms shot them glares.

"What?" Mom asked. "It's true. You can't fit in any of your clothes."

"And you've been eating us out of house and home." Dad finally spoke, and I really wished he hadn't.

"You're both unbelievable." I pushed past them and stormed away, heading toward my abuela's home.

This was exactly why I hadn't talked to my parents about it. They made everything worse.

CHAPTER EIGHTEEN

I huffed and puffed by the time I got to my abuela's. She lived about a mile from my school, but I hadn't walked that far in the longest time.

Mom and Dad had let me walk away. I think they knew I couldn't be reasoned with when anger overtook me. None of us could. We needed to all calm down and clear our heads.

Being in such an angry haze, I hadn't noticed any extra vehicles in front of Abuela's home. When I walked in the door and slipped off my shoes, laughter drifted from the kitchen.

There were two huge pairs of men's Nikes in the basket near the door, along with a smaller women's pair.

Shock slammed into me when I sulked into the kitchen and saw my abuela, my cousin Celeste, Samson, and Neo gathered around the island.

They all paused and turned toward me, probably hearing my heavy breathing.

"Mija? What happened to you?" Abuela asked.

Holding back the tears, I went to the fridge and took out

the pitcher of strawberry lemonade. I slammed the door closed with my foot, took the lid and tossed it on the counter, and chugged straight from the pitcher.

"Oh, dear," Abuela said.

"This isn't good," Celeste said. "I think this calls for caramel flan."

"I like the way you think," Neo said with a smile.

I lowered my pitcher in time to see Neo and Celeste share a sultry look that I so didn't want to deal with at the moment. Just another couple hitting it off within minutes of meeting each other.

Celeste got the flan from the fridge while Abuela retrieved some plates and forks. Neo watched Celeste the whole time, a look of complete infatuation in his eyes, which was completely understandable.

Celeste was gorgeous. She had deep brown eyes, long brown hair, and a body with curves in all the right places. She looked like she'd come straight from the fitness studio she owned. Her red sports bra covered the necessities and highlighted her toned abs. The girl had a major booty, and the tight spandex shorts amplified it.

I set the pitcher on the counter, finding myself right next to Samson.

Samson. He was here. In my abuela's kitchen.

I turned to him, expecting his eyes to be on Celeste like every guy she was in a room with, but his concerned eyes were on me.

Me. Sweaty, ugly, fat me.

I peeled my shirt away from sweat-soaked skin and shook it out, trying to get some air circulating.

Samson's hand landed on my hip, causing my breath to hitch.

"V, what's going on?" Samson asked, his whole body

focused directly on me, like we were the only ones in the room.

I threw my arms around him, and he held me tight. I didn't care that I was a sweaty mess. I wanted to feel his warmth. To go to my happy place and forget everything that had just happened. From one ear, I could hear everyone else shuffling around the kitchen, clinking plates and talking to each other.

My other ear smooshed against Samson's chest, hearing the steady beat of his heart. His lips pressed against the top of my head, and he held them there for a while.

After a minute, my abuela cleared her throat. "Come, mija. Have some flan and tell us everything."

I reluctantly released Samson and slumped my way to the table. They'd cut some slices of flan for everyone and had left the rest for me. I sat down in front of the ginormous piece and picked up the fork.

"First, why are all of you here?" I asked before I stuffed a large piece of flan in my mouth. The smooth caramel melted in my mouth and I almost moaned. Flan was exactly what I had needed. The coolness of it always calmed me.

"Abuela recruited me to help with the food for your parents' vow renewal." Celeste delicately pierced her flan with her fork and then slowly took a bite.

Neo watched the whole time, his Adam's apple bobbing when he swallowed. She seriously made everything sexy.

"Taylor sent us over," Samson said. It was then I noticed how close he sat. He'd scooted his chair right next to mine. "Since Neo and I were both home, she thought we could learn the menu and maybe help with some dishes."

"Mija, spill it." Abuela focused on me, her eyes narrowing as each second ticked by.

I finished off the piece in my mouth and licked my lips.

"Where do I begin? Let's see. Principal O'Shaughnessy made me apologize to the two guys making my life a living hell. Christian whined and cried like I'd ruined his entire life. DeShawn reveled in my apology like he'd won the Super Bowl." I snorted. "Like he ever would. The guy doesn't even have the talent to make the local community college's football team."

Neo put a fist to his mouth and let out an, "Ohhh!"

I stabbed my flan. "Oh, and then Christian's dad called us illegal aliens and said we needed to be kicked back over the border—"

A chorus of, "What?" and "Are you serious?" echoed around the room. I wasn't sure who said what, but it was nice to hear the same reaction that had coursed through me.

"Dad hardly said a word and didn't step up for our family," I rattled on. "Then, my parents blame DeShawn for making me fat, like they agree with him that I'm a disgusting pig."

Silence permeated the room, and I realized I'd told them all what I'd been hiding from everyone. My cheeks flared. What had I done? *Why* had I done that?

"DeShawn called you pig?" Samson asked, his voice a mix of shock and outrage.

"I'd show you the messages if I could, but they're all on my destroyed phone." I had no idea what came over me. I guess I wanted someone to understand. Someone to know what I had been going through.

I pulled up one of my old social media accounts, reactivated it, opened a string of messages from DeShawn, and handed my phone over to Samson.

He scrolled through them, his face growing angrier with each message he read. When he finished, he clenched his jaw and passed the phone to my abuela.

As Abuela read through them, Celeste and Neo stood behind her, reading over her shoulders.

"Veronica, those messages go back months," Samson said. "Months. Why haven't you said anything?"

I pushed the plate of flan away. "Because it's embarrassing! They're pounding away at me, making me feel worthless and like a complete slob. They moo and oink at me at school causing everyone to laugh at me." I pressed my hands to my eyes. "I'm so done with this. Why won't they leave me alone?"

Samson wrapped an arm around me and pulled me into him. He rested his chin on the top of my head as I sobbed and sobbed.

How had I gotten here? How had I let these guys take complete control of my life like that? They'd stripped me of my confidence.

Celeste paced the kitchen, yelling in Spanish all the ways she was going to kill DeShawn. While I was envious of her good looks, Celeste always had my back and never made me feel less than her. She was so kind and loving, which made her even hotter.

When I finally stopped crying and sat up straight, I glanced over at Neo. He wore an over-protective big brother look on his face. His hands rested firmly on his hips.

"What can I do, Veronica?" Neo asked. "Name it, and I'll do it."

I shook my head as I wiped at my tears. "I don't want to resort to violence or stoop down to their level. I want them to shut their stupid faces and leave me alone."

Celeste stopped pacing and grinned madly. "I know exactly what we're going to do."

Abuela waggled a finger. "Not if it's one of the things you were suggesting, mija."

Celeste came to my side and leaned against the table. "Veronica's right about not getting even with them. It's about making them shut up." She pointed to my tee. "Why are you wearing that? It in no way screams Veronica Rodriguez."

I tugged at my shirt. "It's one of the few things that fit."

"Then we are going to get you something that screams your name." Celeste ran her fingers down her hair. "We're bringing the old Veronica back."

I stared incredulously at her. "I can't drop fifty pounds in a blink of an eye."

Celeste jerked her head back. "What does weight have to do with that? You're still Veronica Rodriguez no matter how much you weigh. We are going to find your exact style of clothes in sizes that fit you." She eyed my hair. "We need to bring back your spunk. The fire. You've gone from passionate to angry. While both are fiery, only one is healthy."

Abuela smiled at Neo and Samson. "I truly appreciate your willingness to help, but today's lessons have been officially canceled. We will resume this next week. As for now." She turned her smile to me. "Today is all about my nieta."

CHAPTER NINETEEN

Celeste's friend, Adella, co-owned a boutique for women of all shapes and sizes. I wasn't sure how Celeste talked Adella into it, but she closed down Adelmotique so it was only Celeste, Adella, Abuela, me, and Adella's employee, Shanice.

Adella was a lot like Celeste in the physically fit department. They were all about working out and protein shakes. Shanice, on the other hand, was more like me, which helped me relax.

Shanice wore a beautiful royal blue dress with a red polka dot belt around her middle. She rocked her buzzed black hair. With her bold red lipstick, red polka dot dangling earrings, and red high heels, she looked fierce.

Shanice walked in circles around me, sizing me up. "Girl, why are you hiding your curves?"

I clutched my baggy tee. "No one needs to see my folds."

Shanice waggled her finger at me. "Nuh uh. Everybody needs to see your body. *Everybody.*" She stopped in front of me. "Veronica, listen to me loud and clear. You. Are. Beautiful. Your body is beautiful just as it is. And besides, you know what makes us who we are? Our personalities. The way we approach life. The way we treat others. It all comes down to our attitudes. Our skin doesn't do it. Our eyes, lips, every single feature on our bodies does not define us." She tapped her chest over her heart. "This is who we are, Veronica. Our souls." She took a deep breath. "Now, first we have to find your size."

I groaned. I didn't want to know my size. I'd been avoiding it. I'd been in the low single digits my entire life until recently. I knew I'd stepped into the double-digit world, but did I need to put a number to it.

"Wipe that grimace off your face." Shanice pointed to a chart of positive adjectives on the wall. "This is the scale we use. Words. Not numbers." She glanced me up and down. "I'm thinking you're either *stunning* or *exquisite*, but let's try both to be sure."

Adella nodded her head. "That's what I was thinking, too. Possibly *dazzling*, but I'm betting on *stunning*."

"Okay, I love these sizes," I said with a smile.

Celeste appeared before me with a burgundy off-the-shoulder jumpsuit with a smocked bodice and a glittery gold belt. Her smile went ear to ear. "You *have* to try this on." She glanced at the tag. "It's *stunning*, so it should fit."

With a grin, I snatched it from her and ran to the fitting room.

The second I slipped it on, I almost teared up. It fit me perfectly. I turned around, checking out every angle in the mirror, in complete shock about how soft and comfortable it was.

"Hurry up!" Abuela yelled.

I opened the door and threw out my arms. "I'm *stunning*!"

They all clapped their hands. Abuela sat in a chair near the fitting room, the biggest smile on her face. I hustled to a small platform surrounded by mirrors.

"Knew it," Adella said. She looked at Shanice. "I'm thinking that baby blue tie neck top with marigold shorts with the gold buttons lining each leg."

"Yes." Shanice snapped her fingers. "Where's that white dress we just got in? With the crisscross back?" She looked at me with sparkling eyes. "It has the cutest bow at the small of the back that is somehow adorable and sexy at the same time."

Abuela clucked her tongue. "She doesn't need anything sexy. Adorable will do."

"She needs sexy," Celeste, Adella, and Shanice said in unbelievable unison that made everyone laugh.

"You good with heels?" Adella asked.

"I'm good with all shoes, but wedges are my favorite," I said.

Shanice gasped. "We have those burgundy wedges that lace up the leg! It would go perfect with the white dress." She hustled out of sight.

I shot Celeste a quizzical glare. "Did you tell them my favorite colors?"

She nodded. "Yep. Told them a little bit of your style, too, so they would know what they're working with."

I spun around and looked at the jumpsuit in the mirror again. I couldn't believe how much I loved it. The side straps hugged my arms nicely, not too snug or baggy.

Shanice and Adella came at me with so many outfits until we found the perfect ones. All in all, I probably walked away with ten new outfits, a handful of shoes, plus some jewelry. Celeste insisted on paying for all of it. I knew her business was doing well, so I didn't feel too guilty about it.

After I hugged Shanice and Adella, we loaded up the trunk of Celeste's Audi and headed toward a salon another friend of Celeste's owned. The girl knew everyone.

Gabriel welcomed us with open arms. Like, he gave all three of us hugs. His hug for me lingered like we were old friends catching up.

His curly hair went to his shoulders, the curls loose and silky. He set his hands on my shoulders and smiled. "What are we doing today?"

Celeste hesitantly showed us her phone. "I know it's a little bold, but I think Veronica would rock it."

Gabriel's eyes lit up when he saw the picture. "Yes, she would."

I soaked in the picture of the asymmetrical haircut. One side went barely past the shoulder, and the other side was cut below the ear with the front part buzzed.

I grinned at Celeste. "I love it."

Celeste clapped her hands together and squealed. "This is going to be amazing!"

Gabriel ran his fingers through my hair. "How would you feel about burgundy highlights? I think you'd look stunning."

Celeste and I shared a smile, thinking about how that was now my size.

"I like stunning," I said.

As Gabriel went to work, all I could do was grin at the prospect of being myself again. While he put the color in my hair, I glanced down to see a text from my dad.

Dad: I'm so sorry, Veronica. I handled today all wrong. I'm still trying to find my bearings now that I'm back home. I want you to know I love you with all my heart, just as you are.

I debated for a few minutes before I finally responded.

Thanks, Dad. That means a lot.

It wasn't like everything was now magically fixed, but it was definite progress which I'd happily take.

CHAPTER TWENTY

My hair turned out perfect. When I got home and did a fashion show for my mom, brother, and sister, I forgot for a moment how mad I was at my parents for saying I was fat in front of everyone. They all raved over my clothes and hair. Even Javier.

Javier clenched his fists and shook them in the air. "Why didn't you tell me you were going to do this before you left?"

"Uh, because I didn't know," I said.

He folded his arms. "I could have done a before and after reel. Those transitions are always so awesome." His eyes slowly got wider like a plan formed in his brain. Then he grinned. "Okay, we're going to do the Princess Diaries one where they show two before pictures, hold it in front of the person, and then pull it back to reveal the princess. But we're going to switch it up and change 'princess' to 'diva.'" He looked at me. "Veronica, start by picking your favorite outfit and getting dressed. Ma and Luci, find two eight by ten photos of V we have in the house. I'll set up the equipment."

He took off with lightning speed. If the artist thing didn't work out, the guy could definitely be a director.

I changed into the off-the-shoulder burgundy jumpsuit since it matched with my new hair. I also felt incredibly hot in it.

It was fun getting the whole family involved with the process. Instead of sitting down for the reveal, I stood, with my hand on one hip, my hip jutted to the side, and my face at a tilted angle as I cranked up the Rodriguez smolder as high as it would go.

Javier added some music and posted it to my account. Then he started his own live stream on his account, telling all his followers to go check it out.

I headed back up the stairs, eager to hang all my stuff up in my closet, when my mom stopped me.

"I owe you an apology." Mom teared up and took my hand in hers. "I shouldn't have said that about you. You're beautiful, Veronica. I love you just the way you are. I was so mad at the lot of them and that they put you in this situation."

"I put myself in this situation," I said.

She wiped away a tear. "I want you to be healthy and happy. You deserve the world, Veronica, for how much you've done for this family."

I pulled her into a hug. "I know. I probably should ease up on all the junk food. I get winded going up the stairs."

Mom ended our embrace and put a hand on my cheek. "I'm always here for you. What can I do to help?"

"Maybe we could go for evening walks," I said, the idea suddenly popping into my head. "After dinner or something."

Mom smiled. "I love that idea. It will give us a time to talk. Maybe we should do it as a family."

I cringed on the inside. I wasn't sure if I wanted Dad there. Javier and Luciana would probably drive me crazy as well. It would be nice to have some one-on-one time with my mom. But she looked so hopeful, and she deserved all the happiness in the world as well.

"I like that idea," I said.

The front door opened, and Dad walked in wearing a suit and tie. He frowned when he saw my new outfit and hair. "What on earth did you do?"

My smile faltered. "You don't like it?"

"It's just ... drastic." Dad eyed my jumper and shoes. "How much did all of this cost?"

"Matías!" Mom let out a long breath. "That's what you're worried about? Veronica has been through so much lately. She deserves some new clothes."

"I know." Dad set a hand on his hip. "With the vow renewal coming up, we need to be careful with our money."

I folded my arms. "*Our* money? You act like you actually contribute to this family." He had been ever since he'd moved back in, but I was so furious with him. Guess we hadn't made much progress after all.

"Veronica," Mom warned.

Dad's nostrils flared. "I do a lot for this family. I pay for this house. I put food on the table."

"Let me autocorrect that for you," I said. "*Mom* pays for this house. *Mom* puts food on the table."

"Enough!" Dad roared. "I'm not the villain here, Veronica. I screwed up like you did at school. I've apologized like you did. How is that any different?"

"This is *so* different! I didn't abandon my family!" I shook with anger. "I had to raise my brother and sister while Mom worked and you gallivanted around with a twenty-year-old intern!"

Mom held up her hands between Dad and me. "Enough, you two. I'm not sure what to do, but something needs to be done here. Maybe we should see a therapist."

"Are you serious?" I asked.

Dad shook his head. "I'm not paying money for some hoity-toity shrink to tell me how to fix imaginary problems."

I had to choke back an angry laugh at that.

A sniffle behind Mom made us all turn around. Luciana stood there, tears streaming down her cheeks. When Mom reached for her, Luciana jerked back.

"I hate this family!" Luciana squeezed past us and ran up the stairs, the door to her room slamming shut moments later.

Mom scolded Dad and me with her eyes. "Look at what you've done. Both of you need to grow up." She hurried up the stairs.

Javier came up next to us, complete disappointment in his eyes. I thought maybe it was directed at both of us, but his focus settled on Dad.

"Do you realize you've never apologized to your kids for what you did?" Javier clenched his hand into a fist. "You've spent all your energy on Mom, trying to win her back and make her happy. But we're here too, Dad. Veronica's right. She had to take care of Luciana and me while you were gone, and Mom worked herself to death. You may have won Mom back, and probably Luciana because she's too young to understand, but you have a lot of work to do if you want Veronica and me to forgive you."

At that, he stormed out of the house, leaving Dad completely stunned. I knew Javier wasn't happy with Dad, but his hatred was much stronger than I'd thought.

Our family was so damaged all thanks to Dad. We needed him out of our life for good.

CHAPTER TWENTY-ONE

A hot mess of nerves and excitement coursed through me going over to the Thomas household. I couldn't wait to talk to Ryker and get my plan rolling. But for some reason, I was extremely nervous to reveal my new look. I'd felt so confident at the salon, but worry had sunk in. What if they didn't like my hair as much as I did?

Javier's followers had been so nice about my post. A lot of them commented on how hot I was, or how they loved my hair and outfit. But in the end, their opinions didn't matter much.

I'd worn a royal blue romper since I knew that was BYU's color. I knew their family was big into wearing game day apparel, but I didn't own anything with the university's logo. But the shorts showed a lot of my chunky thighs, cellulite and all.

I'd come an hour early in hopes to talk with Ryker. An unusual number of cars sat parked in front of the house. Maybe a neighbor was having a party.

As I stood at the door, I tugged on the bottom of the

romper, wishing it were longer. I should have gone with the full-length one instead.

With a deep breath of courage, I lightly knocked on the door. I waited a good couple of minutes, and no one answered, so I rang the doorbell.

Moments later, Taylor opened the door with Daphne right behind her. They both wore BYU shirts and earrings, along with glitter tattoos of an oval Y and a cougar paw print on their cheeks.

They both gasped when they saw me.

"Oh. My. Gosh." Taylor wore the biggest smile.

"Bow chicka wow wow!" Daphne jumped up and down. "You look so hot!"

Taylor waved a hand in front of me. "I love all of this. The hair. The outfit." She looked down at my white wedges and grinned. "The shoes! Girl, you are sexy!"

Suddenly they were both hugging me and kissing my cheeks repeatedly, making me laugh.

"You two are being ridiculous," I said through my laughter.

When they released me, I realized how incredibly loud it was in the house.

Taylor took my hand and steered me into the front room. I paused when I saw how many people were there, making Taylor jerk to a stop.

I'd expected Taylor's parents and a few brothers. What I wasn't expecting was her parents, five of her brothers (Neo, Ollie, Quinn, Ryker, and Samson), Ollie's very pregnant wife Charlie and their three kids Pierson, Nixon, and Brighton, Quinn's wife Aria and their brand-new baby, Huntley, Daphne, Weston, Laura, Cody, and my cousin Celeste.

Wait, what? My eyes darted to Celeste, who stood

awfully close to Neo. It looked like he might have had his hand resting on the small of her back.

They'd met yesterday.

"Celeste?" What on earth was she doing here?

Her bright eyes found mine. "Hey, cuz! Neo invited me."

Taylor leaned toward me. "Don't worry. It won't last longer than two weeks. Neo can't keep a girlfriend longer than that."

Aria whistled loud. "Veronica! You look amazing!"

"Yeah, she does." Charlie sat on the recliner with her feet kicked up and a bowl of caramel popcorn resting on her protruding belly.

A series of hoots and hollers rang out as everyone in the room agreed, and I found myself blushing. I wasn't expecting to make a grand reveal to a million people.

Laura rushed over and hugged me. "I can't get over your hair. It's just so ... Veronica. I'm loving it."

As Taylor's mom Maggie chimed in, her words were drowned out by the look on Samson's face. His jaw was practically on the floor. He came toward me, and out of the corner of my eye I could see everyone stepping away, but my eyes were solely on him.

He stopped right in front of me and blew out a deep breath like he'd been holding it. "You've rendered me speechless." He glanced me up and down, his gaze finally settling on my hair. "I've missed this."

"Missed what?" I asked, my voice surprisingly breathy.

"Veronica." He wrapped me up in a hug. "You look stunning."

I smiled at his word choice.

"Thanks." I wondered if he could feel how hot my skin was.

Four-year-old Brighton skipped over to where we stood. She wore an adorable BYU cheerleader outfit and small royal pom-poms in her hair. She held out some temporary tattoos. "Which ones do you want?"

I'd spent hours doing my makeup, trying to get my flawless look. No way I was ruining it with some cheap tattoos. "I'm okay, thanks."

Brighton sighed in disappointment. "Okay, fine." Her eyes lit up when she looked at Ryker. "Uncle Ryker, you should wear some!"

Ryker scooped her up in his arms. "Oh, yeah? Which one?"

Brighton studied the tattoos, her face serious. She tapped the BYU logo with a cougar over it. "This one!"

"Let's go put it on," Ryker said before he carried her out of the room.

Pierson scooped up a football from the floor and he and his brother ran out into the backyard.

I checked the time on my phone. "I thought the game starts at three?"

Maggie sighed. "I know, we're running late." She looked over at her husband. "We should get Porter and Emory on video call and make sure everything is working properly."

Lance pointed his thumb toward the sliding glass door in the back. "Let me go check the grill first. Actually, have Quinn help you. He knows how to do that stuff better than me."

Huntley and Weston gave me quick hugs before they went into the kitchen to help with Taylor, Daphne, and Ollie with food.

Samson chuckled. "Pre-game starts two hours before kick-off."

Everyone wore BYU gear like they'd bought out the

entire fan store. I folded my arms close to me, feeling insecure and out of place.

"Perfect color choice, by the way," Samson said.

"I didn't know this was such a grand event."

Samson's smile calmed me. "We love our football. Also,
it's the rivalry game, so it's going to get intense. Just to warn
you."

Cody slowly came toward us, cradling a sleeping baby
in his arms. Laura's eyes lit up in excitement, making me
glad Daphne was in the other room. She'd flip if she knew
her mom was getting baby hungry and wanted Cody to be
the daddy.

Cody smiled when he got to me. He kept his voice low
as to not wake the baby. "You really do look amazing,
Veronica."

"Thanks, Cody." I stepped close so I could see Aria and
Quinn's new baby girl, Poppy. She had a pink onesie with a
baby cougar on it. Even the baby sported BYU gear. Maybe
I did need those temporary tattoos after all.

"Do you want to hold her?" Cody asked.

"Maybe later," I said. "I've changed my mind about the
temporary tattoos. I'll be back."

I found Ryker and Brighton in the guest bathroom.
Brighton stood on the counter and held a damp towel
against Ryker's cheeks. This family was made of giants.

Brighton grinned when she saw me. "Do you want a
tattoo now?"

I nodded, making Brighton swish her hips back and
forth in excitement.

"I'm almost done with Uncle Ryker," Brighton said.
"Ten more seconds."

I leaned against the counter, trying to act casual. "Hey,
Ryker, do you know of a place where I can get some insects

and such? Like, I don't know, say grasshoppers, bees, and a snake?"

Yeah, that so wasn't casual.

Ryker turned his head as Brighton lowered the towel. "That's an odd request. What do you need those for?"

Brighton peeled the paper backings of the tattoos off Ryker's cheeks and squealed when she saw the results. Then she sat down on the counter and motioned for me to come over to her. "Which ones you want?"

"Surprise me," I said as I stood in front of her.

I'd been thinking long and hard about how I could get Ryker's help, and I'd realized the best thing was to get closest to the truth.

"My family has this weird legend that deals with all those things." I grimaced as Brighton put a towel to my face and wiped at my cheek. "Is that necessary, Brighton?"

She nodded fiercely. "You're supposed to clean the skin first. That's what Mommy always does." She pulled back the towel and saw all the concealer left behind on the towel. Her eyes went wide. "Did I peel off your skin?" Her voice was shrill.

I lightly laughed. "No, it's only makeup."

She blew out a breath of relief before she pressed a tattoo to my cheek.

"What's the legend?" Ryker asked, curiosity in his voice.

"I'll tell you later when there aren't little ears in the room," I said. "But I'm filming a reenactment for a school project."

Ryker pulled his phone out of his pocket. "I know a guy who will have everything you need. His house and backyard have practically every insect and reptile known to mankind."

"Really?" I couldn't hide the surprise in my tone. I didn't know such a person existed.

"Yeah. He's a really cool guy. You'll like him."

I wasn't sure if that was true, but I guess I'd find out.

"Do you think it would be affordable?" I asked. "I don't have a ton of money."

Ryker nodded. "Hank is very reasonably priced. Is it for a film class? He's an amateur director and could probably give you pointers." His thumbs moved across his phone, probably sending Hank a message. "When would you need him?"

"As soon as possible." I grinned as Brighton took the paper off my cheek. "How do I look?"

Brighton clasped her hands together, showing off her blue nails. "So pretty!" She glanced down and saw my newly done orange and black fake nails. Mom said I'd have to change them before the vow renewal, though. Hopefully, my plan would go well and I wouldn't have to change them.

"I love your nails." Brighton picked up my hand. "They're so long!"

I tickled her stomach with my other hand, making her giggle.

Samson popped his head into the bathroom. "Burgers are ready."

Brighton hopped down from the counter and ran out of the room, her voice echoing down the hall. "Yay!"

Ryker's phone pinged. "Hank says you can stop by Monday or Tuesday after seven in the evening."

Those were my last two days of suspension, so I'd be with my abuela all day. It needed to be done at nighttime anyway, so it was perfect.

"Tell him we'll come Monday at eight?" I asked. "The

legend happens during the night, so I thought it would be best to film in the dark. Kind of add an eerie vibe."

"What are you two talking about?" Samson asked.

"Hank's going to help Veronica with a school project." Ryker's phone pinged again. "He says he should have all the critters you need."

Samson jerked his head back in surprise. "Critters?"

I grinned. "Wait until you hear about my family's curse."

As I dove into the story, the more excited I got. It was going to happen. Soon, my mom would be spooked into kicking Dad out of our lives for good.

CHAPTER TWENTY-TWO

Ten minutes before kick-off, everyone crammed into the front room. They had set-up extra chairs in practically every inch of the place.

Porter, the one Thomas brother that couldn't be there, had his family on a video call so everyone could watch the game "together."

The Thomas family seemed to all settle into their normal spots, then everyone else filled the holes.

Samson and Ryker were sitting on the loveseat. When Samson and I made eye contact, he pushed himself into the side and patted the spot between him and Ryker.

I was torn. I mean, the spot was probably too small for my big butt. But Samson looked so hopeful. All the other seats were taken. Although, Celeste was so far on the edge of hers that a few more inches and she'd be sitting on Neo's lap. Which left a lot of her seat open.

When I caught Samson's gorgeous gaze again, I melted and worked my way through the crowd, stepping over the kids sitting on the ground in front of the TV.

"Where's Spencer?" I asked Ryker as I took a seat between the guys.

"Sleeping." Ryker stretched out his long legs. "These games are too loud of him anyway."

Brighton climbed onto Ryker's legs, and he lifted them into the air. She held her arms up like a cheerleader and shouted, "Go Cougars!" Then she jumped off with a flourish.

Pierson, Ollie's eight-year-old son, bounced in front of the TV, demanding everyone's attention. "Let's do the fight song like they do in the stadium before the game."

He immediately began clapping and singing. Everyone else in the Thomas family followed suit in a loud chorus. Even little Brighton had the fight song memorized. She'd grabbed some pom-pom's and worked the room like she was a cheerleader for the university.

Suddenly, everyone jumped to their feet. I'd been slightly leaning into Samson, so his sudden absence left me falling to the side. I quickly righted myself and watched on in awe. This family was no joke.

The more I watched it, though, the more it warmed my heart. It was all something they shared and did together.

Maybe walks every evening with the family would be a good thing. Just a time to bond and talk about our days. Maybe it would help us understand each other.

I looked at the wallpaper of my phone and saw the picture of Dad and me at the 49ers game. Maybe it wouldn't be such a bad thing to start watching the games with my family.

The song ended and everyone collapsed back into their seats. Except Pierson and Nixon who yelled, "let's go!" at the top of their lungs. When they chest bumped, I couldn't help but laugh.

Samson put his arm around the back of the couch, turning his body more toward me. "Two future tight ends right there."

I looked up at him. "I thought your family was all about basketball?"

He motioned to the boys. "Not those two. They've been playing football since they could walk. Their dedication sometimes astounds me. Ollie and Charlie don't have to hound them to practice. If anything, they're having to drag the kids back into the house at bedtime."

The game started, and everyone's attention turned to the TV. Except mine. I had no idea what was going on. What I did know, sitting so close to Samson made my heart race. I couldn't concentrate on anything. White noise surrounded me as Samson's presence pulsed with electricity.

It left me utterly confused. This was Samson Thomas. Taylor's older brother. A guy that I'd known forever who felt like family to me. I shouldn't have been feeling this way. I didn't need another guy ruining my life. I so didn't need the distraction, either.

I had a mission to accomplish. A mission that involved two guys that had ruined my life. I thought of the rule in the picture frame on my nightstand. Never trust guys.

All guys cared about were looks. When my dad had the opportunity to snag someone younger and hotter than my mom, he jumped on it. When I gained a little bit of weight, DeShawn ran for the hills.

But the way Samson looked at me when he saw my new look left me second-guessing everything. It didn't make sense. Samson was hot, smart, athletic, driven, kind, honest, all the traits that could have him scooping up any girl he wanted.

So why was his arm around me? When I leaned forward for a moment to adjust the strap on my shoe, why was his arm now around my lower back when I sat back in place? Why did he have his hand on my hip? Why was he acting like this was all completely normal and natural?

Kylie had crushed him. Maybe it had ruined his self-esteem, and he thought I was the only type of girl he could date.

But the guy never lied.

It was so, so confusing.

At half time, I rushed to the bathroom and locked myself inside. I still had another half to get through. Maybe I could fake being sick and go home. Or say I suddenly remembered a family thing I had to be at.

I stared at my chubby cheeks and double chin in the mirror. Shanice had told me I was beautiful the way I was. Why couldn't I believe her? Or anyone that said I looked hot?

I lifted my arm to smooth out my hair and noticed a huge sweat stain under my armpit. When I check my other armpit, it was exactly the same. I'd completely stress sweated. I quickly stuffed some toilet paper under my arms, hoping to soak some of it up.

I searched the drawers for a hair dryer, but there wasn't one. This was a half-bath. Even if they did have one, anyone on the other side of the door would hear me using it and would wonder what I was doing.

A knock sounded on the door. I yanked the toilet paper out of my pits, threw them in the toilet and flushed it. After washing my hands, I opened the door to find Celeste.

"You okay, V?" Celeste asked. "You looked completely anxious during the first half, and not because of the game."

"It's nothing."

Celeste shoved me back in the bathroom and shut the door so we were alone. "I saw how snuggly you and Samson were. But you looked terrified. Is he making unwanted advances? Because I have no problem shutting that down."

I leaned against the sink and sighed. "I'm confused." I motioned to my sweaty armpits. "Who would want this?"

Celeste rolled her eyes. "I sweat all day at my studio. It's a part of life."

"Do you sweat when you're sitting around doing nothing?" I pointed at my pit again. "Because I do."

"You're sweating because you're nervous. Total difference. And why wouldn't Samson want you? You're gorgeous, V." She smiled slyly. "Guess I should say, you're *stunning*."

"It's a stupid size on a label," I muttered.

Celeste tucked her finger under my chin and lifted it. "I don't want to hear you talking like that. There is nothing wrong with your body. Samson is into you. It's obvious and makes a whole bunch of sense." She put her hands on my shoulders and spun me around so I faced the mirror. "Look how beautiful you are. I've always been so jealous of your lips."

I looked at her through the mirror. "You have? They're always covered in loose skin since I bite them so much."

"Well, yeah, you could use some lip gloss, but they're so plump and luscious. Mine are like two sticks." She leaned her head against mine. "Your problem is you're looking for the bad. You should be looking for the good. None of us are perfect, V."

"Except you."

She pointed to her thin lips. "No, I'm not." She bent down and took off her heel, revealing her left foot. Two of her toes were webbed together. She had a tattoo of a cut line where the toes should have been separated and a pair of scissors under the line. "I have this monstrosity."

"How did I not know that?" I stifled a laugh. "What's with the tattoo?"

She shrugged and slipped her heel back on. "Might as well have fun with a crap situation."

"But you never show it to anyone."

"That's not the point." Celeste set her hand on my shoulder. "If we focused on our flaws all the time, we'd go insane." She turned me to face her. "Do you like Samson?"

"I ..." Did I like Samson? I glanced at my sweaty armpits. "Apparently I do."

"Then get out there and have fun," Celeste said with a smile.

"Speaking of fun, what's going on with you and Neo?" I asked.

Celeste cranked up her smolder. "He's so ... manly, with the beard and broad shoulders. He'd look hot wearing flannel and holding an axe."

"Please keep your fantasies to yourself."

She wiggled her drawn-on eyebrows. "But where's the fun in that?"

When we joined everyone again in the front room, I felt a little lighter. Talking to Celeste had really helped.

Samson's eyes lit up when he saw me, and maybe Celeste was right about him liking me. I mean, what would be the point of faking something like that?

I sat down and cozied up next to him. Samson immediately pulled me close and maybe this whole thing wasn't so bad. Maybe nothing would come of it. Maybe it was some light fun.

Samson's lips pressed against my ear, probably because it was so loud in the room and he wanted me to hear him, but it sent my heart in another frenzy. "Are you having fun?"

"I really don't know what's going on. This game makes like zero sense to me."

Samson spent the rest of the half whispering what was going on in my ear. I never knew football talk could be so sexy.

When the game was down to less than a minute and the teams were tied, an unbelievable intensity sat in the room, and I found myself anxious as well. Knowing a little bit about the game and players really helped.

BYU had the ball and they hurried down the field, trying to get in field goal distance so they could win the game. And now I actually knew what that meant.

Everyone cheered for a moment when they got to a place to send out the kicker, and then it went quiet in the room.

Nixon covered his eyes. "I can't watch."

Pierson tried to yank his arms away. "You don't want to miss this, Nix. You'll regret it if you don't watch."

"He's totally got this," Brighton said with pure confidence. "He never misses."

"Don't jinx it!" Ollie yelled.

Brighton rolled her eyes. "Don't be silly, Daddy. The kicker can't hear me."

Samson chuckled next to me, and I realized our hands were clasped.

A collective inhale filled in the room right as the kicker got to the ball. When it went through, the room erupted in screams.

Ryker scooped Brighton off the floor and held her in the air. Neo and Ollie screamed and hugged. High fives flew.

And Samson.

Well.

He bent down, cradled my cheeks with his hands, and pressed his lips to mine, lingering for a good five seconds. I counted.

When he released me, deafening silence filled the room. Everyone stared at us. Some in shock. Some in glee. Some in confusion.

Daphne had an excited face with her mouth in an "O" like she'd won a lifetime supply of Watermelon Sour Patch Kids.

Taylor's face somehow kept switching from grossed out to excited.

Me? I didn't know what to do. So, I ran. Out of the house, to my car, and I took off without looking back.

Samson Thomas *kissed me*.

CHAPTER TWENTY-THREE

My lips pulsed the entire ride home, the heat of Samson's lips lingering on mine. My phone kept buzzing in my pocket, probably everyone trying to contact me, but I was fully focused on getting back to my room and barricading myself inside. My hands gripped the steering wheel tight as the image replayed over and over again in my head, analyzing it from all different directions like they did on TV when they were reviewing a call at a football game.

He'd kissed me.

Samson had kissed me.

In front of his *entire* family.

They'd witnessed our first kiss.

Our first kiss.

I didn't know how to process it. I mean, it was nothing like Jane and Michael's romantic first kiss. They were alone and had fake snow fall on them like something out of a movie.

I never thought I'd share a first kiss with Samson Thomas. My brain shouted all the things that were wrong with the scenario. My hormones buzzed with the complete opposite view.

I couldn't deny that the kiss had been good. Better than I would have thought. But he was my best friend's brother.

What happened if we started dating, broke up, and then I had to face him all the time?

I groaned as I turned into my driveway.

Mom stood in the doorway waiting for me. She looked as confused as I felt.

"Taylor called me," Mom said as I stepped into the house. "She wanted me to check on you. She said something happened but wouldn't tell me what. Is everything okay?"

"No, Ma." I headed toward the stairs. "Everything is *not* okay. It's far from okay. Okay is like in a completely different country right now having the time of its life."

Mom rushed up behind me, matching me step for step up the stairs. "Well, what happened?"

"I can't." For some reason, I couldn't tell Mom that Samson kissed me. Her reaction would interfere with my thoughts and feelings and would probably influence me in the end. I needed to sort things out for myself first.

"What do you mean you can't?" Mom huffed. "You can tell me anything, Veronica. If it's something that bad, we can work through it together."

I paused outside the doorway to my bedroom. "I need time to sort through my thoughts and then we can talk about it."

"Okay." Mom kissed my forehead. "We can talk in ten minutes or so. That's fine."

I pressed a hand to my temple. "I need more than ten minutes, Ma. Like tomorrow, or next week."

"Next week?" Mom pressed a hand to her chest. "My nerves can't last that long."

I took a deep breath, trying to calm myself. "I really want to start doing evening walks as a family. Maybe we can talk then."

Mom nodded as quickly as a bobblehead. "Okay. I'll go round everyone up." She checked her watch. "Meet down-stairs in a half hour?"

"Tomorrow, Mom." I went into my room and shut the door. Then I pushed my dresser in front of the door.

"That's not necessary," Mom said from the other side of the door.

She probably heard me move the dresser. "Trust me, it is."

"Oh, my stubborn, stubborn girl." Mom's voice faded down the hall as she walked away.

I immediately went to my bed, plopped down face first, and let out a scream.

I had absolutely no idea what to do. I flipped over and gazed at the ceiling. Why was I freaking out? I'd kissed guys before.

This one felt so different, though. Unlike anything I'd ever experienced. And it made me super uncomfortable.

I laid there for a few minutes when I heard footsteps pounding up the stairs. Seconds later, Daphne and Taylor's voice came from the other side of the door.

"Open the door, V," Daphne said. The knob jiggled like she was trying to open it.

"Talk to us," Taylor said. "Let us in and we'll figure this out."

"There's nothing to figure out!" I placed my hands over my face and suppressed another scream that wanted to come.

"Uh, considering what just happened," Daphne said in an incredulous tone, "I'd beg to differ."

"What happened?" My mom whispered the words, but I'd still heard her.

"Uh ..." Daphne trailed off.

"Are we telling your mom what happened?" Taylor asked through the door.

"No!"

"Sorry, Mrs. Rodriguez," Daphne said, "but we've been sworn to secrecy. It's nothing personal."

"I know," my mom mumbled. "You're being good friends. I want to help."

Someone banged on the door.

"So do we!" Taylor said.

"You're not going to leave, are you?" I already knew the answer, but still had to ask.

"Nope," Daphne said. "We'll die right here if we have to. Then you'll be responsible for our deaths and there's no way you want that on your conscience. Also, I'll continue to haunt you in death, so ..."

With a sigh, I got up and moved the dresser enough that Daphne and Taylor could squeeze in. Then I put the dresser back in front of the door.

"They have these things called door locks," Daphne said, staring at my dresser.

"My parents take them away on our fifteenth birthday." I sat down on my bed. "Family tradition."

"That's like really weird." Taylor sat down at the vanity. "So. My brother kissed you."

"What?!" Mom exclaimed from the other side of my door.

"Ma!" Of course she was standing on the other side, eavesdropping.

"Sorry, I'll go," Mom muttered. "But we're talking about

this later. It was Samson, right? The one that brought you flowers?"

"Samson brought you flowers?" Taylor asked.

"Yes, it was Samson," I said. "Now, please go away."

"Fine," Mom said. "But so you know, I really like him."

I waited to make sure her footsteps faded down the hall this time.

Daphne went over to the vase full of orchids on my nightstand. "They're beautiful."

I turned to Taylor. "I assumed you knew about the flowers."

"Nope." Taylor took a lip gloss from my vanity and turned it around in her hand. "He feels awful, by the way." She opened the lip gloss, looked at the color, then put the lid back on. "He got so excited from the game."

Awful because he kissed me? Was the kiss awful? Just because I liked it didn't mean he did.

What if I was a terrible kisser? What if that was the true reason DeShawn dumped me?

Daphne sat down next to me and took my hand. "Do you like him?"

"No!" I flushed. "Yes. I don't know."

Taylor smiled. "It's obvious you do. You only get this flustered when you really like someone."

"I do not." I tried to think of all my crushes. DeShawn never got me flustered. I was fully confident when we started dating.

Daphne held up a finger. "Cole in first grade. You spilled glue all over him when he asked to borrow your pencil." She held up another finger. "Austin in second grade. When he asked you to play soccer with him you started yelling at him in Spanish and scared him away."

Taylor raised one of her fingers. "Carlos in middle

school. He asked you to a dance, and you started muttering things in a language that doesn't even exist."

Daphne made an 'O' with her mouth, her eyes lighting up. She stayed like that for a moment before she spoke. "I wasn't here for that one! Oh, man, sounds like I missed a good one."

"It was priceless," Taylor said through her laugh.

I folded my arms. "Okay, okay, I can get flustered."

"Over guys." Daphne squeezed my hand. "So, what are we going to do about Samson?"

"Nothing," I sputtered, making them both break out in giggles. I sighed. "There's nothing to do, okay? Taylor pointed out that he did it out of excitement over the game—"

"Well, and the fact that he likes you." Taylor set down the lip gloss and rifled through my mascaras.

"I thought he said it was a mistake," I said.

She grabbed my waterproof mascara and read the front. "He did. But I think he meant, like, I really shouldn't have kissed Veronica in front of my whole family. I should have done it when no one was around."

I pressed a hand to my lips.

Taylor put the mascara back in its place. "I know my brother, V. I've seen the way he's looked at you over the last few months."

"A few months!" Daphne put her hand on her hip. "He's been crushing on V for months?"

"I hadn't really thought about it until Huntley pointed it out," Taylor said. "But the more I looked back, the more I saw the signs."

That made no sense at all. All I had done in the past couple of months was gain weight.

"Is Samson some sort of a chubby chaser?" The second

the words left my mouth, I regretted them. I'd meant to think it, not say it.

"What? No." Taylor came over and sat on the other side of me. "Weight has nothing to do with it. Samson's all about the personality."

I stood. "So, he's not actually physically attracted to me. He only likes my personality?"

Taylor jumped up. "That's not what I meant! Of course he's physically attracted to you. No one can date someone they're not attracted to. It would never work out."

"Why not?" Daphne asked.

Taylor threw up her hands. "It's logic. Beauty is in the eye of the beholder. We're all attracted to different people. You can't sit there and tell me you'd want to make out with a guy you're not attracted to."

"I only want to make out with Weston," Daphne said with a confused look.

"Yeah, and you're attracted to him, right?" Taylor asked.

"Bow chicka wow wow." Daphne wiggled her eyebrows. "You know it. The guy is hot."

"Can we ever get you to stop saying that?" I asked Daphne.

She shook her head. "Nope. In fact, I'm going to do a recording of it so someone can put it in my casket and anytime someone reaches in and touches my hand they'll hear me say it."

Taylor snorted a laugh. "I can totally see you doing it."

"Because I'm going to." Daphne took her phone out of her pocket. "Hey, Google, remind me to record myself saying, 'bow chicka wow wow' tonight. Also remind me to put together my will."

"*Okay,*" the automated voice responded. "*I'll remind you tonight.*"

"Which one of you wants my Care Bear onesies?" Daphne asked. "Or should I give them to Weston?" She tapped her lips with her finger. "I guess I have plenty to go around. You can all get one."

Taylor pushed Daphne on the arm. "We're getting off topic. We need to focus on Veronica and Samson."

I paced in front of them. "I'm not ready for a relationship right now. DeShawn put me in a bad place, and I really need to focus on sorting that all out." I also needed to break up my parents for good.

"Samson will understand that," Taylor said. "He'll never pressure you into anything. If you want to wait, he'll wait."

I stopped in front of my vanity mirror and stared at myself.

But was I, Veronica Rodriguez, really worth the wait?

Daphne suddenly appeared behind me, making me jump. "We need some music up in here." She slinked out of view and then started playing "2 Be Loved" by Lizzo on her phone.

After slipping off her shoes, she jumped on my bed and motioned for Taylor and me to join her as she danced and sang along to the song.

Taylor didn't even hesitate. She was up next to her in seconds.

They both used their pointer fingers to beckon me up until I finally caved and joined them. We ended up borrowing Javier's ring light and filming some videos for TikTok. Singing and dancing on my bed with my two best friends was the exact therapy I needed.

CHAPTER TWENTY-FOUR

I knew I couldn't avoid Samson forever, but I wasn't ready to talk about our kiss. I texted him telling him I needed some time to think everything through. He responded with:

> Samson: Take all the time you need, V. I'll still be here when you're ready.

That made him even more likable.

It was still a couple of weeks until the vow renewal. The curse said they came the three nights leading up to the wedding. Javier and I decided we would probably be too busy around that time, so maybe we needed to do it earlier. That way Mom could call it off sooner than later and put everyone out of their misery.

After spending the day cooking empanadas with my abuela, I told Daphne to meet me at Hank's place. I so didn't want to make the trip alone, and Ryker had already gone back to UCLA. Javier's job was to keep an eye on everyone at home and make sure they didn't leave the house.

Hank lived in an average one-story house, nothing flashy, but also not run-down like some of the homes in his area. A white gate surrounded his front yard, so we opened it and slowly shuffled down the walkway. We weren't in the biggest hurry to meet to guy. I mean, his house was full of insects and reptiles.

A bunch of pumpkins carved with spiders, snakes, roaches, and bats sat on the porch.

We stopped in front of the door and stood still.

Daphne pushed my arm. "Knock already."

I pushed her back. "You knock already."

"We're here because of you."

I couldn't argue with that.

Daphne sighed. "Remember, this was your idea. If you want your dad out of your life for good, you have to do something about it. Otherwise, let's go get some ice cream or something."

I lifted my hand to knock when Daphne leaned in toward me. "Also, for the record, I still think an intern is the way to go. Not bugs." She stood straight with a satisfied smile.

With a roll of my eyes, I knocked on the door.

Moments later, the door swung open and a thin guy in his thirties stood there. He wore jeans and a polo and looked nothing like I'd expected. The guy looked ... normal. Just an average thirty-something living a blue-collar life.

"You must be Veronica." Hank stuck out his hand. "I'm Hank."

I quickly shook his hand and ended contact as quickly as I could. I pointed to Daphne. "This is my friend, Daphne."

Daphne waved. "Hello, insect man."

Hank chuckled and opened the door wide for us to

come in. The inside of his house took me by surprise. Again, it was totally normal. An average front room and kitchen with very plain furniture. There really wasn't a theme going on, but it worked.

"Everything you'll need is in the back." Hank turned and walked down the hall, expecting Daphne and I to follow him.

Daphne patted the bag strapped around her and whispered to me, "I brought some mace in case he turns out to be a serial killer. I'll probably be frozen in horror if he is, so you might have to take the reins on the mace."

After that completely non-comforting advice, we hurried after Hank.

He glanced over his shoulder at me. "Ryker told me about your family curse. That's quite the story."

"You should hear my abuela tell it," I said. "Way more interesting coming from her."

Hank pulled a key from his pocket and opened a door at the end of the hall. The second it swung open, that was when the chaos happened.

Everything hit me at once. The weird smell I couldn't pin down. The chirps, caws, rattles, buzzing, basically every sound an insect or reptile could make carried through this enormous room.

Hank had taken the whole back of the house and turned it into an exhibit hall. If I didn't know any better, I'd think I was at a museum with the smooth dark gray concrete floor and areas glassed off with snakes and other reptiles behind them.

A ginormous bird cage took up the corner, housing practically every bird imaginable. Rows of aquariums and cages of all sizes lined the middle of the space.

Daphne bent down and looked wide-eyed at some

tarantulas in a terrarium. "Hey, fellas. Good news! You're not part of Veronica's family curse. Which leads to the other good news, I never have to see you again." She stood straight, shuddered, and continued down the aisle.

"Tarantulas are very misunderstood creatures," Hank said, looking inside the terrarium.

"My mom tried to tell me the same thing about clowns," Daphne said. "She was totally wrong. They're all serial killers." She paused in front of a glass enclosure and lightly clapped her hands. "V! I found your grasshoppers!"

I hurried down to be at her side. I wanted this whole thing over with, and I didn't want to be out of arm's reach of Daphne. That way I could grab her and run at a moment's notice in case this Hank clown turned out to be a serial killer himself.

A grasshopper jumped onto the glass.

"Patience, young grasshopper," Daphne said in a horrible accent. "Your turn to terrorize the Rodriguez household will soon come."

"Those are actually camel crickets." Hank's sudden voice behind us made Daphne and me jump in the air and scream. Hank took a large step back. "Sorry. I'm really bad with personal space."

"No worries," I said with a strained smile.

Daphne glanced in the glass enclosure. "Did you say these were camel crickets? Where are their humps?" She looked at Hank, totally serious. "Do you think they'd let other crickets or insects ride their backs if they were in the desert? Like camels let humans ride them? Also, do these guys drink a lot? And spit?"

Hank chuckled. "There's actually a different camel cricket that lives in the desert. And, technically, camels don't spit. It's more like they throw up. It's food along with saliva."

Both Daphne and I scrunched our faces in disgust.

"TMI, Hank," Daphne said with a shake of her head.

I bumped her arm. "You're the one who asked."

Hank pointed to the enclosure next to us. "Those are the grasshoppers."

There were at least a dozen inside. I had no idea how many grasshoppers were said to roam the house of my ancestor so hopefully this would do.

"Is this all you have?" I asked.

Hank shook his head. "I have another dozen or so out back. You thinking all of them?"

"I was hoping for a decent amount," I said.

"Okay. I'll round them all up for you." He disappeared out into the back, leaving Daphne and me alone with a bunch of random creatures.

Daphne rounded the corner, heading down another aisle, so I hurried to keep up with her. She stopped in front of a glass enclosure with soil taking up half the space.

"What do you think is in the soil?" Daphne asked.

I leaned toward the case. "A plant? It's soil."

Daphne's fingered hovered next to the glass. "Should I tap it? See if it wakes up?"

I slapped her hand down. "Are you crazy? Isn't that like the number one rule of these things? Don't tap on the glass?"

"Only one way to find out." Daphne tapped on the glass with her pointer finger before I could stop her.

I held my breath, waiting for something to jump out or press itself against the glass, but nothing happened.

Daphne sighed. "Well, that was a total letdown."

She turned to walk away when I saw a black horn come

up from the soil, sticking into the air. I grabbed onto the back of her shirt and yanked her back to me.

"Something is in there," I said.

Daphne leaned down, resting her palms on her slightly bent knees. "That's a shiny horn. What has a horn?" Her eyes lit up. "Do you think it's a unicorn?"

I rolled my eyes. "Obviously not."

Daphne nodded. "True. That horn is pure black and curved on top." She squinted. "The underbelly of the horn is covered in fur. That's so weird."

We continued to watch it emerge from the soil.

Another horn came out, below the other. Beady eyes blinked at us, and we took a step back.

"What kind of insect *is* that?" Daphne asked.

The back was yellow with black spots, with three legs on each side.

"Looks like some sort of beetle," I said, watching it walk across the soil.

"A mutated one," Daphne mumbled.

The beetle took flight, causing us to cry out and take a jump back.

"It flies?" Daphne shrieked.

"They're called the Hercules beetle." Hank's sudden voice at our side made our screams double.

Daphne and I clung to each other as we stared at Hank and screamed.

He waited patiently, holding two cages of grasshoppers, until Daphne and I both stopped screaming.

"I smuggled Hercules in from Mexico. I've wanted one since I was a kid." He held out the cages of grasshoppers. "I found thirty-seven. Hopefully that will work."

I took a shaky step forward and retrieved the cages. I tried to speak, but my mouth was completely dry. I licked my lips and swallowed a few times before I found my voice again. "Thanks, Hank."

"Anytime." He motioned to Hercules' enclosure. "Either of you want to hold him?"

Was he serious?

"No, sir," Daphne said, "we most definitely would *not* want to hold him. But we appreciate the strange offer."

I pushed the cages of grasshoppers into Daphne's chest until she finally took the handles. After digging some cash from my pocket, I slapped it in Hank's hand, and Daphne and I took off, getting out of that house as fast as humanly possible.

"Take care!" Hank shouted after us, all happy, like people darting from his house with fear in their eyes was an everyday occurrence.

When we were outside, we put the grasshoppers in my trunk and slammed it shut.

Hank stood in the doorway to his house and waved. "Let me know when you need the bees. I've got a whole bunch out back."

"Thanks!" I yelled.

We jumped into our cars and hightailed it out of there.

CHAPTER TWENTY-FIVE

With Monday Night Football in full swing and 49ers playing tonight, it was the perfect time to unleash the grasshoppers in my home. My dad, brother, and sister were avid Niners fans. Like, you didn't interrupt them during a game unless you had a death wish.

Mom would watch, but her focus was providing the snacks and beverages. She made sure everyone was comfortable throughout the entire game.

Any time they played, I always locked myself in my room. Since it involved football, it always made me think of DeShawn—although, Samson had sure changed that, and now I was thoroughly confused. So, instead of locking myself in my room tonight and trying to wade through what my heart wasn't ready to figure out, I could finally begin the process of getting my dad out of our lives before he had the chance to break my mom's heart again.

Our plan was for me to join my family inside while Daphne unleashed the grasshoppers. Our doorbell had a camera, so going in that way was out of the question. If the garage door opened, Mom and Dad would be alerted on their app.

Instinctively, my hand went to my wrist, wanting to take a band and throw my hair in a messy bun, but my new hairstyle didn't allow it. I'd need to come up with a new way to prep myself for action. "I think it would be best if you went around to the back of the house and waited. I'll text you when it's time."

Daphne slipped a black mask over her face. It only had openings for the eyes and mouth. With her pink Care Bear shirt, it was quite the look and obvious it was her. When she saw me staring, she patted the top of her head. "What? Should I have made jailbird Mickey ears?" She slapped her forehead in frustration. "Of course I should have. What was I thinking?"

I placed my hand on her shoulder. "That would have made it even more obvious it's you behind that mask."

Daphne scoffed. "I know tons of people who dress like I do."

"Name one."

She paused for a moment. "Oh! That little girl that lives down the street from me."

I lowered my hand. "I worry about you sometimes." I picked up one of the containers of grasshoppers and handed it to her. "Try to be as quick as you can and make sure you aren't seen. Just release and go."

She did one firm nod. "Got it." She grabbed the second container. "Uh, where do I go after I release them? Head home?"

"That's why I had you bring your car, remember?"

"Right. But you have to call me after and give me a play-by-play of what happens."

"I will."

She turned around, crouched, and quietly tiptoed toward my backyard, holding a container of grasshoppers in each hand.

Even though it was my own house, my heart raced like I was doing something totally illegal. I took some deep breaths and reminded myself it was for my mom. She didn't deserve to be hurt by my dad once again.

After shaking off the last of my nerves, I went inside and joined my family in the front room.

Mom's eyes lit up when she saw me. "Veronica! Are you going to join us?"

"Sure, why not?" I plopped down next to Javier on the loveseat.

Mom, Dad, and Luciana were all on the couch, like we'd planned. We wanted them facing the TV and not the back of the house. Dad and Luciana hadn't peeled their eyes from the screen as to so much as glance at me, so it probably didn't really matter where they were sitting in the end.

Mom stood and hustled toward the kitchen. "Good thing I made extra salsa and queso!"

A bowl of each, plus a bowl of tortilla chips, sat on the coffee table in front of us.

Javier leaned toward me and whispered. "You have the goods?"

"Daphne has them out back."

Javier's leg bounced, his nervous tick. "Is she releasing them now?"

I shook my head. "I thought I'd wait until half-time. Otherwise, I don't think Dad and Luciana will even notice they were surrounded by grasshoppers."

Javier chuckled. "Good point."

Mom hurried back in the room and placed more chips,

salsa, and queso on the coffee table. Her eyes narrowed in on Javier's bouncing leg. "You okay, Javy?"

His leg went still. Then he licked his lips. "I gotta pee." He jumped and ran toward the downstairs bathroom.

Mom's skeptical eyes landed on me, so I smiled warmly at her and grabbed a bowl of salsa and chips.

"Are these Abuela's tomatoes or ours?" I asked as I casually scooped some salsa with a chip.

Mom's demeanor loosened. "Ours. Just picked them tonight."

"Shhh!" Luciana hissed at us, though she didn't look away from the TV.

Mom and I lightly laughed before we turned our attention to the game.

When Javier rejoined us, I kept a close eye on his leg. The second it started bouncing, I quietly slapped his leg. Eventually, he got sucked into the game and the nerves left him.

When it was almost half-time, I texted Daphne, telling her it was time. I felt bad making her wait so long, but she insisted she'd be fine. She created a playlist for this occasion with songs like "Smooth Criminal" and "Pumped Up Kicks."

Javier and I went into the kitchen to grab some sodas, and when we came back out, we deliberately stood so we were blocking the view of the backdoor.

The TV was loud enough to cover the sound of Daphne sliding the door open. I desperately wanted to turn around and watch, but I kept my focus on the TV. Javier held his phone at his side, catching the whole thing on video. We'd have to settle with watching the unleashing later.

Dad and Luciana got up from the couch, finally out of

their trance-like states. Mom went about combining the bowls of salsa into one.

Dad stretched his arms over his head. "I really like that Warner kid. Best linebacker on the team." He looked at me. "Did you know he played at BYU? I bet Samson knows who he is."

I shook my head, trying to be casual even though I wanted to check on the grasshoppers. "I didn't know that. I'll have to ask."

Luciana rolled her neck. "I always end up so stiff after these games."

Javier and I shared a light laugh. Dad used to always say that when watching games because he was so rigid.

Dad's eyes narrowed in on the ground near my foot. "Is that a grasshopper?"

I looked down and jumped back in fake surprise. "Uh, yeah. Why is it in the house?"

Two more hopped into view, heading toward the coffee table.

With a shriek, Luciana pounced onto the couch and clung to Dad's back.

Mom hurried over, her eyes springing wide as her attention went to the kitchen. I spun around to see grasshoppers everywhere, covering the table, chairs, and floor.

I quickly glanced out back, but I couldn't see any sign of Daphne. The sliding glass door was firmly back in place, making it seem like the grasshoppers had come out of nowhere.

With a startling roar, Mom rushed toward the kitchen and fetched a broom. As she swatted at the grasshoppers, Javier filmed the whole thing, choking back a laugh as he did. Dad held a still-shrieking Luciana in his arms as he watched on in shock.

Mom paused her whacking to glare at me. "Why are you just standing there? Open the back door!"

I sprang into action, leaping over the grasshoppers as I headed toward the back door. As soon as I slid it open, Mom used her broom like a golf club, hitting the grasshoppers out of the house one by one. Dad shook out of his shock, set Luciana down, and then slapped the grasshoppers closer to Mom, like he was setting them up for her swings. I couldn't believe how efficiently they were working together.

When the last one was out of the house, I slid the door closed and locked it. Mom huffed and wiped some sweat from her brow.

Luciana crept into the kitchen. "Are they gone?"

Mom nodded. "Yes, mija."

Dad checked all the windows in back, jiggling them for good measure. "Where did they come from?"

"I don't know." Mom panted and rested her arm on the top of the broom. "The backdoor was sealed shut."

"That can't be a good sign," Dad said, making Javier and me share the slightest of smiles.

I really hoped Mom saw it as a bad sign. She knew the legend of the curse better than I did. Even if it didn't register at first, she'd talk to my abuela who would definitely instill the fear in her. In fact, that option would probably be best. My abuela was very convincing.

It would also mean mom would make the choice herself to end it with Dad instead of blaming it on other people, like her children.

Dad folded his arms, his impressed eyes on Mom. "You've got a good stroke, Kemena. I should take you golfing with me next time I go."

Mom's eyes lit up. "I'd love that."

"It's a date." Dad's smile couldn't have gotten any bigger.

And my hopes were crushed. Total backfire. They weren't supposed to make a date of the situation.

Mom put the broom back in its spot. "We should probably call an exterminator. We could have an infestation."

"Of grasshoppers?" I asked. "How many homes get infestations of grasshoppers?"

Mom swept out an arm. "Well, what do you call this? They could be living in the walls or something." She put an arm around Luciana. "There probably isn't anywhere open tonight. I'll call someone first thing in the morning."

My only remaining hope for some good to come of this would be that Mom would talk to Abuela. She'd let her know it was a sign of the family curse.

Then I could move on to step two.

CHAPTER TWENTY-SIX

*A*buela showed up at our house with a priest in tow in the early hours of the morning. She barged into the house, not bothering to knock. She had a key, but she still usually announced her presence before she entered our home.

Mom and Dad were in a heated discussion in the front room as I descended the stairs, wanting to get some breakfast before school.

Abuela made the sign of the cross as she glanced around. Then she motioned to the priest next to her. "Father Ambrose is here to cleanse the house of the Torres brothers."

Perfect. Mom had talked to her and Abuela had pieced it all together.

Dad scratched his head in confusion. "The Torres brothers?"

Mom rolled her eyes. "Ma, this has nothing to do with them. It's some grasshoppers that got into the house."

Abuela nodded. "Exactly. They got into the house because the Torres brothers let them in."

Mom sighed and rubbed her forehead. "This isn't helping, Ma. The exterminators will be here soon."

Abuela motioned to Father Ambrose. "I have an exterminator right here!"

Dad stepped between the two women. "Who are the Torres brothers?"

Mom's eyebrows raised. "Are you serious, Matías?"

"Are they neighbors?" Dad asked. "Did they move in while I wasn't here?"

Abuela looked like she wanted to straight-up slap my dad. She shot a glance at Father Ambrose like she remembered he was there and relaxed her stance. She settled with clucking her tongue. "My ancestors. Have you already forgotten all the stories I've shared about them over the years?"

Realization passed over Dad's eyes. "Ah, yes, that's right." Then he frowned. "Wait, is this in reference to the curse?"

"Yes, because it's alive and well!" Abuela took a deep breath like she was calming herself.

Father Ambrose, to his credit, stayed quiet the entire time. He wore a soft smile and held his bible in his right hand.

"First the crows, now the grasshoppers." Abuela rubbed the small gold cross hanging around her neck between her thumb and forefinger.

I froze, worried my parents would ask her about the crows, but it appeared they hadn't registered what she had said.

"There's no curse!" Dad said. "That's some silly myth."

Now it was Mom's turn to be mad. She rounded on Dad. "You know full and well that the curse is real."

Someone knocked on the door. I checked out the peephole, surprised to see my dad's brother Rubén and his wife Malena, who held a bucket of cleaning supplies. I willed myself some courage before opening the door. I wasn't sure why they were here, but my mom and auntie didn't have the greatest relationship.

"Good morning," I said with a forced smile.

Malena swept down and kissed my cheek before she came into the house, followed by Rubén, who kissed my forehead.

"Sorry, Matías." Rubén was dressed for work, wearing an expensive-looking suit. His tie and pocket square were pink paisley. "I barely got your message. I had the phone turned off last night. Otherwise, we would have been here sooner."

"Why did you call them?" Mom asked with a hand on her hip.

Dad pointed to the front room like there were still grasshoppers roaming around. "We were invaded. I needed another opinion."

Mom motioned to Rubén and Malena. "What insight could they possibly offer?"

Malena, who wore spandex pants and a tee, held up her bucket. "I brought stuff to clean. I know sometimes life gets away from me and the house gets a little messy. Lets the critters come in."

I sucked in a breath as Mom's cheeks went scarlet. "I keep my house perfectly clean, thank you."

Malena smiled sheepishly. "I'm sure you do. I thought you could use an extra pair of hands since you're so busy."

Mom huffed. "Do you even know how to clean? Don't you have housekeepers at your estate?"

"Kemena," Dad said under his breath. "They're just trying to help. We need to focus on the problem at hand."

Rubén unbuttoned his blazer and stuffed his hands in his pants' pockets. "Walk me through what happened again."

"Somehow, a whole bunch of grasshoppers were in the kitchen ..." Dad started.

Abuela huffed. "*Somehow?* We know how."

Rubén and Malena shared a confused look.

Abuela looked at Father Ambrose. "Shall we get started?"

Rubén turned to where abuela looked and jumped a little. He apparently hadn't noticed Father Ambrose when he came in the house.

To be fair, Father Ambrose had stood there in content silence, not making a sound or even a movement.

Malena set her bucket down on the entryway floor. "Wait a second. Is this about the curse?"

Rubén rubbed his forehead. "Oh, I forgot about that. It's not real." He lowered his hand. "Hold on. Are you comparing Matías to Cristobal?"

Abuela lifted her chin. "He's the one who chose to climb in another woman's bed."

"Ma," Mom said softly.

Rubén opened his mouth, a look of fury on his face, when the front door flew open.

"We're here!" Dulce squeezed her way into the house. "We're here."

Celeste was right behind her but stopped abruptly when she saw everyone crowded in the entryway.

Dad looked at my mom. "Does anyone in your family knock?"

Dulce ignored Dad, her sole focus on my mom. "We brought Father Nicholas in case you need him. He's waiting in the car."

Abuela smiled at her daughter. "Great minds. I brought Father Ambrose. Maybe they can combine efforts."

"This house is not plagued by a curse!" Dad said.

At that, all my family members went off in Spanish, yelling over one another so it was difficult to make out what any of them were saying.

I smiled apologetically at Father Ambrose before I crept upstairs to my room. Everything was going as planned, but I really didn't want to witness any more of the fallout.

I also needed to get ready for school. With it being my first day back since the suspension, I wanted to look my best.

As the yelling continued downstairs, I prayed I hadn't created a war in my family.

CHAPTER TWENTY-SEVEN

It took forever to conceal the bags under my eyes, but I got the job done. Every inch of skin on my face was smooth, the color even. I went with smoky eyes to add some flare to my new haircut.

Before I left, I stuffed a folder filled with messages from DeShawn and his friends in my backpack. If DeShawn left me alone at school and we'd moved passed this whole thing, then I wouldn't give them to the principal. I really wanted to wipe the whole thing from existence and never think about it again. But I also wanted backup in case DeShawn tried anything stupid, which I wouldn't put passed him.

As luck would have it, I didn't see him or his friends all morning. We never crossed paths, which made me hopeful that they'd moved on from following me around. Maybe talking with the principal and our parents had really helped them.

Taylor, Daphne, Weston, Bentley, Sierra, and I sat on the steps of the outdoor amphitheater having lunch. Daphne and Weston were all snuggled up like they'd been glued together.

Bentley and Sierra had a noticeable distance between them. I hadn't seen them fight or seem upset with each other, but they'd kinda drifted apart romantically. They hadn't officially come out to say they weren't together anymore, but they also didn't act like they were still a couple. The whole situation was awkward considering all the drama getting them together in the first place. Not all relationships lasted, though. As long as we could all remain friends, I didn't care what their relationship status ended up being.

Taylor finished off her sandwich and crumpled up the bag. "Okay. So, I have a favor to ask of Weston, Bentley, and Sierra."

They all paused what they were doing and stared at her with curious expressions.

Taylor reached over and patted my arm. "As you know, Veronica's parents are renewing their vows next weekend."

Was it that soon? The whole suspension had messed with my time frame. Maybe I needed to do the bees tomorrow or the next day. Get it in before this weekend so Mom had some time to really let everything sink in.

"Yeah, are we excited about this, or no?" Sierra kicked her legs up on the step and crossed her ankles before leaning back on her palms. "I can't really get a vibe from Veronica."

I sighed. "I'm not happy about it but there's nothing I can do about it."

Daphne winked dramatically at me.

"What was that?" Taylor asked, motioning between Daphne and me.

"What was what?" Daphne asked in a not-so-nonchalant manner.

She really was the worst at keeping secrets. I'd bet she'd

even told Weston when I'd told her not to. By the way he awkwardly checked out the sky to avoid making eye contact with anyone, she'd told him.

"That wink." Taylor turned toward me. "What did you do?"

"Nothing." I snatched an apple from my bag and took a huge bite, letting the crisp sound fill the air.

"You better not ruin this for me, Veronica," Taylor said. "This is a huge deal for our business."

"What business?" Bentley asked.

Daphne clapped her hands together in glee. "Veronica, Taylor, and I are opening a business! Well, when we graduate from UCLA."

I took another bite of my apple. Someday I'd have to tell them I was applying to USC as well. At the moment, it didn't matter since neither application had been submitted. With a suspension now on my record, I might not get into either college. The thought crushed me.

"Gotcha." Bentley closed the lid on his pizza box and chucked it toward the trashcan near us. He grinned wildly when it went in. "So, Taylor, what's the favor?"

Her excitement came back, which I hoped meant she'd forgot about Daphne's over-the-top wink. Taylor clasped her hands together in a plea. "I was hoping the three of you would be servers at the after party."

Sierra arched a pencil-thin black eyebrow. "What would that entail?"

Taylor glanced at her notebook next to her. "Making sure everyone's waters are always topped off. Clear empty plates and silverware off the tables when someone finishes. Bring people desserts they request. Stuff like that."

"How much are we getting paid?" Bentley asked.

Taylor flipped the paper on her notepad. "I have two

hundred dollars budgeted for that and I want to get one more person, so, like fifty a piece. It will only be a few hours. The party starts at seven and will probably go to around ten."

I snorted back a laugh. "You don't know my family." I looked at Bentley, Sierra, and then Weston. "My family will be there until *at least* midnight. But by that point, they'll mostly be dancing so you won't have to do much."

Weston scratched his nose before nodding. "Yeah, okay. I can help."

Daphne kissed him on the cheek. "You're the best."

He smiled, his nose inching up. "No, you're the best."

"No, yo—" Daphne started.

Sierra reached over, snatched one of Bentley's bunched up napkins, and threw it at Daphne and Weston. "Please don't." She sat up and brushed off her hands. "Sure, I'll help. Money is always good."

"Count me in," Bentley said with a grin.

Taylor waved her hands like they were pom-poms. "Yay! Thank you!" She flipped through her notebook, looking over all the details.

The sight was too much, so I stood, gathered my trash, and took it over to the bin. I felt bad about doing this to Taylor. Whether or not my parents went through with it, they'd pay her for her work, so I wasn't worried about that. It was that I knew she'd be super disappointed if it got canceled. All her hard work for nothing.

But it was practice, right? Good prep for her next client.

I spun around right as a huge bucket of white paint tipped over my head, falling all over me and taking me by complete surprise. Thick paint covered my face, making it difficult to open my eyes, but I could hear DeShawn and

Christian's laughter, along with some of their friends. Including the disgusting Jaylen.

A mixture of horror, anger, and complete embarrassment swept over me as the laughter continued. Taylor, Daphne, and Sierra started yelling at the guys, but I couldn't see what was going on. I could only hear all the commotion around me. I froze in place, not knowing what to do. The paint was heavy on me, ruining my hair and probably my brand-new clothes and shoes.

I fell to my knees and wiped at my eyes, trying to get the paint off them. My fake eyelashes came off, sticking to my fingers, and I wanted everything to end. I wanted to be magically in my room, safe from stupid, stupid guys.

The paint fumes overwhelmed me as I struggled for air.

The last thing I heard before I passed out was Daphne screaming at the top of her lungs, "I'm going to murder *all* of you!"

CHAPTER TWENTY-EIGHT

My eyelids tried to open, but the paint held them in place. Even with my eyes closed, dizziness overtook me. Someone scooped me into their arms. I drifted in and out as they carried me across campus. I assumed it was Bentley since he was close and strong enough to carry me.

Wait. Carry me? Wasn't I too heavy? I'd think they'd all need to band together and create a trust grip to heft me all that way. But he walked with surprising ease. Maybe it wasn't Bentley. But then, who was it?

They took me inside and set me down on a rock-hard bed. I must have been in the nurse's office. I couldn't see a thing thanks to the paint.

"Thanks, Victor," Taylor said.

Victor? The lineman on the football team? Why would he help? Maybe he was the only one in the school who could physically carry me, and they'd had to bribe him to do it.

"No problem," Victor's deep voice rumbled. "Sorry, Veronica. Once I figured out what they were up to, it was too late to stop it. What they've been doing to you isn't right."

Okay. Maybe he was a nice guy.

"Take care, Veronica." Victor's large footsteps faded down the hall.

A wet towel pressed against my face.

"Let's scrub off this mess," Daphne said.

Scrub it off? That meant removing my makeup as well, and that so wasn't happening. No way I was revealing all my blemishes to the world, especially right now. I ripped the towels from her hands and pressed them against my face, covering every possible inch, including my eyes since my fake eyelashes had come off.

"Are you okay?" Daphne asked. When I didn't respond, she shook my arms. "Say something, woman!"

"I'm—" The word burned in my throat.

Daphne dropped her hands and ran out of the room, her footsteps fading away.

Taylor's musky smell suddenly embraced me as she wrapped me in a tight hug. I tried to push away, knowing I was getting paint all over her, but she wouldn't budge.

"I can't believe they did that to you." Taylor's voice shook with rage. "Daphne and I tried to maul them, but Bentley and Weston intervened. Said something like we didn't need to get suspended too." She huffed. "Stupid boys."

"I have water!" Daphne's voice bounced as she pounded back into the room. "Tay, let her have some water."

"Oh!" Taylor immediately stepped back.

"Uh, you might want to take the paper towels off," Daphne said.

I shook my head. They were so not coming off.

"Are your eyes burning?" Taylor asked with concern in

her tone. "Maybe we should rinse them off in the sink or something. Daphne and I can help."

I reached my hand out, keeping the paper towels firmly in place with my other hand. The cup landed in my hand, and I wrapped my fist tightly around it. I'd never been so grateful for water in my life. I downed the cup in seconds.

Daphne snatched the cup from me and yelled, "Refill!"

There was a moment of silence before I heard Weston's voice. "Guess that was my cue. Sorry." His quiet footsteps faded.

"He's been suspended." Mom's voice was right in front of me, making me jump. "Both of them! Those two *monsters*!" I hadn't even heard her come in.

"Please lower your volume, Mrs. Rodriguez," Principal O'Shaughnessy said.

"My daughter will use whatever volume she wants!" Abuela? Why was she here too? "Her daughter was attacked by those bullies!"

"I know," Principal O'Shaughnessy said. "But they have been escorted off campus. There's no one left here to yell at." There was a slight pause. "How are you doing, Veronica?"

I picked at the skin on my lips with my teeth, then stopped myself after tasting paint. How was I? Awful. Completely humiliated and standing around with paper towels covering my face so no one could accidentally see me without makeup.

"Did the paint ruin your vocal cords?" Mom asked.

I rolled my eyes, even though she couldn't see them. "No, Ma. I'm stunned."

She tugged at the paper towels. "Why are you holding those there?"

I jerked away. The back of my head collided with the wall, and I sharply inhaled. "Can I go home now?"

"Of course." Mom's voice was soft. "Why are you acting so weird?"

"Weird?" I huffed. "Ma, I just had a five-gallon bucket of paint poured on me. I'm a sticky mess."

A warm arm wrapped around me. "Let's get you home, mija," Abuela said. "I think a hot bubble bath would do you good."

"Did you need more water, Veronica?" Weston asked. "I have some."

I shook my head. "No, thank you. I'll wait until I get home."

"I'm whipping you up a fresh batch of raspberry lemonade the second we walk in the doors," Abuela said.

I suddenly remembered all the messages I'd printed. After what happened, I was definitely handing them over to the principal. "Does someone have my backpack?"

"I do," Bentley said. He was there too? Was *everyone* there, watching me be completely humiliated?

"There's a folder in there," I said. "Can you give it to Principal O'Shaughnessy? It has printouts of all the message DeShawn and the others sent to me."

I heard him unzip my backpack and shuffle through it. I waited in agonizing silence until Principal O'Shaughnessy spoke. "There are messages from other students besides DeShawn and Christian?" Another long pause as papers shuffled. "There are at least a dozen students. Veronica, why didn't you bring this up sooner? This is completely unacceptable and not tolerated at our school."

Tears welled in my eyes. The paper towels absorbed them right away. "I thought they'd stop."

Abuela rubbed her hand along my arm. "I think it's time we get you home and cleaned up."

I slowly nodded and leaned into my abuela as she escorted me to the car and helped me in the front seat.

The second we got home, Mom started the bath for me and Abuela went to making the lemonade. I scrubbed off all the paint—and my makeup—from my face until the true me was revealed.

I checked my phone to see a text from Dad.

> Dad: I heard what happened. I hope you're okay.

Dots danced across the screen before another text came in.

> Dad: Veronica, we really need to talk. All the fighting won't get us anywhere. When you're ready, I'm here.

With a sigh, I sat on the edge of the tub, waiting for it to fill. I wasn't sure when I'd be ready to talk. Right now, all I felt like doing was crying and screaming.

I received an incoming video call from Samson on my phone. With tears in my eyes, I hit ignore and tossed the phone on the counter. No way he was *ever* seeing me like this. He'd see the full, ugly truth. Which meant, Samson and I could never be together. He deserved a model.

Even though I knew my stupid rule of never trusting guys, the thought of Samson being with someone else tore at my heart way more than it should have.

CHAPTER TWENTY-NINE

I soaked in the tub until my skin had gone way past wrinkly. Thank goodness the paint was water-based, so it was easy to get out of my hair. I'd read up on it and saw people mentioning using dish soap and tooth-paste to get it out and I so didn't want to go to that extreme.

Daphne and Taylor stopped by that evening. I hadn't bothered with putting makeup back on, so I told my mom to not let them in the house. I was currently snuggled under my covers, holding a pillow close to my chest. I'd brought up *Jane the Virgin* on the TV but couldn't force myself to press play. I'd been watching it with Samson and didn't want to continue without him.

Mom came upstairs with a huge brown wicker basket in her arms. Her face barely peered out behind the cellophane so she could see where she was going. She plopped it down on my bed with a grunt.

"They were so upset when I told them they couldn't come in." Mom sat down on the bed next to me. "Why do you not want to see them?"

"I'm not in the mood for company." I slowly sat up and set the pillow next to me.

My family had all seen me without makeup, so it didn't bother me to have them see me looking like that.

"Do I have to go to school tomorrow?" I asked, though I already knew what my mom would say.

"Yes, mija." Mom placed a hand on my cheek. "Running away from your problems won't do you any good." She lowered her hand. "Do you know why I named you Veronica?"

She'd never told me the story. "I figured you liked the name."

She softly smiled. "I do. But it means, 'she who brings victory.' It represents being saintly, sensuous, and strong. Three traits you have flaunted since birth." She took my hand in hers. "I've always admired how fierce you are. You cannot let these silly boys strip that from you. You're a good person with a good heart." She chuckled. "I heard Daphne tried to do some sort of karate chop on DeShawn but completely missed the mark. But it's the thought that counts. You picked friends who would fight for you as much as you would fight for them. You need to learn to let them fully in."

I pulled back in surprise. "I do. I've always been honest with them."

Her gaze traveled to my massive makeup collection. "Veronica also means 'true image.' Have you showed them your true image, mija? The beautifully flawed flower you are?"

"Flawed?" That cut to the core.

Mom rolled her eyes. "No one is perfect, Veronica. That's a lie spread by all these big companies pushing their products. We are all beautiful in our own right. Embrace your true beauty, mija." She leaned in and kissed me on the forehead. "Get some rest." She left the room, closing the door behind her.

I sought out the flower image of me on the wall. What was the point of letting my friends see me at my worst? There was no harm in making sure I was always presentable around them.

With a deep breath, I tugged the gift basket toward me. "Wow, this is heavy."

I untied the ribbon and opened the cellophane. The basket overflowed with presents. All my favorite chips and candy. Bottles of lemonade. Nail polishes, lip glosses, facial masks, lotions, and bath bombs. Tears filled my eyes to the point I couldn't see. I brushed them away.

I really did have the best friends. They'd always been there for me. Especially when my dad first left. Daphne was in a completely different state at the time and she video called me every single day to cheer me up with a dance, song, or some crazy story.

I'd done the same when her dad died.

Why couldn't I let her see me like this? Or Taylor? Would they really stop being my friends if they found out I wasn't pretty?

I noticed a card tucked into the side of the basket. When I pulled it out, a gift card to my favorite Indian restaurant fell onto my lap.

With a smile, I read the card. It began in Daphne's handwriting.

VERONICA!

We love you so much and want you to know that we will kill anyone you ask us to. Or if you call us one night and say, 'grab a shovel and come help me move a body' we will be there, no questions asked.

At this point, it switched to Taylor's handwriting.

OR we could all go to dinner at Veronica's favorite restaurant on Saturday night. Samson's paying. Huntley and Weston will be there, too.

We got your back, girl.

Back to Daphne's handwriting.

Ugh, boring and gross, but fine. We'll go eat dinner instead. But if we take a detour past a certain football's players hou—

It abruptly cut off and switched back to Taylor's handwriting.

Clear your Saturday night! You're going to have the night of your life. That doesn't involve

killing anyone, btw.

Back to Daphne.

I'm sending you a playlist to cheer you up.
Listen to them, V. Really listen.
Kissy noises!

Their names were in their own handwriting.

Daphne agreeing to go to an Indian restaurant was a huge deal. She hated the smell and spices. But she also knew it was my favorite.

Samson was paying. He'd be there.

Wait. There would be six of us. Three girls, three guys. Was this a triple date?

I shoved the thought right out of my mind as quickly as it came. No, it wasn't. It was two couples and then two friends hanging out. No big deal.

My phone charged on the nightstand, so I reached to grab it. The orchids Samson had gotten me were still in the vase. They'd wilted, but I couldn't get myself to throw them away.

I brought up the playlist on my phone and scrolled through the songs. "Victoria's Secret" by Jax, "About Damn Time," by Lizzo, and "Made You Look" by Meghan Trainor were some of the songs.

There was one I didn't recognize. "Body Image" by Madilyn Paige.

I pressed play and laid down on my bed, closing my eyes. The tears came on the very first line.

Why was it so hard to tell myself I was beautiful or accept me the way I was?

One line really made me pause as I let the words sink in. *'Imagine me loving me, what would that be like?'*

I thought back to before my dad left, before I'd gained all the weight, before DeShawn had crushed my self-esteem in his stupid hands.

I loved me then. I was confident and strong.

I needed to find that Veronica again.

CHAPTER THIRTY

Dad wanted to finally sit down and talk, but a problem came up at work and he spent most nights in his office trying to put out the fire.

Since the guys weren't at school, the next few days were completely uneventful, which was perfect.

Victor and some of the other football players came over and apologized on behalf of their stupid teammates, which I thought was nice of them. Even the coaches sought me out on campus to let me know they didn't condone that kind of behavior and that the guys had been suspended from the next game, which happened to be our rival, so I knew that was a big deal.

On Friday night, I found myself smiling when I sat down for dinner with my family. Things had kind of simmered and gone back to the way things had been before Dad's big exodus.

It also helped that Mom made Khao Soi (a Thai coconut curry noodle soup) which she knew was one of my favorite dishes. It did make me think of Samson since we'd both gotten it from a restaurant when we were helping prepare for his father's grand birthday party.

I'd learned that day how much Samson and I had in common. I'd started looking at him in a different way after that but didn't realize it until now.

"What are you smiling about, mija?" Mom asked.

I looked up from my soup. I hadn't realized I'd been smiling. "Oh. I love this soup."

Her eyes narrowed in a knowing way, but she dropped it. She turned to Javier and Luciana. "How was school today for you two? Veronica already gave me a rundown of her day."

We'd been doing it every day this week. Mom and Dad wanted to know everything that happened at school to make sure I wasn't being bullied. All of it had stopped with DeShawn's and his friends' suspensions, but a part of me worried it would start up again when they were back in school.

Luciana swirled the noodles around in her soup. "It was okay. Someone farted during math, and it totally smelled like rotten eggs. No one would admit it was them, though."

Mom and Dad both chuckled.

Javier grinned. "It was you, wasn't it?"

Luciana swatted him hard on the arm. "No! Most of us think it was Daniel, but we aren't certain."

Javier set his fork and spoon down. "I got an A on my latest drawing in Art. It's from my new collection titled 'Social Media.'"

"That's wonderful, Javy!" Mom practically burst with joy.

"How many images do you have in the collection so far?" I scooped some of the soup onto my spoon.

"Only three so far." Javier wore the biggest smile. He

had such a passion for his art. "But my goal is ten. That's how many I do for each collection."

"Can I see some of them?" I asked.

Javier pulled out his phone.

"After dinner, Javy." Mom looked at my dad. "We have such talented kids, don't we Matías?"

Dad shook his head. "An artist is not a real job, Javy. You need to aim higher."

"It is a real job, Dad." Javier folded his arms. "I thought you were finally starting to support my art."

Dad sat tall in his chair. "It's only a hobby. It won't put food on the table."

"Dad, Javy is a really good artist," I said. "He's already making money from it."

"Creating paintings for an art museum is one thing," Dad said. "But doing some scribbles for some teenage girls online is a waste of time." He waved a hand toward me. "You should follow the example of your sister. She's getting a business degree from UCLA. She's going to move mountains one day."

I set my spoon next to my bowl, my sole focus going to Dad. "I haven't been accepted to UCLA yet."

"You will," Dad said with determined eyes.

I sighed. "Maybe. But I also want to go to the Institute of Culinary Education." I swallowed. "Which is actually really close to USC."

Dad harrumphed. "Being a chef is a risky business. And none of this USC talk. I think Samson is corrupting your mind."

"This has nothing to do with Samson!" I took a long, shaky breath. "This is *my* choice."

Mom scolded Dad with her eyes. "Maybe we shouldn't

talk about this right now." She jerked her head toward Luciana, whose eyes had filled with tears.

"Then what would you like to talk about, Kemena?" Dad asked. The steel tone of his voice brought me back to when they were fighting before Dad had walked out on the family.

The sting in Mom's eyes told me she noticed. She composed herself before speaking. "We have about a week until the vow renewal. I'm picking up my dress tomorrow."

The tension at the table grew. That wasn't really the happy conversation turner she'd been hoping for. Half of the people at the table didn't want the renewal to happen.

It was comforting knowing I wasn't the only one seething at this prospect. Javier was right there with me.

Javier moved his full attention to his bowl of soup. Luciana gazed into her bowl, her eyes unfocused as tears slid down her cheeks.

"You're all acting like someone died," Dad said with obvious annoyance.

"You know our feelings on the matter." I tried to hold back the anger in my tone, but it dripped through.

Mom slammed her palm down on the table. "Everyone to their rooms." When no one moved, she stood. "Now!"

The three of us kids scurried out of the kitchen and up the stairs. I went straight to my room but when I went to close the door, both Javier and Luciana stood there expectantly.

I motioned for them to come in and shut the door behind them.

Luciana immediately flopped down on my bed and grabbed one of the decorative pillows. Javier took a seat at the vanity. I'd expected him to maybe take a photo of himself through the mirror for his followers, but he sulked instead.

"Why do you hate Dad so much?" Luciana asked.

Javier opened his mouth and by the look in his eyes I knew it wouldn't be nice, so I spoke before he could. "He's put our family through so much, Luci." I sat down on the bed, and she set her head in my lap. "I think we're scared he's going to do it again."

She sniffed. "He said he was sorry."

Javier scoffed at that but didn't say anything.

I combed my fingers through my sister's hair. "I know he did. But people sometimes make the same bad choices over and over again. We can't trust him like we used to."

Her voice was so soft. "Don't you want to be a family again?"

I looked over at Javier. His demeanor softened.

"Of course we want that," Javier said. "But it's not that simple."

"All I want is for everyone to stop fighting," Luciana whispered.

Javier and I shared a long look. It would be nice if we could wave a magical wand and fix everything, but life was never that easy. I needed to ramp up my plan.

As soon as my brother and sister left the room, I texted Hank to let him know I was ready for some bees. Stage two was about to commence.

CHAPTER THIRTY-ONE

I pulled into Daphne's driveway and honked my horn. I usually got out and went to the front door, but I was eager to get this over with.

I'd thought about being inside the house when the bees were released, but I wasn't sure if Daphne could handle the bees all on her own. I'd have to watch Javier's recording afterward.

Daphne waddled out of her house in what appeared to be a beekeeper outfit. She drowned in it, like a little kid playing dress-up. She held something big and bulky in her arms.

She bent in front of the closed passenger side window, her voice coming out muffled. "Pop the trunk!" Then she waddled away.

After Daphne had stuffed everything in the trunk, she awkwardly climbed into the front seat.

"What are you wearing?" I asked, trying to contain my laughter.

Daphne tried to shut the door, but it got caught on her pants. She gathered up the material then tried again, the door closing that time. "My neighbor, Terry, is a beekeeper. He let me borrow some outfits." She bunched all the excess material in her arms. "He's like six foot five and about four hundred pounds, so he only had them in four XL. I'm realizing I should have waited to put this on once we got there."

With a chuckle, I pulled out of the driveway.

"Laugh now, lady," Daphne said with a huff. "But when we're surrounded by bees, you'll be thanking me." She suddenly gasped, making me jerk to a stop. "I should have made bee Mickey ears! Missed opportunity."

"And that caused you to gasp like I was about to hit something?" I didn't mask the annoyance in my voice as I started driving again.

She tilted her head toward me, the angle awkward. "Uh, yeah."

I busted out in a laugh that felt so good. I loved my best friend and was beyond glad to have her back in the same state with me.

When we got to Hank's house, I had Daphne stay in the car. Mostly because I wasn't sure if she'd be able to get out and back in with the ginormous outfit on.

Hank carried out a box of bees and put them in the trunk. I ended up putting the other beekeeper outfit into the back seat so there would be room for the bees.

Hank gently closed the trunk. "You sure you don't want help with this? Bees aren't something anyone can handle."

No way I was letting Hank help. It would blow my operation wide open. "Thanks, but my friend's neighbor is a beekeeper. He's meeting us to help film." Total lie, but Hank didn't know that.

Hank blew out a breath of relief. "Good. I was a little worried. Bees can get aggressive when they're moved from their normal location to another."

That didn't bode well, but there was no going back now. "Thanks again, Hank!"

He saluted me and then went back inside his house.

When I got back in the car, Daphne had "Honey Bee" by Blake Shelton playing via Bluetooth. She serenaded me all the way back to my house, putting the song on repeat as she cranked up the twang in her voice.

By the time we pulled along the curb in front of my neighbor's house, I'd be happy if I never heard the song again.

I opened the trunk and stared at the box of bees. A light buzzing drifted from the box.

Daphne shuffled up next to me and tugged on a beekeeper hat. "What's the plan?"

"We're going to take this box to my dad's office and release them." I bent toward the box. "Help me carry it."

Daphne clucked her tongue. "Not until you put on your beekeeper outfit, young lady."

I stood upright and rolled my eyes. "I'm not putting that stupid thing on."

She folded her arms. "Then I'm not helping you."

We glared at each other, her eyes getting wider and crazier with each passing second. I finally gave in and put on the outfit that was four sizes too big, along with the stupid hat. I had to roll up the arms and legs on the uniform so I could function.

Daphne and I carried the box to the side of my house, setting it down outside the window to my dad's office.

I burned up inside the uniform and couldn't wait to get it off.

"You go in first," Daphne said, lifting the window open, "and then I'll hand you the box."

I looked at the hole I needed to crawl through and

wished I would have waited to put on the uniform *after* I'd gone through the window. I lifted one leg inside and tried to shuffle across the desk, but the uniform got stuck on the windowsill. Daphne wrestled the material free and then gave my booty a little push until I was fully inside the office.

I was a sweaty, panting mess by the time I stood up and held my arms out for the box. With a grunt, Daphne lifted the box and pushed it through so it sat on the office table.

"I think I'm going to take off the lid here," I said, looking over the top of the box at Daphne.

"But what if they all fly outside?" Daphne asked.

I sighed. "I really don't want to move it to the floor. It's heavy and I'm tired."

"Then we should at least close the window." Daphne set her gloved hands on the lid of the window. "I know I'm not inside with you, but I am in spirit." She closed the window before I could respond.

The buzzing in the box grew, and I really, really hoped I didn't regret this. With a silent prayer, I tiptoed over to the office door and cracked it open. Mom and Dad were curled up together on the couch watching a movie. Guess they had worked through their fight.

When I got back to the box, I slowly lifted the lid, squinting my eyes like bees were going to zoom out into my face. The screen from the hat protected my face but the thought of one sneaking through terrified me.

To my dismay, the bees mostly stayed in the box, attached to the honeycomb. A few drifted out but didn't go far.

"Come on, guys!" I pleaded quietly. "I know that honey is sweet, but I need you to go out into the front room. Just fly around a bit and then you can come back and have all the honeycomb you want."

The bees stayed put.

Gritting my teeth—mostly out of fear—I slipped out one of the walls of honeycomb and held it far away from me as I carried it over to the door. Bees buzzed all around it not drifting too far.

Using my foot, I opened the door a little more so the bees would have room to escape. I swung the honeycomb back and forth, trying to get them to leave.

The buzzing grew like they were getting ticked off at me. They finally left the honeycomb, heading into the front room. I swished the honeycomb a little more until most of the bees were gone, then shut the door, slid the wall back into the box, replaced the lid, and had Daphne help me get it out of the house and back to my car.

My throat cried for water when I sat in the front seat of my car. I'd removed the stupid uniform and thrown it in the back. Even Daphne had ditched hers.

"What are we going to do with the extra bees?" Daphne asked.

"Would your neighbor want them?" I started the car and pulled away from the curb.

"I'll ask." Daphne went to hook her phone back up to my Bluetooth, so I slapped her hand away.

"We're keeping it connected to my phone. If I hear that 'Honey Bee' song one more time, I'm kicking you out of my car."

She maneuvered her phone so I couldn't see the screen. "I have no idea what you're talking about. My plan was to play some Post Malone."

"Uh huh." A smile spread on my face, not because of Daphne, but because I'd completed phase two. I couldn't wait to watch the playback from Javier.

I figured Mom would use the same tactic. Grab a

broom, have Javy open the back door, and swat all the bees out of the house.

We were almost to Daphne's when an incoming call came through on my Bluetooth. It was my mom.

Daphne mimed zipping her mouth close and then pressed answer on the screen.

"Hello?" I asked.

In the background, Javier screamed at the top of his lungs.

"Shh!" Mom said. "Veronica? Uh, there's been an incident. We're taking Javier to the hospital, but it's not a big deal, so I don't want you to panic."

Hospital?

"I'm going to die!" Javier shrieked.

"It's only a few bee stings," Dad said. "You'll live."

"He's allergic!" Luciana yelled.

Daphne pressed mute on the call. "Javier is allergic to bees?"

My hands gripped the steering wheel tight. "I didn't know that!"

"Okay, well, maybe it's like a minor allergy and not like a he's-going-to-die allergy."

Dad and Mom didn't sound too worried. Javier was freaking out, but that was typical for him. The guy was all about the theatrics.

As I pulled in front of Daphne's house, I hoped and prayed I hadn't royally screwed my brother.

CHAPTER THIRTY-TWO

It didn't take me long to find my family when I got to the E.R. Javier's wails could be heard the second the double doors swooshed open. Some relief washed through me when I realized they were his dramatic wails that he saved for end-of-the-world type things that weren't actually end-of-the-world to normal people. Just him.

"How can I ever go out in public again?" Javier cried, his fourteen-year-old voice cracking.

A nurse stepped out from behind the closed curtain with an amused smile on her face. She paused when she saw me. "Are you the sister?"

"Not sure I want to claim that at the moment," I said. "Is he going to be okay?"

She nodded. "Oh, yeah. His face is completely swollen, but with some rest and Benadryl, he'll be as good as new in no time."

I lowered my voice. "Any way we could keep a little permanent swelling? The kid needs to be kicked off the pedestal he's put himself on."

The nurse chuckled. "I remember that age. Everything seemed like the biggest deal."

"Doesn't help that he has hundreds of thousands of followers online."

Her thin eyebrows shot up. "Impressive." She paused. "Oh, that makes sense now what your dad has been doing. He's been live streaming the whole thing and saying all these weird things about Hottie Javy."

Oh, no. Javier would *kill* Dad if he posted this online. I hurried past the nurse and into the curtained off area.

Mom stood next to the bedside, trying to console Javier. The nurse downplayed the swelling. I couldn't even recognize Javier. Most of his features merged into one big lump.

Javier clutched Luciana's unicorn, Sparkles, in his arms as he thrashed about. Luciana grimaced like Javier was actually hurting Sparkles by squeezing her so hard.

Off to the side, Dad filmed the meltdown. I ran over to his side and checked over his shoulder. The nurse had been right. He was live streaming it to Javier's followers.

I quickly snatched the phone from Dad and ended the live stream.

"What are you doing?" Dad asked through his laugh. "This is priceless!"

I hurried to Javier's homepage and deleted the video, though the damage had been done. It was then that I noticed Javier had almost a million followers. And it was climbing. He'd been at five hundred thousand a couple of weeks ago. I wasn't sure if it had been steadily growing or if this was all because of the video.

I scrolled through his feed. So many people were commenting and sharing screen shots of his tantrum. Javier might never recover from this.

I glared at Dad. "What were you thinking?"

Dad waved a hand. "Calm down. It's all in good fun."

I was pretty sure Javier would beg to differ.

I went to his side. "What happened?"

Mom stroked his damp hair. "We were sitting in the living room when bees trickled in. I screamed in panic, which caused Javier to bound down the stairs. He very heroically swatted at them, but it made them sting him." She pulled back the blanket and showed me his swollen arms. "His legs are the same. The nurse says all his vital signs are fine. His skin had a weird reaction. It could take a week for his skin to go back to normal."

"A week!" Javier's wails—that had lightened—increased tenfold as he clutched Sparkles.

Luciana covered her ears with her palms.

Javier's phone buzzed in my hand. I pulled up his feed to notice he'd hit a million followers. Maybe something good had come from it. Although, seeing all the mean things people said and how they mocked him wouldn't be good to Javier. He would be devastated to see it.

So many people tagged him in their posts. Memes had already been created.

Did I delete his account? Maybe temporarily disable it until things settled? I wasn't sure the best way to approach it.

Suddenly, Abuela ran in with Father Ambrose at her side.

"We're here!" Abuela pushed my dad out of the way so she could be at Javier's side. "Father Ambrose will fix everything, mijo." She went to kiss him on the forehead but stopped herself short, probably at the sight of his skin. "The curse is back." She rounded on my dad. "You must leave, Matías. At once."

Dad's face went scarlet. "I'm not leaving!"

"Ma!" Mom's wide eyes were on my abuela. "There's no curse!"

"First grasshoppers and now bees?" Abuela shook her finger at my mom. "It's the curse, Kemena. This is what you get for letting *that man* back into your home. If you don't put an end to this now, a snake will be next. Our family will be doomed."

Luciana's chin quivered. "A curse? Snake? Doomed? I don't like any of those words!"

Mom wrapped an arm around her. "It's okay, Luci. Your abuela is spouting nonsense."

At that moment, I saw some doubt in Mom's eyes. Her confused gaze settled on my dad.

Dad threw up his arms. "Oh, come on, Kemena. This is crazy. Your family is way too superstitious."

"Superstitious?" Abuela seethed. "You can't ignore the signs, Matías. They're all there!"

Luciana cried, tears streaming down her cheeks and neck. The whole thing twisted my stomach into a knot. I was happy that my plan was working on my mom and abuela, but I hadn't taken my siblings into consideration. Especially Luciana. For someone so feisty, she had a very sensitive heart. She wore her emotions on her sleeves.

Dulce suddenly slid into the packed area around Javier's bed. "I came as soon as I could." She looked at Father Ambrose. "I'm so glad you're here."

Dad rubbed his forehead like a headache was forming. "Kemena, are you going to keep involving your family in all our problems?"

Mom huffed. "I wasn't aware our child being in the hospital was a problem!"

I tucked Javier's phone into my bag slung across my body. "Why don't I take Luciana home?" I turned to my dad. "Maybe you should come, too. We've already created quite the scene."

Mom kissed the top of Luciana's head and then gently pushed her toward me. "I think that's a good idea. It's way too crowded in here."

"So, you're choosing your family over me?" Dad asked.

Mom let out a tired sigh before she motioned to Luciana. "I'm choosing *our* family."

Dad softened at that, finally realizing how all the fighting affected Luciana.

I took Luciana's hand and turned around, only to jump. Father Ambrose quietly stood there, a serene smile on his face. I'd totally forgotten about him.

"Uh, good luck in there," I said to him before I steered Luciana out of the E.R.

Luciana clung to my hand like if I let go, she'd fade away.

"Everything's going to be okay, Luci," I said. "I promise."

She leaned into me as we walked. "Will the fighting ever stop?"

The only way it would stop was if we got rid of Dad for good. With Abuela's reaction to the curse, we were definitely on the right course.

A phone in my bag buzzed, and it didn't take a genius to figure it was probably Javier's and not mine. When I pulled it out, I saw he had some messages from his friends seeing if he was okay.

His followers may have turned on him, but at least his friends hadn't.

CHAPTER THIRTY-THREE

*J*avier locked himself in his room when he got back from the hospital. Any time someone knocked on his door and tried to talk to him, he'd either ignore them or yell at them to go away.

It wasn't until the next day when I was getting ready for my not-triple-date that Javier opened his door and exited his room.

"DAD!" Javier's voice was on the verge of madness.

I only had one eyelash on, but the other one would have to wait. I ran out into the hall to see what was going on.

Javier stood there fuming. "DAD!" His swelling had gone down, so he was recognizable once again.

"What's wrong, Javy?" I approached cautiously, not wanting to get the brunt of his wrath.

He held out his phone so the screen faced me. The main page of his social media account was up. Uh oh. The last time I checked, his phone was in my room. I hadn't wanted to give it to Javier quite yet. That meant someone went in my room when I wasn't around.

"Who gave that to you?" I asked.

He shook in anger. "That doesn't matter! What matters is Dad filmed the ENTIRE THING FOR MY FOLLOWERS TO SEE!"

Yes, he had screamed it at the top of his lungs. I'd be surprised if the neighbors didn't hear.

I held up my palms, hoping to calm him. "I know, Javy. I stopped it as soon as I got there. The good news is you have over a million followers now. Hasn't that been your goal?"

With his puffy face, his dyed-red hair in devil horns, plus his old Pokémon shirt that he slept in, Javier was quite the sight. I kind of wanted to snap a picture but knew I'd be dead if I did.

Loud footsteps pounded on the stairs and seconds later Mom appeared in the hallway. "Why are you yelling?"

Javier rounded on her. "Did you know? About the livestream?"

"I was too busy focused on you!" Mom took a deep breath. "I was trying to calm you down in the stressful situa-tion. I wasn't paying attention to your father."

Javier showed her his screen. "Have you seen this, Ma? All the reels of me writhing with 'Bones' by Imagine Dragons playing." He pressed play, so I hurried over to see. The reel had Javier in the midst of his tantrum, arms and legs flailing, combined with the part of the song that says, "My patience is waning. Is this entertaining?"

Javier scrolled to another video. "They've done this to 'Shivers,' 'Maniac.' Oh, and 'World's Smallest Violin' by AJR." He brought up another video. "This one they did in slow motion so all my movements are in sync with 'Glimpse of Us' by Joji. I look like a freak!"

His followers had really gotten creative.

"Isn't this a good thing?" Mom asked with a confused expression. "You're famous now, right?"

"Not for the right reasons!" Javier yanked at his devil horns. "Everyone is making fun of me, Ma. I'm the laughingstock of TikTok!"

"Javier, calm down," Mom said. "You're overreacting."

"Where is he?" Javier asked.

Mom set a hand on her hip. "He and Luciana went to run some errands."

Javier spun on his heels and marched toward Mom and Dad's bedroom.

Mom hurried after him. "What are you doing?"

"Getting his stuff." Javier slammed the bedroom door open. "I'm kicking him out of the house."

"You can't do that." Mom ran in front of Javier and gently put her hands on his heaving chest. "You don't run this home, Javy."

"You do," Javier said. "You should kick him out. He doesn't deserve to be here."

"That's not fair—"

Javier threw up his hands. "He ruins *everything*. Our lives are better without him in it."

Mom flinched like she'd been slapped. "Don't say that."

I stood in the doorway and whistled. They both turned to me.

"This is getting out of hand," I said. "Ma, Javier has a point. Our lives have been chaos since Dad came back in the picture."

Mom's eyes welled with tears. "It's been chaos because of you stubborn kids. I love your father. I want him in our home. Neither of you get to choose for me. We're the adults and both of you need to remember that. You live under *our* roof."

I hated seeing her so upset, but I didn't understand where she was coming from at all. "Mom, maybe if you helped us understand why you took him back, we might be more open to the idea."

Mom sat on her bed, tears flowing freely down her face. Javier softened and grabbed a box of tissues from the dresser before he sat next to Mom and put his arm around her. I sat on the other side of her.

"It's difficult to put into words." Mom took a shaky breath. "When your father and I met, we had an instant connection. I'd never felt anything like it. It was like everything aligned in the world. It was like ... like ..." She sighed and rubbed her forehead.

"Like you'd found your person," I finished for her. Stupid Daphne.

She turned to me and nodded. "Exactly. We were meant for each other. No one has ever made me as happy as he has."

"No one has ever broken your heart like he has," Javier said.

Mom wiped at her cheeks with a tissue. "I know. You're right about that. It was like my heart had been ripped out. But when he came back? It tucked safely back into place. I know it's not going to be easy, but I'm hoping that with time your hearts will do the same."

I leaned my head on her shoulder. "I'm sorry, Ma. But I do need to know that Dad feels the same about you. We love you so much and you deserve someone who will treat you with respect."

"Have either of you thought about sitting down with your father and talking to him about it?" She rubbed the tissue under her nose and yanked another tissue out of the box.

Javier and I exchanged a glance before he spoke. "Dad doesn't really show an interest in us."

I thought back to all the texts Dad had been sending me. He'd been trying to reach out, and I'd been shutting him down. Had he not been sending Javier texts as well?

"He loves all three of you very much," Mom said. "He doesn't know how to show his emotions sometimes. I guess quality time and words of affirmation aren't his love languages."

Javier smiled at that, but it quickly faded. "He hasn't apologized to us for leaving. His sole focus has been you. We're here, too."

"Sounds like the three of you need to sit down and talk this out." Mom wrapped her arms around us and pulled us close. "I know you don't trust your father, but do you trust me?"

"Yeah," Javier said at the same time I said, "Of course."

"Then trust me to make the right decision for our family. I believe your dad being home is the right choice. You two need to open your hearts."

Silence sat in the air as we let everything sink in. We needed to stop putting off our talk with Dad. Or maybe we needed family therapy.

"Why do you only have one eyelash on?" Javier suddenly asked.

I jumped from the bed. "I have to get ready!"

The whole fight had distracted me. I checked my watch. Only fifteen minutes until they picked me up.

"Ma, I need your help!" I said as I sprinted from her room.

Her footsteps pounded behind me. "What can I do?"

I turned the corner into my room and ran to the vanity. "Can you do my hair while I finish my makeup?"

Mom smiled. "Of course, mija."

In record time, my hair had been styled, my makeup

perfectly done, and I had slipped into a burgundy jumper that matched the highlights in my hair. I almost wore a dress, but I wasn't sure what the night entailed. No one had given me specifics, just that we were going out. And I'd been too busy to really reach out and ask.

For a fleeing moment, I'd totally forgotten about the argument.

Then I saw Javier in the hallway, and it all came rushing back.

"You okay?" I asked.

Javier shrugged. "I will be. Eventually. I'm completely humiliated." He leaned against the wall. "It's probably a good thing Dad wasn't here when I first saw what he'd done. I was *so* mad."

I wasn't sure if asking would open another can of worms, but I decided to risk it. "Javy, has Dad been sending you texts?"

He nodded. "Yeah, but I ignore them. They are so random and weird."

"Like memories from growing up?"

"You, too?"

"Yep," I said. "I've come to the conclusion that he's trying to help us remember the good times."

"That makes sense." Javier paused, his expression thoughtful. "Maybe I can have a rational conversation with him when he gets home. Make him see our side of things."

"Good luck." I went to my brother and hugged him tight. "Things will work out the way they're supposed to."

Javier sighed as we ended our embrace. "I'm afraid I'm not going to like the way."

I nodded. "Same."

"I forgot I have something to give you." Javier went into his room and came back out holding a small present.

With a smile, I unwrapped the sky-blue paper. It was a phone case for my new phone. I turned it over and noticed Javier's original artwork on the back. *The Veronica.*

"This way you can have a constant reminder of who you are." Javier stuffed his hands in his pockets.

"Thanks, Javy." I cleared my throat, trying to stop the tears that wanted to come. "I love it."

"Have fun tonight." Javier slunk past me toward the bathroom but then paused and turned back around. "For the record, I like Samson. He's a cool guy. About a million times better than DeShawn."

My face heated. "Samson and I are just friends."

"If you say so." Javier slipped into the bathroom and closed the door.

Samson and I *were* just friends. I didn't need another guy in my life so soon after the last, especially when the last one had sucked the life out of me. I needed to find myself again before I started dating again.

CHAPTER THIRTY-FOUR

The Thomas family's huge van—aka *the shuttle*—stopped outside my house right at six o'clock, but only Samson came to the door. He handed me a gift bag with all my favorite goodies.

I hadn't seen him in person since our kiss. I wasn't sure how I'd feel, but seeing his fun-loving smile made my heart melt. I found myself grinning wildly and kind of wanting to kiss him again.

"Are you okay with a hug?" Samson asked.

"Of course." I wrapped an arm around him—my other arm held the bag.

I breathed in his light breezy scent, like the ocean. I wasn't sure it if was his soap or cologne, but I liked it.

"I can take the bag for you." Mom suddenly stood there, holding out her arms.

I handed her the bag. "Thanks, Ma."

"Hi, Samson," Mom said with a bright smile. "It's nice to see you again."

"You, too, Mrs. Rodriguez." Samson still had an arm

around me. "Is there a certain time Veronica should be home?"

If my mom's smile was bright before, it turned blinding. Samson definitely knew how to score points with the parents.

"Around ten is fine," Mom said.

"Ten?" Using my eyes, I pleaded with her. Taylor and Daphne both had midnight curfews on the weekends.

She finally gave in. "Eleven, but not a minute later." She looked at Samson. "We'll have to have you over for dinner again. We all had such a lovely time."

I held in my eyeroll. Dad definitely hadn't had a lovely time but a lot of that was thanks to Samson going to Dad's rival college.

"I'd be honored," Samson said.

"You kids have fun!" Mom kissed my cheek and then winked at me.

Samson escorted me to *the shuttle* and held open the passenger door for me as I got in.

"Girl, I *love* that jumper," Taylor said from the bench behind me.

She and Huntley snuggled up, looking totally hot together.

Daphne and Weston sat on the bench behind them, also snuggled up in their adorkable way. They really both had found their perfect match.

Samson slid into the front seat and started the engine.

"What's the plan?" I asked.

Samson put the van in drive. "How do you feel about roller skating?"

I hadn't been since I was a little girl. I wasn't sure if I'd remember how.

"She *loves* the idea and thinks we're all brilliant for suggesting it," Daphne said.

Samson stared at me, waiting for my response. I had this nagging feeling that it would go horribly wrong, but I didn't want to let everyone down.

"Roller skating it is," I said.

Samson turned on some Post Malone and then pulled away from the curb.

Butterflies rushed to my stomach when we stepped onto the skating rink. Trying to bend over, reach my feet, and wrestle on the skates made me break out in a sweat.

The second we got onto the rink, my legs spread, going in opposite directions that would surely leave me doing the splits on the ground and never being able to get back up.

Samson's hand landed on the small of my back as his other hand steadied my arm. "You need to do a few laps and you'll get the hang of it."

"If you say so." I really appreciated his being there to keep me from making a fool of myself. "But you can't let go until I'm ready."

He leaned toward me. "And if I don't want to let go?"

"Then don't." The words flew out of my mouth before I could properly analyze them and evaluate the weight they carried.

The smile on Samson's face made me forget my worries.

He slid his hand into mine, interlocking our fingers. I lost my balance for a second—why was his touch driving me crazy?—so I latched my other hand onto his arm and stayed as close as I possibly could to him.

"This brings me back to what, your seventh or eighth birthday?" Samson grinned. "You sure knew how to skate back then."

I knew exactly what party he was referring to. I wanted so hard to impress Taylor's older brothers that day. Well, mostly Samson. "I think that was my eighth birthday." My hip swung to the side, so I used him as a support to right myself. "And I most definitely did not know how to skate. I think I fell like ten times." I had been so embarrassed and never wanted to go roller skating again.

Taylor and Huntley lapped us, skating like professionals. I swear they were seconds away from Huntley lifting Taylor into the air.

"Well, I remember an extremely confident Veronica. She owned the rink."

How did he remember so much from our past? At least he remembered the good parts, not the bad.

I hadn't seen Daphne and Weston since we got onto the rink. Not that I'd really been looking for them. My whole focus had been Samson. And also not making a fool of myself.

I risked peeking behind me and saw Daphne and Weston sprawled on the ground, laughing hysterically. At least if I fell, I wouldn't be the only one.

Although, whenever Daphne or Weston did something clumsy, it was adorable and made people smile.

When *I* did something clumsy, I looked like a beached whale trying to find their way back to the water.

"Only a week until the vow renewal," Samson said.

It took me a moment to register his words. Then it took

me another moment to collect my thoughts and respond. "Yep."

"How are you feeling about it?" His tone held so much interest like he wanted to know my real thoughts and feelings.

My relationship with DeShawn had been so superficial. DeShawn had never wanted to talk about personal things or get deep. It could have been because Samson was older and wiser, but I think it mostly came down to the fact that he was an all-around better person.

"Not good." I stumbled a little, but Samson kept me on my feet. He'd been doing that a lot lately. I sighed. "I don't understand how my mom could forgive him so easily."

"Have you asked her about it?"

"Yeah, and her response didn't satisfy my heart."

We turned a corner on the rink, so I clutched onto Samson. He'd been right. I was getting the hang of it after a few laps, but I liked having a reason to cling to him.

"What response would satisfy you?" Samson stared down at me, somehow skating flawlessly without even looking where he was going.

I thought about his question for a while. What would satisfy me? Mom kicking Dad out for good would do it.

Luciana's cute, sassy face entered my mind. It would devastate her, though. I hadn't realized how much she'd shut down with Dad gone until he came back and her lively-self surfaced again.

If Mom and Luciana were happy about it, shouldn't I be? Why couldn't I be?

"I want to know he won't leave again." My voice came out shaky, and I realized I was crying.

Samson steered us off the rink and over the side, so we were out of the way of traffic. I stumbled on my skates, slipping around. Samson's warm hand landed on my waist as I clutched his arm, not wanting to fall, putting our faces unbelievably close together.

Clearing my throat, I stood straight and created enough distance that I could think properly. This was such a serious topic, and yet my mind—and eyes—kept wandering to Samson's lips.

I wiped some tears from my eyes. "I want him to take responsibility for his actions. He's never apologized to Javier and me. Or Luciana. His whole focus has been my mom."

Samson brushed back my bangs that were sticking to my eyelashes. "Does he know you feel this way?"

"He knows." Most of it, at least.

"Have you two sat down and talked about everything?" Samson leaned against the wall next to us. "Maybe you need to lay some ground rules or lay out your expectations of him being home."

"I don't think I get a say in that."

"You should. You're as much a part of the family as everyone else. It kind of sounds like everyone is on different pages." Samson lightly smiled. "Growing up with so many siblings, our house was complete chaos. When everyone was off doing their own things, not checking in with each other, life would get a little turbulent. It was like we were off our game. But when we made time for each other, scheduled out a day and time for everyone to get together and hang out, things went so much smoother." He looked over his shoulder at the skating rink where Taylor and Huntley spun in circles. "Our dad has this saying. 'You can go things alone and be miserable, or we can work through them as a family and succeed.' Even now with everyone scattered, we'll do group calls when someone hits a big bump in the road. Not everyone will be on the call, but whoever can. It's actually helped us to understand each other."

I thought about how I wanted to do walks as a family. Maybe I needed to schedule one instead of thinking about. I thought about Javier and wondered if he'd had a talk with Dad yet and how it went.

I patted Samson's chest. "When did you get all wise and stuff?"

He chuckled. "I always have been. You weren't paying close enough attention."

"I am now."

"I'm glad you are."

He leaned toward me, closing that comfortable gap that I needed to function properly.

A loud thump sounded behind me as someone slammed into the wall.

I looked over my shoulder to see Daphne smiling sheepishly.

Daphne motioned to her skates. "These things should come with brakes."

"They do." I pointed at the rubber brake at the heel of skate.

"Oh." Daphne folded her arms. "Can we eat now? I'm starving and I already have a massive bruise forming on my butt from falling so many times."

Samson wrapped an arm around my shoulders. "Sounds good to me."

CHAPTER THIRTY-FIVE

After dinner, we walked around an outdoor mall in the area, laughing and having a good time. Samson and I held hands most of the time, and I couldn't believe how natural it felt. Maybe it was because we'd known each other for so long. Samson was familiar, which was exactly what I needed right now.

Taylor suddenly squealed. "Puppies!" She dropped Huntley's hand and ran toward one of the shops.

Through the window, a couple of puppies rolled around on the ground. A bunch of puppies and kittens ran through the store, chasing each other.

"We *have* to go in," Taylor said to no one in particular before she opened the door and hustled inside.

Huntley turned to us with wide eyes. "Taylor can't walk out of there with a puppy, okay?"

"Why not?" Daphne asked. She leaned down and cooed at the little golden retriever who had its paws on the glass. "Who's a cute little doggie?"

Samson chuckled. "She's been asking for a puppy since

she was a toddler. My dad is allergic, and my mom doesn't want pets."

Weston looked inside where we could see Taylor holding a black lab in the air. "Why don't you tell her no?"

Huntley gazed adoringly at her. "I don't have the willpower to say no to her hot face. I'll give in like I always do when she wants something."

Samson clapped him on the shoulder. "Don't worry. No way Veronica and I are letting her leave with one."

"We'll drag her out if we have to," I said.

"Aww, kitties!" Daphne ran inside.

Weston blew out a deep breath. "Oh boy. We're in trouble."

We joined Daphne and Taylor inside the shop.

Taylor mauled the black lab with kisses, and it definitely didn't mind. It kept licking her face and barking.

"Listen to his bark." Taylor had completely melted. "It's so cute!"

"Just remember," Huntley said in a soft tone. "We are only here to play with him. That's it."

Taylor stuck her tongue out at him. "You ruin everything." She sat down on the ground, her anger disappearing as she played with the lab.

Samson rested his arm along my shoulders. "Are you a cat or dog person?"

"I've never really thought about it." I went over to the golden retriever near the front window. He immediately came to me and swatted at my wedges. I leaned down and picked him up. He tried to lick my face, so I quickly put him back down. "Okay, not a dog person."

Samson laughed. "Did you ever have pets growing up?"

I shook my head. "My parents are the same as yours.

Dad is allergic and Mom doesn't want another kid to take care of."

Daphne slowly slid toward me with a black kitten on one shoulder, a white kitten on the other, and an orange kitten on top of her head. "Look. I have a shoulder angel and devil." She pointed to the orange kitten. "And the one I actually listen to because he's a little spastic."

"Which one is the devil?" Samson asked.

Daphne shrugged, making the kittens slide against her neck. "Not sure yet. So far they've both just purred."

Weston walked over to us holding a gray, black, and white tabby kitten against his chest. "Look at her! She's precious."

Daphne's eyes widened. "I need her."

Weston's smile faltered. "Uh, what?"

Daphne held out her arms. "I need that kitten. Now."

Weston reluctantly handed her the kitten. Daphne kissed it on top of its head and then set it on her arm. The kitten curled up and closed its eyes.

I pulled out my phone and snapped a picture of Daphne with all four cats on her.

"Oh, send that picture to my mom," Daphne said. "Just say, 'which one?'"

Weston signed in defeat. "Why did I show her that kitten?"

I sent it off, curious as to what Laura would say.

Taylor joined us, holding the black lab in her arms. "What should I name him?"

"Nothing," Huntley said, cautiously coming up behind her. "Because you're not getting him."

Taylor pouted. "Aww, come on." She held the puppy close to his face. "Look at him."

Huntley's panicked eyes found Samson, and he mouthed, "*Help me.*"

Samson gently took the puppy from his sister. "No puppies, sis. Mom and Dad would kill you."

Taylor folded her arms and jutted her hip to the side. "The first thing I'm doing when I move out is get a dog."

My phone buzzed. I looked down to see Laura had responded.

> Laura: Cody says the orange one. I say the gray and black one in Daphne's arms.

I stared at the message in shock before I finally got myself to respond.

> Are you serious? I don't want to say anything to Daphne if you're not serious.

Laura, seconds later:

> Laura: Why not?

Dots danced across the screen before the next text came.

> Laura: Her last cat died a little after her dad did, and she's never asked for one again. If she's really excited about, tell her yes.

I looked up at Daphne who currently sang "I Like You" by Post Malone and Doja Cat to the kitten in her arms. "Hey, Daph, do you really want a cat?"

She nodded. "It's weird. I hadn't really thought about since Sour Patch passed away, but the second I saw this kitty, my heart instantly wanted it."

Weston's eyes went wide in panic. "I'm not sure how happy your mom would be if you randomly brought a cat home."

I texted Laura.

> She's serious.

> Laura: Okay. Get the orange one for Cody and then whatever one she wants

"Well, Weston," I said with a smile. "You're off the hook. Mrs. Richards gave the green light."

Daphne squealed, and then quickly shut off when all the kittens looked at her with terrified eyes. "Seriously?"

"Yep." I reached up and retrieved the orange kitten from her head. "Cody wants this one."

Daphne glanced at the three kittens she had left. "Sorry, Angel and Devil, but I'm going with Cherry here." She held up the gray and black kitten and kissed it on the nose.

Taylor clasped her hands together in a plea. "Hey, Veronica. You want to reach out to my parents as well?"

Samson shook his head. "It's not happening, Tay."

My phone rang. Luciana was calling. She wouldn't call unless she really needed me. I handed Samson the orange kitten and went outside to answer the phone.

"Luci?"

She sniffed on the other end. "Javy and Dad are fighting. Can you come home? They're scaring me."

Guess the talk wasn't going so well.

I glanced inside at my friends. They would all understand. "I'm on my way, Luci. Stay in your room until I get there, okay?"

"Okay. Thanks, V."

I was about to tuck my phone into my pocket when a girl stopped.

"Is that Hottie Javy's artwork?" She checked out my new phone cover. She was probably fourteen or fifteen, but she wore so much makeup it was difficult to tell.

"Yep." I held up the phone so she could see it better.

"I didn't know he sold these. Where did you buy it?"

I'd never been so proud to tell someone that Javier was my brother. "Actually, he gave it to me."

Her eyes bulged. "What? Why? How?"

The Rodriguez smolder almost surfaced, but I shut it down. I didn't want to appear too conceited. "I'm his sister."

Her eyes widened in an entirely different way. Her jaw dropped as she looked me up and down. "*You're* Javy's sister?" The condescension practically dripped out of her mouth and left a puddle on the cement.

I stared at her in shock. Why was it so hard to believe that I was his sister?

She snorted and flipped her long hair behind her. "Nice try, but I'm not buying it. No way you're his sister. She would be so ...." Her gaze traveled my body once again. "Well, she'd be hot."

She strutted away and all I could do was watch as my cheeks heated. Had she really said that? To my face?

Samson strolled out of the shop with his carefree smile. "Is everything okay?"

I gathered my wits and turned to him. "Uh, yeah. I mean, no." I sighed. "Luci called. Apparently, my dad and Javier are fighting. I hate to do this, but I think I need to go home."

Samson took my hand. "No big deal. Family comes

first." He looked through the window where Daphne and Taylor held the kittens Daphne was getting. "They're almost done in there anyway, and it's not like we can take kittens around with us everywhere we go."

I put my arms around him. "Thanks Samson."

He held me tight. "Always, V. Always."

CHAPTER THIRTY-SIX

Samson dropped Daphne and Weston off at Daphne's house since Weston's car was there. I expected me to be the next stop, but Samson dropped Taylor and Huntley off at his house and then drove me back to mine so we were alone. He said he wanted to be there in case we needed him for any reason which was another sign of how much he cared.

I'd dated a lot of guys, but they'd never made me this nervous. I was completely unsure of myself and what to do. That girl outside of the puppy store hadn't helped, either. She'd kicked my already low confidence down another peg or two.

Samson had opened up to me about Kylie. If she'd crushed his self-esteem, he might have thought he needed to settle for some fat high schooler who would be too insecure to cheat on him.

But as Samson walked me to the door and we stopped on the porch, it all fell into place. We'd grown up together. The transition from friend to boyfriend could be weird and confusing. In my mind, he was Taylor's brother. How did I naturally shift that line of thought to seeing him as my boyfriend?

"I had fun tonight," Samson said, cutting through my thoughts.

The weight of everything came crashing down, and it was way too much. I turned to open the door so I could rush inside and hide away in my room, but Samson gently set his hand on my arm and froze me in place.

"I never apologized for kissing you like that in front of everyone," Samson said with all the sincerity in the world. "My emotions got the better of me."

I couldn't look him in the eye. "No big deal. It's fine."

"I somehow always seem to lose my cool around you." His voice became slightly breathy like he was having as difficult a time finding air like I was.

I finally looked at him. "Samson—" I wasn't even sure what I wanted to say.

"Can we try again?" Those gorgeous brown eyes of his held all the hope in the world and it took my breath away. How could he look at me like that? What could he possibly see in me?

"Why?"

His head jerked back in surprise. "Why? I'm sorry, am I reading this wrong? I thought there was something between us."

What was between us? Was it real? Was it a rebound for me and a settlement for him?

"I like you, Veronica." Wow, he said it. No hesitation. What was happening? "But if you don't feel the same way, just say so. I'll back off."

What did I feel? I needed to talk to Daphne and Taylor. I needed to sort through my thoughts and feelings. I needed to figure *myself* out.

Why couldn't I get myself to speak? This guy was totally opening up and being honest and I couldn't form a single word.

"V, I'd never force you to do something you didn't want, if that is what your hesitation is about. I respect you and your values. Mine are the same."

And I completely melted into a puddle on the ground. DeShawn was the total opposite. He didn't quite grasp the concept of 'no.' I think he expected every girl to give him what he wanted, no questions asked. But I wasn't one of those girls.

"Honestly, Samson, I don't know what I want. Everything is confusing to me right now."

He nodded. "No problem. There's no rush, V. Just know I'll be here when you're ready." He scratched his indented scar near his eye. "The only thing I ask is if you don't ever want something with me, just say so. I'd rather move on than hang onto a hope of something that won't happen."

I took his hand in mine. "You'll be the first to know."

He flashed his all-is-right-in-the-world smile, and I wished I had his confidence. Maybe it was his maturity, and I needed time to get there.

"Oh, before I forget," Samson said, "my dormmate's cousin is having a Halloween party. I thought it would be fun if you, Taylor, and the others go."

"Like a college party?" I wasn't sure I was ready for that.

Samson squeezed my hand and let go. "It's not a kegger if that's what you're worried about. Just some music, snacks, and games. Oh, and you have to dress up."

Dress up? What could I even be for Halloween? Maybe I could get one of those inflatable ones, like a dinosaur. That way I could cover up all my fat.

"Uh, sure, that sounds fun." Maybe I could do the Kool-Aid guy. Or the Pillsbury Doughboy.

Samson reached down and lightly kissed my cheek, releasing all the crazy thoughts in my head and sending my heart into a frenzy.

"Night, Veronica."

"Night, Samson."

He made it two steps before a high-pitched squeal erupted inside my home, reminding me why we had come home early in the first place. He spun around, his eyes wide. I fumbled to get my keys in the lock and open the door. We stumbled into the entry way, frantically looking around.

Seconds later, my mom came barreling down the stairs holding a squirming snake in her outstretched hand. She pushed past Samson and me and hightailed it out the front door, squealing the whole time.

Had I seen that right? Mom was holding a *snake*? I ran out the door in time to see her chuck the poor snake across the lawn.

"And stay out!" Mom shouted. She brushed off her hands with a satisfied nod.

I had to give my mom credit. She was one tough lady. She'd easily handled each part of the curse.

Wait. Where had that snake come from? I hadn't done it. Had Javier taken matters into his own hands?

Mom marched back into the house, so I followed, closing the door behind us. Samson stood in the entryway, completely baffled.

Dad, Javier, and Luciana scattered on the stairs, their focus on Mom.

"What happened?" I finally asked.

Mom pointed at the door. "That snake was in our bed!"

Luciana shrieked and threw herself at Dad, trying to get

her feet off the ground. She buried her head into Dad's neck as he held her and rubbed her back.

Dad's angry eyes landed on me.

I shrunk back. "Why are you looking at me like that?"

"You want to tell me where that snake come from, Veronica?" Dad asked.

I threw up my arms. "I don't know. I wasn't even here!"

"Yet you've conveniently handled every situation with ease." Dad clenched his jaw, and I could tell he was doing everything in his power to stay calm.

"There's no way Veronica was responsible for that," Samson said, making all eyes turn toward him. "I've been with her all night. Taylor and Daphne can back that up."

"Why do you think *I* had something to do with it?" Okay, so I was the one that put the ball in motion, but I didn't like the way he glared at me.

"You've been against your mom and I being together since I came back." Dad kissed Luciana on the forehead and set her down. "Luci, go to bed."

"But what if there's a snake in my bed!" Luciana tugged on my dad's shirt. "I don't want to go in there!"

Dad gently put his hands on her shoulders. "I promise there is no snake in your bed. This has all been a sick prank. Now, please, go to bed."

Luciana huffed. "Fine. But I'm not happy about it!" She stormed up the stairs, shoving past Javier.

Javier who casually rested against the banister, calm and not in the least bit shocked.

I narrowed my eyes at him. He *had* done it. I wished he would have told me.

Dad stomped down the rest of the stairs and stopped in the entryway. "Samson, I think it's time for you to go home.

Thank you for bringing my daughter home safely and on time."

"Yes, sir." Samson gently squeezed my arm and then let himself out of the house.

Mom's accusatory gaze settled on me.

"Javier," Dad said. "Veronica. In the front room. Now." His tone had gone from angry to complete disappointment, which was somehow worse.

CHAPTER THIRTY-SEVEN

Javier and I sat down on the couch in the front room. We were close, clinging to one another almost in solidarity. The hammer was about to slam down.

Mom stood near the couch with her hands on her hips. "Has this been you two the whole time?"

"No!" We both said, I think out of reflex more than anything. I always wanted to defend myself when someone accused me of something, even if they were right.

"Do not lie to your mother." Dad slumped onto the loveseat, his sad eyes on Javier and me. "She deserves the truth. You may hate me, but your mother has done so much for this family."

He was right. Mom didn't deserve any of this. She'd always been the strongest one in the family.

I sighed and sat back on the couch, my head resting against the cushion. "I thought if I reenacted the curse, Mom would have second thoughts about getting back with Dad."

Mom sat on the coffee table and placed her hands over

her face, hiding her emotions. Was she upset? Sad? Tired of it all?

"But technically," I said, "I had nothing to do with the snake."

"That was me," Javier said.

I turned to him. "Why?"

He slumped back next to me. "Dad and I talked tonight, and it didn't go well. So, I thought I'd finish it off for you."

Mom removed her hands covering her face, revealing red eyes filled with tears. "I raised you better than this."

With that, she stood and went to the bottom of the stairs. She placed her hand on the rail and let out a full-body sigh that I could feel deep in my heart. With a shake of her head, she ascended the stairs, leaving all of us in stunned silence.

After a moment, I stood, wanting to follow her and explain myself, but Dad held up a hand to stop me.

"Sit down, Veronica. We all need to talk."

I fell back onto the couch, dread settling into my stomach.

"This all stops now," Dad said. "Your mom and I are renewing our vows, and there's nothing you can do to stop it." He rubbed his eyes with his thumbs. "You both owe your mother an apology for doing this to her."

Javier stood. "Fine. I'll apologize to Mom. Can we go now?"

"Sit down, Javier," Dad said in a sharp tone.

Javier scoffed. "Why? So, you can spew some more nonsense about a mid-life crisis? Continue to put the blame on anyone but yourself?"

Dad stood, throwing out his arms. "What do you want from me?"

"I want you to acknowledge what you did to this family!" Javier yelled.

I put my hand out, trying to tell him to calm, but he shoved me away.

"I want you to take responsibility for your actions." Javier had his hands clenched into fists.

Dad looked at me. "And what do you want from me, Veronica? How do we make this all stop?"

"By doing exactly what Javier asked for." I sat tall. "Apologize to us."

"I'm sorry!" Dad yelled so loud, Javier and I flinched. "I did a horrible thing and ruined this family! I took the complete cowardly way of handling my insecurities."

Javier and I shared a look before I spoke. "Insecurities?"

Dad pinched the bridge of his nose like he was trying to stop himself from crying. "I think we all know how amazing your mother is. I've dealt with depression since I was a kid. There's this voice in my head that tells me I don't deserve her, or you kids." He sat back down on the couch, complete defeat taking over. "I thought if I left, you'd all be better without me. That intern meant nothing. I was hoping to fill the void of not having you in my life, but obviously it was the worst way to handle it. It only made things worse. And your mom, instead of shutting me out continued to be there for me and love me despite it all."

Javier sat next to me. "What do you mean she continued to be there for you?"

Dad licked his lips. "She knew I was having a breakdown. Your mom worked so many jobs so she could send me money and make sure I was eating and taking care of myself. Every single night she'd text me to tell me she loved me, and the front door was always open."

If I thought I'd been shocked before, I was way wrong. I didn't know how to process everything my dad was saying.

"Mom did that?" Javier asked in disbelief.

Dad wiped at the tears that fell down his cheeks. "Yes. I've always struggled with my mental health and have been too proud to admit it, especially to you kids. I wanted you to think I was strong and a real man."

"Dad." I took a deep breath. "A real man would own up to his shortcomings. He would show his children that he's not perfect and doesn't expect them to be."

"I know that now." Dad choked back a sob. We sat in silence as he collected himself. "I'm so sorry, Veronica and Javier. I've been seeing a therapist and trying to work through my issues. She has me on medication that has been doing a decent job of regulating my system."

Javier and I shared a stunned look. Dad had been going through *all* of this and we knew nothing about it. We thought he was an overbearing jerk.

"Your mom makes me a better person," Dad whispered. "She makes everyone she touches a better person. If it weren't for her, I'd ... I'd be dead."

I went to his side and sat next to him, putting my arm around him. "You tried to commit suicide?"

"Multiple times." Dad's voice shook.

Javier stood, left the room, and came back with tissues. He grabbed a couple for himself before handing the box to Dad. Javier sat down on the coffee table in front of us and wiped at his wet cheeks.

I rubbed my hand up and down Dad's arm, unsure what to say. Depression didn't justify poor choices, but what he went through must have been difficult and our anger toward him only made things worse.

Dad blew his nose and then bunched the tissue in his

hand. "Every time I tried to end things, your mom would magically show up wherever I was. She has some crazy ability to sense when I'm at my worst."

"You have a tell." Mom's sudden voice startled us. She sat at the foot of the stairs. "You always send the same text. *Forever and always, mi amor.*" She leaned against the railing. "Also, I have a tracker on your phone, so I always know where you are."

Dad wiped at his tears, smiling. "I still think you have magical powers. You've always been able to sense when something has been going on with one of the kids."

"That's called a mother's intuition." Mom softly smiled. "I've always thought of it like the mom and baby leaving a bit of each other's souls behind before the baby leaves the womb. Just a way to always stay connected."

There was a pause before Javier said, "That's really weird, Mom."

We all laughed at that, easing the tension in the room.

I leaned against my dad's arm. "I'm sorry, Dad."

"Me, too," Javier said. "I wish we would have known all of this."

Dad cleared his throat. "I've always been a proud man. It's difficult for me to admit my faults or when I'm wrong. But I was so very wrong for ever abandoning this family. You kids—" He cleared his throat again. "You kids are the best thing I've ever done. I'm proud of how independent and strong-willed you are." He took a shaky breath. "I hope one day you'll be able to forgive me."

"I hope you can forgive us, too," I said. "We messed up as well."

"I like Veronica's idea of going on family walks in the evenings," Mom said. "I think that will benefit everyone in multiple ways."

Javier nodded. "I'm in."

"Same," Dad said.

"Me, too!" Luciana appeared on the stairs, bending at the stomach to look into the front room.

Dad stood and motioned for everyone to come over. We all huddled close, hugging as a family. We had a long way to go, but we'd made definite progress. Which meant the vow renewal was officially on.

CHAPTER THIRTY-EIGHT

The next day, Mom, Luciana, and I went shopping for dresses. Mom obviously already had hers, but Luciana and I had nothing.

Since red and white were the renewal colors, we'd found Luciana a cute frilly red dress at the first place we stopped. Everywhere Mom offered to take me for a dress had nothing that fit me well ... or at all.

I finally suggested going to Adelmotique. I didn't remember seeing anything super fancy there, but maybe they had something that would work.

Mom and Dad wanted the kids to look as fancy as they did since it had become more of a family renewal than vow renewal. We were all starting over and figuring out how to be a family in a way that worked for everyone.

Dad and Javier had matching tuxes. Mom had a white dress covered in rhinestones that made her sparkle. Even Luciana's red dress had rhinestones on the bodice in addition to the frill the bottom had to offer.

When we stepped inside the store, someone gasped. Shanice stopped in front of me with her jaw dropped. She said nothing, just walked over and analyzed my hair, nodding her head up and down.

"Yes, yes, yes." Shanice waved a hand over my head. "Love it. Celeste told me she took you to Gabriel but seeing it in person is so—" She kissed the tips of her fingers. "Perfect." She looked at my mom and sister. "And who are you lovely ladies?"

I introduced them to Shanice who greeted them with air kisses on their cheeks.

"Is Adella here?" I asked.

Shanice shook her head. "She stepped out for dinner but should be back soon. Now, what can we do for you today, my *stunning* girl?"

"She needs a dress for my upcoming vow renewal," Mom said with a bright smile.

Shanice clicked her nails together. "Oh, loving the sound of this. How big are we going?"

Luciana held out her arms as wide as they'd go. "Like huge."

Shanice rubbed her buzzed head. "And how bold?"

"All the bold," Mom said.

Shanice tapped her thick lips until her eyes suddenly lit up. "I have the perfect thing. It's in red. Will that be okay?"

Luciana giggled. "More than okay. That's the color she needs!"

"I knew I was holding this for something." Shanice moved toward the back of the store, her ample hips swaying. "And, it's in *stunning*. Veronica, fate has smiled upon you once again."

Shanice disappeared into the back.

Luciana looked at me. "Why does she keep saying *stunning* that way?" She tried to mimic Shanice's sultry voice and failed miserably.

"It's their sizing," I said. "My size happens to be *stunning* on their scale."

Luciana snapped her fingers. "I don't like. I LOVE."

Mom and I both laughed. Though she drove us wild, sassy Luciana was the best version. We'd seen too much of the broken-hearted Luci lately.

"We might need to clear some room." Shanice's voice was muffled by an alarming amount of red fabric in her arms as she came out from the back.

She took the dress to the center step that the mirrors surrounded and held it up for us to see in all its glory.

It was now our turn to gasp.

Luciana squealed next to me, jumping up and down in excitement.

Mom clasped her hands together and said a little prayer. Her words came out breathless. "Oh, V."

Beaded lace appliqués covered a lace-edged, three-tiered tulle ballgown that poofed out far. The sweetheart neckline was perfect. The bold red took my breath away.

"Shall we try it on?" Shanice asked.

"Yes, please!" I went straight for it, eager to get it on.

With all the lace and material, it took all of us to get me into the dress. Mom and Shanice helped me onto the step in the center of the room so I could see the full dress from every angle.

Mom stepped back and pressed her hands to her mouth as her eyes filled with tears. I found myself doing the same. I hadn't felt so pretty in the longest time. The dress fit like it had been designed for me.

Shanice left the room for a second and sauntered back with some strips of red clip-on hair. "I know you have burgundy in, but maybe for the event you can clip in some red. Really help pull everything together." She held it up to my hair and nodded. "Yes. I think that will be the perfect addition. You can cut it to size."

I rested my hands on my warm neck. "Thank you, Shanice. I always leave here feeling beautiful."

Shanice placed a hand on her hip. "Girl, we talked about this. You should always go everywhere feeling beautiful, because you are."

Luciana leaned against the side of my dress. "I hope I grow up to be as beautiful as you, V."

I looked at my sister in shock. She thought I was beautiful? I wasn't sure if I ever heard her say that. I think my family really needed to work on being communicative with each other. It would probably solve so many problems.

"You'll be even more beautiful, Luci," I said, smiling at her. "You already are."

She blushed. "Am not. But one day." She grinned wildly. "Wait until Samson sees! He won't be able to take his eyes off you!"

"No, he won't," Mom said.

Shanice's eyes sparkled. "Oh, who's Samson?"

"V's boyfriend," Luciana said. "He's super tall. Like a giant."

"He's not my boyfriend, Luci," I said.

"Not yet." Mom winked at me. "It will happen. Your father and I fully approve, by the way. He's such a great guy."

Shanice held out her hand. "I need to see a picture."

Luciana skipped over to my phone sitting on a chair and brought it back to me. I opened to the picture of him and Ryker laughing. "That's him. The one on the left."

Shanice waved her hand in front of her face. "Oh, yes please. You two would be a power couple." She held out her arms. "I have chills." And she did. Goosebumps covered her skin. She handed back my phone. "I'm going to need pictures from the event."

"Why don't you come?" Mom blurted out. "Veronica and my mother are making the food. There will be plenty of dancing and laughter. Celeste will be there. I'm sure she'd love to see you. And you've done so much for my daughter."

Shanice shimmied her shoulders. "Count me in. I do love a good party." She stepped back and analyzed me. "Would you mind if I take photos of you in the dress for our website and social media? I think our clients will eat it up!"

"Uh, sure," I said. "On Saturday, right? When my hair and makeup will be done to match?"

"Of course, sugar." Shanice wiggled her eyebrows. "Will this Samson be there?"

"Yes," I said with a smile.

She clapped her hands. "Please tell me he has a brother."

Mom, Luciana, and I laughed.

"He's got a lot of brothers," Luciana said through her giggling.

"But only two that aren't married," I said. "Celeste is currently dating one, and the other is very much not your type."

Shanice snapped her fingers. "Not with *that* attitude."

I tried to picture Shanice and Ryker together and it made me break out in a loud laugh that hurt my stomach.

"Well, you better like geckos, then," Mom said.

Shanice looked thoroughly confused. "Geckos?"

Mom flicked my arm, cutting off my laughter. "Speaking of geckos, I hope Ryker knows he can bring Spencer to the ceremony. We're allowing all creatures to be there."

Luciana folded her arms. "I take it Uncle Alfredo wants to bring his dog?"

"Bought him a tux and everything," Mom said with a smile.

"He'll be the cutest one there," I said.

Shanice held up a palm. "Wait. So, this Ryker guy brings a gecko named Spencer with him everywhere he goes?"

"Yes," I said.

"Interesting." Shanice tapped her lips. "I'm not exactly sure what to do with this information."

"Well, you'll meet him on Saturday." Mom smiled up at me. "Now, let's get you out of this dress and go have dinner. I'm starving."

I took one last look at myself in the mirror. I really felt confident in the dress. I somehow needed to carry that confidence around with me no matter what I was wearing or looked like.

CHAPTER THIRTY-NINE

After dinner, my family decided to go on our first walk together. It was quiet for the first couple of blocks. Though we'd talked things through with Dad, some awkwardness hung in the air. So much had been revealed in a small amount of time. Forgiving needed to be done on all sides.

While we understood Dad's struggles, he'd still humiliated Javier in front of all his followers. I thought Javier would be excited he'd reached over a million followers, but the kid was only fourteen with a very fragile ego.

I turned and looked at him. We had more in common than I thought. Other people's opinions of us practically ran our lives.

Javier patted his slightly puffy checks. The swelling had gone down considerably. "Why are you looking at me like that?"

"Why do you care what others think about you?" I scratched at an itch on my arm, then kept it up since my artificial nails felt good against the skin.

Javier adjusted the large cross hanging around his neck.

With the two red spikes in his hair that looked like devil horns, the sight was funny. "Other people decide your social status. I want to be somebody that makes a difference."

Dad snorted a laugh. "Showing off your abs isn't going to make a difference in the world."

Javier shot him an angry glare but reeled it in when he saw Mom's disapproving scowl. He finally sighed. "It's about my art. I started the account to get it out there in the world. Which meant drawing on myself a lot." He smirked. "I can't help it if the ladies like what they see."

I rolled my eyes. "At least you haven't let it go to your head."

"I will say your 'mood' series is really good," Dad suddenly said.

Javier turned to him in shock. "You looked at my work?"

Dad nodded. "I decided to check out the website. You've really built yourself a business. I'm proud of you for that." He chuckled. "All I could think about at your age was girls and sports."

"Don't get me wrong," Javier said with a smirk. "I think about those things, too."

Luci threw up her hands. "Now I have to find something to be good at. Javy can draw and dance. Veronica can sing and cook. I've got nothing going on over here."

"You can dance?" Mom asked Javier at the same time Dad asked me, "You can sing?"

"Ay, ay, ay." Luciana sighed. "This family really needs to comminate more."

Everyone chuckled.

"I think you mean communicate," I said to her.

She placed a hand to her forehead. "I can't even get my words right." She stopped and picked a dandelion from the grass.

"Maybe you could become a writer," I said. "It would make you work on your words and spelling."

We turned a corner, and I came to an abrupt stop, making Luciana bump into me.

Luciana slapped my back. "What the heck, V?"

We were on DeShawn's street. I so didn't want to walk in front of his house.

"Uh, let's go another way." I moved across the street, hoping my family would follow. "I heard there's a house that went all out on their Halloween decorations."

My family hurried to catch up with me.

Javier swatted my arm to get my attention. "We know why you don't want to go down that street. Which makes me wonder, why do *you* care so much about what other people think?"

"I don't!" I snapped.

My entire family wore expressions that knew full well I did.

I sighed. "I don't know. I guess I want people to like me."

I mean, really, what did it boil down to? What others thought of me shouldn't define my life or choices. Only I should.

"People love you, mija," Mom said.

"I can name a bunch of people who don't," I muttered.

Javier stuffed his hands in his pockets. "Those guys are idiots, Veronica. They are the last people you should be worried about."

"Trust me, I know," I said. "I can't get them out of my head. Every time I see myself in the mirror, all their mean comments fill my brain to the point it might explode."

Dad stopped walking, causing all of us to turn around.

"Matías?" Mom went to his side.

Dad's eyes swirled with frustration, anger, and determination. "No more."

"No more what?" Luciana asked.

Dad swept out his arms. "We've been letting other people control us for so long. We are letting society decide our fate. We are the Rodriguez family. We are strong, smart, capable, and worthy of love. No more letting others tell us how we have to feel. No more letting others control our lives. *We* are in control. So, the next time someone tries to take control, we say, no more!"

Mom nodded in approval. "No more. I like it."

"No more cyberbullies making me feel horrible," Javier said.

"No more bullies making me feel small," I said.

"No more demons telling me I'm not worth it," Dad said.

Luciana stomped her feet on the cement. "We are the Rodriguez family!"

CHAPTER FORTY

A huge spray of Cherry Coke came rushing out of Daphne's mouth. She wiped at the corners of her mouth as I wiped off my phone with a napkin with a disgusted grimace.

We sat in the outdoor amphitheater at school having lunch, enjoying the lovely fall day.

"That is seriously the most gorgeous dress, ever," Daphne said with her hand on her chest. "I mean, you can't get married now. No dress will ever top that."

Weston reached over and handed me a wet wipe with an apologetic look in his eyes before he stuffed the bag back into his backpack.

"Do you carry those everywhere you go?" Taylor asked.

Weston nodded his head at Daphne. "Ever since I started dating her, yes."

Daphne didn't even seem phased by everyone's comments. She took my phone from me and held it out for Bentley and Sierra to see. "I mean, look at this." She held it right in front of Sierra's face. "Look!"

Sierra swatted Daphne's hand away with a smile. "We see, Daph. And yes, it's gorgeous."

Taylor bumped my arm, bringing my attention to her. "What shoes are you going to wear?"

"Technically, no one will see them with all that material," Bentley said.

Taylor took a sip of her Dr Pepper. "So? She still needs shoes."

"Can't you wear flip flops?" Bentley asked. "Since no one will see them?"

Daphne gasped. "How dare you, Bentley!"

Weston had mouthed the words at the same time, coming to know Daphne so well.

Daphne pointed at Weston. "And I saw that, and you're lucky I love you."

Weston answered with a chuckle.

"Girls and their clothes, man," Bentley said with a shake of the head. "They're just shoes."

Weston faked gasped, his eyes reflecting his fake shock. "You're unbelievable, Bentley."

Daphne threw a watermelon Sour Patch Kid at Weston, hitting him on the nose, making everyone laugh.

I'd been putting off the topic of college, but I knew I had to tell my friends sooner or later. I took a deep breath to steel myself. "I think I might apply to USC."

Everyone turned their attention to me. Daphne, Taylor, and Weston were planning on going to UCLA. Sierra had a basketball scholarship there, so she was definitely going. Bentley hadn't talked about it much.

Taylor and Daphne looked at each other but didn't say anything.

Bentley let out a loud breath of relief. "Oh, thank goodness. So am I."

"You are?" Sierra asked him with shock in her eyes.

He nodded. "Yeah. And Stanford. I'm torn on where I want to go."

I looked at Taylor and Daphne, trying to catch their eyes. I had no idea what they were thinking.

Daphne crumpled her empty Watermelon Sour Patch Kid bag. "May I ask why?" She had a very diplomatic tone.

"Well, Samson, obviously," Taylor said as a smile grew on her face.

I quickly shook my head. "No. It's because it's closer to the Institute of Culinary Education."

All five of them let out a collection, "Ohhhhhh."

"That makes a lot of sense," Weston said. "You could work on both degrees at the same time."

"Bingo," I said.

Daphne kept her head held high. "I understand and accept your logic. However ..." She suddenly threw her arms around me. "I'll just miss you so much if you're not at UCLA, but if it makes more sense to go to USC, then you should do it because it will benefit you and our business and Samson—"

"Why do you keep bringing him up?" I asked. "This has nothing to do with him." But it was definitely an added perk.

Taylor winked dramatically. "Sure." Then she smiled. "Girl, do what you gotta do. We'll support you no matter what."

Daphne fake sniffed. "Yeah, abandon us if that's what you feel is best."

I shoved her on the arm, making her laugh.

Daphne leaned her head against mine. "UCLA and USC are less than fifteen miles apart. I think we'll survive."

"You've calculated?" Taylor asked.

"Well, duh," Daphne said. "I figured we'd be going to see Samson a lot. Now we'll just be going to see Veronica and Samson." She grinned at Bentley. "And maybe you. But if you go to Stanford, which is about three hundred and eighty miles away, you're on your own, kid."

Bentley chuckled. "Noted."

"I don't know if I'll get into USC," I said. "Or UCLA for that matter. And I haven't made my mind up yet. I just wanted to let you know I was thinking about it."

Out of the corner of my eye, I saw DeShawn and his friends coming toward our area. My heart leaped straight into my throat wondering what he possibly wanted. When they stopped a few yards short of us and started talking with one another, my breathing calmed. Maybe it had nothing to do with me and I was being overly paranoid.

Daphne leaned toward me and began singing the part of "Bohemian rhapsody" where he tells his mom he killed someone.

I elbowed her, making her laugh.

"Should I have gone with 'Earl's Gotta Die' by The Chicks?" Daphne pursed her lips. "Yeah, should have gone with that one. I mean, Freddie Mercury was like, 'Hey, I killed a man but I'm not going to give you any details.' The Chicks were like, 'Earl's a total loser and abuser and his death is totally warranted and let's poison him, wrap him in a tarp, and put him in the trunk.' They had a plan and followed through, you know?"

Weston kissed Daphne on the cheek and smiled. "You're looking so beautiful today and I love you with all my heart and please never kill me, okay?"

Daphne poked him on the nose. "Don't be an abusing loser and everything will be fine."

Sierra sighed. "It's so weird that Daphton is relationship goals, but it totally is."

"It's like next-level," Bentley said with awe in his voice.

For a moment, I'd forgotten about DeShawn until I heard his voice.

"Man, the party this weekend is going to be lit," DeShawn said loud enough for my group to hear. "I'm gonna have Autumn Masters at my side. Everybody who is *anybody* will be there."

Autumn Masters? She was undoubtedly the hottest senior on campus. And well on her way to becoming the valedictorian. Why would she want to go with DeShawn Mack of all people?

"Do you have your costumes picked out?" Christian asked.

I didn't have to be looking at them to know who was talking. They each had their unique obnoxious voice that could be noticed in a crowd.

"Yeah," DeShawn said. "I'm going as Lucas from Stranger Things. I'm going to slay his basketball uniform." His voice somehow went up another notch. "And Autumn is going to be Max. Like that scene where she's suspended in air and her eyes and limbs go all weird. But like a sexy version."

"How on earth could anyone make that sexy?" Taylor asked our group.

"*Why* would anyone *want* to make that sexy?" Sierra asked.

"At least you won't have that *other chick* at your side," Christian said, again being purposefully loud.

Daphne sighed. "I thought we were behind this."

"So did I," I said quietly.

"What would she even go as?" DeShawn asked. "Ursula? Miss Piggy?"

"What's that fat character from Encanto?" Christian asked. "Louise or something?"

I wasn't sure why that was my breaking point, but it was. My dad's voice saying, "No more" kept replaying in my mind.

I was so done with all of this.

I stood and marched over to the guys. "It's Luisa, and she's strong enough to beat up both of you losers."

DeShawn opened his mouth to say something that would surely get him punched in the face, so I stopped him short.

"Enough, DeShawn," I said. "This whole thing? It's over. For someone who claims to not like me, you're super obsessed. Everywhere I go, there you are. You follow me around like some creepy stalker. I've been over you for a long time. You're the one still hung up."

"Oh!" Daphne suddenly shouted. "I still have the stalker playlist I made for Sierra last year if you want it, DeShawn!"

"It is a really good playlist," Sierra said.

DeShawn forced a laugh, his focus solely on me. "No, I'm not."

I motioned to where my friends sat a couple of yards away. "Then why are you talking right here? You never come to this area."

"You don't own the school," Christian said.

I rolled my eyes. "Obviously. But he knows where I sit at lunch." I rounded on DeShawn and pointed my finger into his chest. "Stay out of my life. Stay away from me and my friends. Get a life, DeShawn. One that doesn't involve me. Because this is old." I started to walk away but stopped short in my tracks. "Maybe focus on your studies for once so you can go to college and make something of yourself. It's more than obvious your lack of skills on the football field, and abhorrent personality won't be getting you a ticket in."

DeShawn mouthed *abhorrent* with a confused look on his face.

"Look it up! Maybe you can walk away today actually learning something." I headed straight back to my friends and sat down.

Daphne leaned toward me. "That was the coolest thing I've ever witnessed."

"Same," Weston said with admiration.

Taylor grunted. "Why wasn't I recording that?"

"Seriously," Sierra said, "the transformation on his face from smug to embarrassed was monumental."

Bentley placed his hand on Sierra's arm. "Easy on the big words there. We wouldn't want anyone getting confused."

Daphne threw her arms around me and squeezed tight as we all laughed.

I hadn't felt so light in the longest time. DeShawn Mack no longer owned me. He should have never in the first place, but I let him get to me.

But that chapter was now closed and sealed for life.

CHAPTER FORTY-ONE

Daphne invited Taylor and me over to her house, and she wouldn't tell us why. Laura greeted us at the door holding a pair of blindfolds.

"Hey, girls." Laura twirled the blindfolds in her hands. "I've been instructed to put these on you before you enter the house."

"Why?" Taylor asked.

Laura sighed. "You know Daphne. She can't do anything halfway."

"Can we at least come inside first?" I asked.

"No!" Daphne shouted from somewhere in the house. "You do as you're told, young lady!"

With a look that said, "I'm so sorry about my daughter," Laura stepped onto the porch and blindfolded Taylor and me. Then she helped escort us into the house to somewhere in the front room.

"Wait right here," Laura said.

Taylor slapped my hand before she held it, like she'd been searching for it through the dark. "What do you think this is about?"

"I have absolutely no idea."

It wasn't near anyone's birthdays. Aside from Halloween, there weren't any special events coming up. Well, except my parent's vow renewal, but I had a suspicion that had nothing to do with this.

Unless Daphne made us matching Mickey ears for the ceremony. If she did, that would be a hard no from me.

A small meow came from near my feet.

"Aww," Taylor said. "I wanna see the kitty!"

"Don't you dare take your blindfold off!" Daphne shouted.

A lot of shuffling and mumbling filled the front room while Taylor and I awkwardly stood there.

Someone stepped in front of us and by the bounce in her step and the quirkiness somehow radiating from her, I knew it was Daphne.

"I'm so excited to show you this!" Daphne said.

"You're being ridiculous," I said through my smile. "Why are we blindfolded?"

"For the grand reveal," Daphne said incredulously. "Duh."

"The grand reveal of what?" My smile slowly faded, along with my patience.

"So, I've been working on a secret project for a while," Daphne said, her tone full of excitement. "It's our senior year, and I wanted to have our last Halloween in high school be a knock-out."

"Okay," Taylor said in a curious tone.

"I made us costumes!" Daphne blurted out.

Costumes?

"What kind?" I asked, not able to hide the worry in my tone.

Were we all going to be Care Bears? Or maybe in true

Daphne-horror-fashion she made zombie Care Bears, which actually wouldn't be a bad idea. Their blood could be rainbow colors. Maybe toss a little sparkle in the blood for extra pizzazz.

"Don't sound so scared," Daphne said.

"This is *you* we're talking about," Taylor said.

Daphne dramatically sighed. "Don't ruin this for me. I spent countless hours working on these, wanting them to be absolutely perfect. Like so perfect, people would think we were the real-life ones."

Taylor tapped her foot impatiently. "Daphne, let us see!"

"Okay," Daphne. "Take off your blindfolds in three ..."

I ripped mine off and noticed Taylor had done the same.

"Two, one," Daphne said with a frown. "Impatient much?" She held Cherry in her arms.

Taylor gasped and ran to a costume laid out on the couch. "Is this Black Widow?"

Daphne jumped up and down in glee, causing Cherry to look at her with frightened eyes. "Yes!" That poor kitty was going to have to get used to Daphne's outbursts.

Daphne herself was in a Captain America outfit. Well, a female version. The uniform was molded to her body like in the movies. She wore a utility belt and boots that were exact replicas.

Daphne saw me staring and grinned. "I picked the one from Civil War. It's my favorite uniform." She grabbed something from the couch. "I have the blue helmet with the chin strap." She put it back on the couch, along with Cherry, and then went around the back of it and held up a shield. "I have the leather straps that will hold this on my back." She pointed to some claw marks on the shield. "Those are from Black Panther. That crazy kid."

I leaned over the couch and ran my fingers along it. "This is incredible, Daph."

She squealed. "Thanks!"

Cherry climbed up my leg using her little claws. I took her off and set her back on the floor.

Taylor held up the black leather jumpsuit. "I'm going to go put this on!" She darted out of the room.

Daphne put down the shield and held out her hands toward the other costume made for me.

Wonder Woman.

I slowly went to it, picking up the red and gold bodice. It was so ... big. Wonder Woman was tiny. Gal Gadot who played her in the movies was a freaking super model.

I was so far from that.

Daphne clasped her hands together and held them under her chin. "Do you like it?"

"I ..." I didn't know what to say.

The huge smile on Daphne's face slowly disappeared. "But you love Wonder Woman."

I motioned to myself. "Yeah, but I look nothing like her."

"Says who?" Daphne asked.

I huffed. "The entire world."

Daphne lowered her arms and put a hand on her hip. "Well, the world sucks, in case you haven't noticed. You're strong, beautiful, brave, feisty, and a genuinely good person. You're freaking Wonder Woman to me."

I wasn't sure if I could work up the courage to put it on. Even though Daphne had worked so hard on it, I felt ridiculous even toying with the idea of being Wonder Woman.

Laura came forward and picked up Cherry who meowed for attention. "I think it will look great on you, Veronica. Give it a try."

Taylor bounded into view with a huge smile on her face. The leather jumpsuit fit her flawlessly.

Daphne clapped her hands. "You look amazing!"

Taylor pointed at her. "You're amazing!"

Daphne scooped up some things from the couch and handed them to Taylor one by one. "I have the belt with the red center because that's my favorite. There's the waistband with the holsters attached to hold your guns." She turned them over in her hand. "Don't worry, they aren't real. They just look it." And they totally did. "Let's see, there's also a band that clips around your thigh to secure the holsters. Oh, and the fingerless gloves with the cuffs attached to that." She shrugged. "I figured it would be better for those to slip on and off, so they don't get in the way if you have to go to the bathroom or something."

Taylor shook in excitement. "I can't believe you did this, Daph."

Laura picked up the red wig from the couch. "Also got you this."

Taylor slipped it on. "How do I look?"

"Like Black Widow," I said with complete awe. Daphne was *really* good.

Everyone stared expectantly at me. I didn't want to let Daphne down. Not after all she'd done. The least I could do was try it on. If I looked ridiculous, she'd see it and realize I shouldn't wear it.

With a tight smile, I scooped the costume off the couch and headed to the bathroom in the hall. I stared at the costume a good five minutes before I worked up the courage to take off my clothes and slip on the skirt.

A soft knock sounded on the door.

"How's it going in there?" Daphne asked.

I held the bodice against my chest and zipped up the side. I took a few deep breaths before I opened the door and let her in.

Daphne came in with a sleeping Cherry on her shoulder. She grinned over my shoulder and looked at me through the mirror. "You look so good, Veronica. Wait until we get everything else on you!" She ran her fingers over my hair. "When I started making this, you had your long dark hair, which I figured would be perfect. We could get a wig, but I really like this edgy vibe to Wonder Woman. I could totally see her rocking your haircut."

I gazed at the asymmetrical shape and shaved side. The burgundy did go with the outfit.

The outfit. I ran my fingers along the bodice, surprised at how soft it was. It fit my body perfectly.

"How did you know my size?" I asked.

"I'd been trying to figure that out since you've been kind weird about it lately," Daphne said with a sheepish smile. "I waited to do yours last. When I found out about that boutique you went to, I stopped by there and asked what the *stunning* measurements were."

My cheeks flared. She knew my measurements. Like the inches and everything.

She gently placed her hands on my shoulders. "Veronica, I'm being totally serious when I say you're beautiful. This costume is gorgeous on you."

I took myself in. With the gold trim and belt, shiny blue skirt, and lined bodice, I did feel pretty amazing. Daphne had done a phenomenal job.

"Come on," Daphne said. "Let's get the rest on."

After a couple of shaky breaths, I forced myself to leave the bathroom and go into the front room.

Taylor whistled. "Seriously, Daphne, did you break into DC's costume department? This is an exact replica."

I held in my eyeroll. It obviously wasn't since it was much bigger, but I appreciated the sentiment.

Daphne helped me put on the gold arm band, long metal arm cuffs, and the gold head piece. Somehow, Cherry stayed sound asleep on Daphne's shoulders the entire time.

Daphne attached the lasso to my side before I sat down and pulled on the tall boots. They went over my knees, bending perfectly where they needed to.

Daphne held up a strap and shield. "We can't forget the cherry on top."

As soon as we got it on me, she stepped back. Daphne, Taylor, and Laura all grinned wildly.

"You look so hot," Taylor said.

"Absolutely gorgeous," Laura said.

"You look fierce," Daphne said.

Fierce. That was by far the biggest compliment.

Steeling myself, I went into Daphne's bedroom so I could see myself in the full-length mirror.

I took in the entire costume and all the accessories. A huge smile broke out on my face, and I couldn't tame it.

"Told you," Daphne said, coming into the room. Her shoulders were empty, so she'd probably put Cherry down somewhere to sleep.

Taylor was right behind her. "If you don't say it, Daphne, I will."

Daphne shimmied up beside me. "Bow chicka wow wow."

I threw my arms around her and held her tight. "Thank you, Daph."

She held me close. "You know you're my hero, right? You helped me with my dad's death. You've talked me down from all my anxiety attacks. You've stuck by my side through everything. I love you always, sis."

Tears welled in my eyes, and I let them cascade down my cheeks. I didn't care if it ruined my makeup.

Taylor wrapped her arms around both of us. "You ladies are my absolute favorite. I don't even care that I'm the third wheel in this relationship."

Daphne and I gasped and pushed away from each other.

"You are *not*!" Daphne said.

"Why would you even think that?" I asked.

Taylor pressed her lips together and then finally broke out in a laugh. "I know. I know. You're both so fun to rile up."

Daphne and I both pushed Taylor on the shoulders before we laughed as well.

Daphne wrapped her arms around us. "Love you both so much."

Taylor leaned her head against Daphne's. "Aww, love you, too."

"Always and forever." I glared at Taylor through the mirror. "Including you, third wheel."

Laura softly knocked on the door. "Would you super-heroes mind if I snapped a quick picture?"

The three of us posed so she could. Then we all paused and looked down at our outfits.

"I kinda don't want to take it off," Taylor said.

"Same," I said.

Daphne grinned. "Wanna watch a movie?"

When Taylor and I both nodded, Laura spoke. "I'll make some popcorn."

I turned back to the mirror. Maybe it was all a mind-set. I needed to be more positive. Which meant loving myself as I was.

CHAPTER FORTY-TWO

Taylor, Daphne, and I got ready at Daphne's place for the Halloween bash. A mixture of nerves and excitement flitted through me. My confidence had skyrocketed, and I couldn't wait to see Samson.

Cherry napped in Daphne's hammock chair, looking completely adorable.

Taylor stood in front of the mirror on the inside of Daphne's closet door. She slipped a clip in her hair, pinning it back for the wig. "So, Veronica, I know you've been super closed-lipped about Samson, and I know he's my brother, but we need all the juicy details." She scrunched her nose, thinking. "Okay, maybe not the *juicy* details, but the mild details. Like, what's happening with you two?"

I was currently putting on some eyelash extenders, so I took the time to complete it and work through my thoughts.

"Seriously, V, what's the hold-up?" Daphne asked. She'd already finished with her costume, so she ratted the top of my hair, trying to add some volume to my short hairdo. "You two like each other."

I fished my concealer out of my makeup bag. "I'm not looking for a relationship right now."

Taylor slid in another clip, securing more hair in place. "Lame excuse. Try again."

I looked at her through the mirror. "Why is that lame? I don't have to be in a relationship all the time."

"Well, duh." Daphne picked up a bottle of hairspray and doused my hair. "But if you really like someone, and they like you back, why not be together? I mean, think of all the kissing you could be doing."

Taylor faked gagged. "Or not. You could snuggle or hold hands, or always have someone to turn to when you need to unleash your feelings."

"I can do all of that with you two." I applied an extra thick layer of concealer. I'd broken out thanks to all the stress lately.

"What do you have against kissing?" Daphne asked Taylor. "You and Huntley are always stealing kisses when you think no one is looking." She batted her eyelashes. "And it's adorable."

Taylor rolled her eyes as she slid her wig over her head. "I have nothing against kissing. I just don't like to think about any of my brothers kissing."

I placed my concealer back in my bag. "You two are obsessed with kissing."

Daphne and Taylor shared a look before they both nodded.

"That's true," Daphne said. "It's super fun. But beyond that, I think you and Samson are good for each other. You seem to really understand each other, which is difficult to find."

Taylor came up next to us. "No one has ever made you

laugh or smile the way Samson can. It's this completely different, carefree version of yourself that glows."

"She's right," Daphne said.

Taylor flipped her long red hair. "Always am."

"Red is a good color on you," Daphne said to her.

I turned in my chair so I could face them. "It really is."

Taylor snatched my handheld mirror from the table and ran her fingers through her wig as she stared in the mirror. "It is kinda fun. Maybe I should dye it sometime." She set the mirror back down. "Will you please tell us what's really going on, V?"

They both sat down on Daphne's bed and faced me.

They wouldn't drop it until I told them.

I folded my arms close to my chest. "I'm used to guys walking out of my life. I really like having Samson in my life. I don't want to lose what I have with him now."

"Samson is not your dad or DeShawn," Taylor said. "When Samson loves, he does with all his heart. He would never do anything to hurt you."

"There's no way to guarantee that," I said with an irritated huff. "He could find someone hotter and more mature at college. He could get bored of me. He could cheat—"

"You know for a fact Samson wouldn't cheat on you," Taylor said with obvious hurt in her tone. "He told me that he told you about Kylie. He knows how much that hurts and would never inflict that upon someone else, especially someone he loves."

Daphne leaned forward. "Uh, what's this about Kylie?"

"She cheated on Samson," Taylor said, her hurt eyes still on me.

"Stupid Kylie," Daphne muttered. Her eyes lit up. "Oh! If you kill DeShawn, and he kills Kylie, you could bury them next to each other and it could be a bonding moment for you two."

Taylor blinked at Daphne with a blank face.

"I feel like your humor has grown more morbid," I said.

Daphne shrugged. "I think it's Halloween. And probably that horror novel I recently read about a serial killer couple."

Taylor continued to blink at her until she finally turned her straight face back to me. "Veronica, you can take cheating off the table. He won't do it."

I wiped at a smear of concealer on my acrylic nail. "And when he gets bored with me? It's going to completely suck. I won't be able to come over to your house anymore."

"He won't get bored," Taylor said.

"You don't know that!" My frustration flew out of me.

Taylor stood. "So, you're not going to take a chance because you're worried about something you don't even know will happen?"

I stood so we were standing toe-to-toe. "I don't want to risk having another guy rip my heart out!"

"Samson won't do that!" Taylor growled.

"You're only saying that because he's your brother!" I said.

Daphne awkwardly worked her way between the two of us, put her hands on our shoulders, and gently pushed us back. "I think we can all agree that Samson is a great guy. I think we can also agree that there are always risks in relationships. Nothing is guaranteed." She turned her soft eyes to me. "But is that how you want to live your life? Not giving love a chance because of two stupid dudes? Veronica, this world is full of stupid people but not *everyone* is stupid."

I collapsed onto the chair. "I'm scared."

Daphne and Taylor both kneeled in front of me and took my hands in theirs.

Taylor had completely softened. "Relationships are scary. But they can also be the greatest things in the world if you let it."

"I know you hate when I talk about *your person*," Daphne started.

I snorted an awkward laugh.

"But I really believe that Samson is *your person*," Daphne went on. "And I'm not talking about someone to kiss and go on dates with. I'm talking about someone you can turn to at any hour of the day with any problem. Someone to be by your side as you go through messy things and all the awesome things. Could you go through things alone? Of course you could. You're Veronica freaking Rodriguez. But why would you want to when you have *your person* right in front of you?"

"What if Samson doesn't feel *that* strongly?" I whispered.

"He does." Taylor took a deep breath. "We've had a lot of long talks lately. He told me to keep everything he said to myself, so I will, but what I can guarantee is that now, in this moment, he is very much infatuated with you."

Daphne wiggled her eyebrows. "*Infatuated.* I really love that word."

I wanted to believe Taylor. But that voice in the back of my head told me she was wrong.

Then I remembered what my dad said. No more. I needed to say *no more* to the negative thoughts invading my life.

I grinned. "Then we better get going."

CHAPTER FORTY-THREE

We picked up Weston on the way to the party. We decided I would drive since we had a ways to go, and while I loved Daphne and Taylor with all my heart, I was hands-down the best driver of the bunch.

Daphne had made Weston a Captain America suit as well, and by the way they kept making googly eyes at each other, it was obvious those two were going to be all over each other all night in their totally adorable way.

"What's Huntley wearing?" Daphne asked from the backseat. She sat in the middle so she could sit next to Weston.

Taylor playfully glared over her shoulder at Daphne from the passenger seat. "Since you didn't make him anything, I told him to do whatever he wanted."

Daphne scoffed. "Well, excuse me for not having time to do it. I barely got ours done in time."

Weston chuckled. "I feel honored I even made the list."

We ended up having to park a few blocks away. Tons of cars lined the curbs.

The second we climbed out of the car, both Daphne

and Weston were making sure their Captain America helmets were in place.

"I wished these covered more of the face," Weston said, tugging at the side of his leather helmet.

"I know, right?" Daphne slapped her forehead with her palm. "Why didn't I think of that before?"

"Why?" Taylor asked. "They're fine the way they are."

Daphne motioned to the bottom half of her face. "But people can still see me. I prefer anonymity at these kinds of shindigs."

I shook my head with a smile. I loved the random words Daphne used. "At least you two have each other."

Daphne snatched Weston's hand, and they huddled close together.

"Thanks for coming," I said, mostly to Daphne and Weston. I knew how uncomfortable huge social scenes made them, especially when they wouldn't know many people there.

"Always." Daphne shrugged one shoulder. "Being in a costume really helps, though. I can be someone else for a night. That way, people will be saying, 'Did you see that one incredibly stupid thing that Captain America did?' instead of, 'Did you see that one incredibly stupid thing that Daphne girl did?'"

I popped the trunk so we could grab our shields. Daphne helped strap mine to my back and then I strapped hers to her back. We turned to find Weston already had put his on himself.

He scrunched his nose. "What?"

"You're so freaking hot," Daphne whispered.

Taylor's phone buzzed, and she pulled it out of her pants' pocket. "Let's go. Huntley is already there."

"Just Huntley?" I asked.

We told him to make Ryker come, even though it was a long shot.

Taylor sighed. "You know Ryker. He'd rather stay in with Spencer than go to a crowded party."

"I knew I always liked him," Daphne and Weston said at the same time, making us all laugh.

The closer we got to the house, the more my confidence slipped. We were about to attend a college party. The only reason all our parents agreed was because we were going together, and Samson had invited us. They all loved and trusted him. He'd never take us somewhere we shouldn't be.

Taylor stopped walking a couple of yards ahead of me and turned around. "Why did you slow down?"

"I did?" I hadn't realized I had. But we had been walking side-by-side moments ago.

Daphne and Weston were taking their sweet precious time as well, not in a hurry to get to the party. I think Taylor was the only one who was actually excited.

The second we turned onto the street, the music and chatter drifted from the house, practically vibrating the entire area.

A guy leaned against the streetlamp outside of the house. He wore a Miles Morales costume, with the blue and red jacket and gray shorts over the jumpsuit. As we neared, he turned his head toward us.

"Huntley!" Taylor ran and threw her arms around him.

He picked her up from the ground and spun her around. When he finally set her down, he was all smiles. "I almost didn't recognize you." He took in her whole outfit and whistled. "Wow, Daphne. This is legit."

"Thanks!" Daphne said in a strained tone.

Huntley looked at her with furrowed eyebrows. "You okay?"

Daphne's head bobbled wildly. "Yeppers! Not freaking out at all about going into a home I've never been in, in a city I've never been in, surrounded by a whole bunch of people I've never met and probably don't want to meet."

"Maybe we could stay out here." Weston looked toward the sky. "It's a nice night. We can still hear the music." He glanced at the large porch where about a dozen people hung out. "Smaller crowd."

"I like where your head's at," Daphne said.

I frowned at her. "You can't stay out here. I need you inside."

Daphne waved a hand in a nonchalant manner. "You'll have Samson in there."

"We're not officially together or anything," I said. "He's not going to hang at my side the entire night."

"He might," Taylor said with a smile. "Just gotta get in there and charm him with your sexy Veronica ways."

Heat rushed to my cheeks, and I was super glad I'd caked on the concealer. I had a feeling I'd be blushing a lot tonight.

I picked at the skin on my bottom lip with my teeth. Maybe we could leave. It wasn't too late. The five of us could grab something to eat or go see a movie.

I was about to suggest leaving when Taylor suddenly grabbed my hand and yanked me up the walkway.

"You're not talking yourself out of this," Taylor said as she tugged me up the porch steps.

The front door hung open, the energy from the people inside electric. An onslaught of chatter and laughter slammed into me the second we walked through the door.

I glanced around the packed house, eagerly looking for Samson. Unfortunately, in the process, my eyes wandered over all the hot college girls in sexy Halloween costumes.

"Uh, is that girl dressed as a sexy janitor?" Daphne asked, leaning in close so I could hear her over the crowd.

I jumped, not realizing she'd come in behind me.

Daphne didn't flinch at my surprise. She kept staring at the girl. "Just because you can make something sexy doesn't mean you *should* make it sexy."

Taylor squeezed my hand to get my attention. From the look on her face, she hadn't heard a thing Daphne had said. Taylor pointed somewhere in the front room. "There's Samson!"

I followed her line of sight until my gaze finally settled on Samson. My breath caught in my throat. For starters, he was dressed as Clark Kent with the glasses, hair curl, dress shirt, loose tie, and slacks. Some of the buttons on the shirt were undone to expose the Superman costume underneath. Second, he looked unbelievably gorgeous.

Third? A breathtaking girl stood next to him dressed as Lois Lane. She had her arm linked with Samson's as they both laughed at something another guy had said.

Taylor's smile evaporated as she took in the scene as well. She swallowed. "It could mean nothing. It could be a total coincidence that they're both dressed like that."

Someone gasped next to us, catching my and Taylor's attention.

"Those costumes are amazing!" A girl dressed as a sexy nerd smiled at all of us. "Where did you get them?"

Weston pointed at Daphne. "She made them."

"No. Way." The girl pulled out her phone. "Can I get a picture with all of you? My twin is in a fashion design program in Paris and will die when he sees these."

Since only the top half of Daphne's face was covered, the deep red blush that covered her cheeks and necks were more than obvious.

"Of course!" Taylor said.

The girl handed Huntley her phone. "Mind taking the picture?" She didn't wait for his response. She worked her way between Daphne and me, putting her arms around our backs.

"Uh, sure." The laughter in Huntley's eyes told me he didn't mind. Guess it was obvious his had been store bought.

Taylor awkwardly squished against my other side, trying to avoid the shield strapped to my back.

Huntley arched an eyebrow at me. "Smile, everyone."

It was then I realized I'd been biting at my lip with probably the most worried expression on my face. I plastered on a smile, trying to appear somewhat happy.

When Huntley handed the camera back, the girl scrolled through the photos. "Thanks so much!" She looked at Daphne. "Seriously, these are amazing. You're amazing!"

"Thanks," Daphne said with a sheepish smile.

The girl wandered off into the crowd, typing on her phone, probably sending the picture to her twin.

The distraction had pulled my attention from Samson. Went I turned back to find him, my breath caught in my throat again for the worst reason ever.

Samson and Lois Lane were posing for a picture. Samson stood tall with a smug expression on his face. Lois had one arm draped around his neck, the other holding onto Samson's tie as she kissed his cheek. A guy near them snapped the picture then handed Lois the phone. She and Samson huddled close together as they looked at the photo on the screen, both wearing the biggest smiles.

Lois looked up at Samson and laughed. She placed her hand on his jaw and turned his head to reveal a big, red kiss mark. She went to wipe it off, but Samson swatted her hand away and shook his head. I wasn't sure what he said to her, but they left the lipstick stain where it was and took another picture.

"I'm sure that's totally innocent," Daphne said in a strained tone. "I mean, who doesn't kiss their friends on the cheeks and leave a red lipstick mark behind?"

"Can we go now?" I asked.

"Yep," Daphne said as she took my hand.

Taylor moved toward Samson, her hands balled into fists. "I need to take care of something really quick."

Huntley grabbed her arm and yanked her back. "I think we should leave. No need to make a scene."

Taylor mumbled something under her breath that I couldn't understand before she let Huntley guide her out of the house. Daphne, Weston, and I were quick at their heels, all eager to get out of the house for our own reasons.

As Daphne and I hurried through the front door, the shields strapped to our backs got jammed in the doorway.

We both tried to wriggle free, but we were stuck.

"Let me try pushing you," Weston said from behind us. With a grunt of effort, he pushed into our shields, trying to set us free.

Huntley and Taylor had gotten to the sidewalk when they turned back to see us stuck. They sprinted back to the door—and I couldn't deny how hot Taylor looked in her Black Widow costume and a look on her face that said, "I'm about to do some serious damage."

Taylor took my hand, and Huntley took Daphne's.

"Both of you turn to the right," Huntley said.

We turned, only moving an inch before we got caught again.

Huntley looked over us at Weston. "We'll pull, you push."

"One," Weston said. "Two. Three."

Taylor and Huntley yanked at our arms as Weston shoved with all his might. We broke free and toppled forward, landing on top of Taylor and Huntley.

Weston had pushed so hard that he fell on top of us.

Taylor let out an audible, "oof," beneath me and Huntley grunted his pain.

Weston scrambled to get up, then helped Daphne before they helped me up. When all five of us stood again, I turned to see we had an audience. Everyone on the porch, plus a ton of people gathered in the entryway, held up their phones as they laughed.

Taylor bowed, sweeping out her arms.

Daphne and I shared a panicked look before we hurried down the porch steps, trying to get as far away from the house as we could.

CHAPTER FORTY-FOUR

By the time we made it back to my car, we were all panting. We quickly stuffed our shields into the trunk before we hurried into the car, everyone slamming their doors closed.

Huntley had run with us, so he was in the backseat with Daphne and Weston.

Taylor pulled out her phone and furiously typed something with her thumbs.

"What are you doing?" I asked through labored breaths.

"Yelling at Samson for being a dirtbag." Taylor's face flared in outrage.

I gently set my hand on top of her phone and pushed it down. "How about we not tonight, okay? My worst fear had been confirmed—guys are total losers. But we're dressed in the coolest costumes ever and need to flaunt them."

"Aren't you too upset?" Daphne asked, leaving forward from the backseat.

I shook my head. "I'm just done."

"Done?" Taylor asked.

I sighed and sunk back in the driver's seat. "I'm done

trying to impress other people. I'm done putting any ounce of faith in guys. I'm done wasting my breath on things that don't matter or aren't going to happen. I want to be myself again."

Daphne smiled. "I've really missed Veronica."

"Me, too," Taylor said. "She's like my favorite person ever."

Daphne held up a finger and then another. "She's fierce and fun."

"Hot," Taylor said.

Daphne's finger went up. "Extremely hot. Super smart." Another finger.

"Independent," Taylor said as Daphne's thumb went up. "Courageous. Compassionate. Loving. Kind. Hilarious. Driven—"

"Hold on!" Daphne yelled with all her fingers in the air. "I've run out of fingers. Let me take off my boots." Her eyes widened. "Wait! We can use Weston's hands. And then Huntley's. Then we can pull out all the feet." She slapped her forehead with her palm. "Wait, we have Taylor's hands, too. Duh."

I reached out and set a hand on her arm. "There's no need, Daph. I got it."

She placed her hand over mine. "We want you to realize how awesome you are. See what we see."

"I know what you see in me." I leaned my head against the headrest. "I'm so exhausted. This whole thing has drained me. I've never realized how much energy it takes to impress someone." I thought of my dad and DeShawn. "Or to hate someone."

Huntley cleared his throat, making us turn our attention to him. "I know I really don't have a voice in this discussion—"

"You do have one," I quickly said. Then I looked at Weston. "So do you. You're my best friend's better halves, so your opinions will always be gold to me."

Daphne nodded, and then frowned. "Wait. *They're* the best halves?"

Taylor shrugged. "Well, look at them."

Daphne turned to Weston who did his adorable inched-up-nose-crooked-smile thing. Then she looked at Huntley who turned on a smolder that put the Rodriguez one to shame.

She sighed in defeat. "Yeah, okay, I see it."

"Veronica," Huntley said, "You know the first thing that came to my mind when I saw you?"

"Nooooo ..." I said. "Do I want to?"

"Yeah, does she want to?" Taylor asked with a fake glare.

Huntley chuckled. "Bold."

I sat back letting that sink in.

"Bold." Taylor smiled at him. "I like it. It's so fitting."

"Confident," Weston said. "You carry yourself with a confidence that blows my mind. I've never seen anyone wear it and rock it as well as you do."

Tears welled in my eyes. I wiped at the tears that escaped down my cheeks. "Really?"

"Honestly," Weston said, "I was straight-up intimidated by you. But in the best way possible, if that makes sense."

"It does." I leaned around my headrest so I could look at him. "Thanks, Weston."

"That's why I sat by you in math," he went on. "I took one glance around the room and saw you and said, 'Now, there's a person who knows how to get things done.'"

Daphne flung her arms around Weston and kissed his cheek repeatedly, making him blush.

Taylor and Huntley both laughed, making me do the same.

"I guess all guys aren't bad," I said when I'd calmed.

"Don't get me wrong," Huntley said, holding up a hand. "There are a lot of stupid guys out there. And stupid guys tend to do stupid things." He smiled. "Heck, smart guys do stupid things. Especially when it comes to girls."

"I gotta find the right one," I said.

Huntley glanced at Taylor before he spoke again. "Look, I've known Ryker for well over a year now. I've heard him talk about his family a ton. I'd even talked with Samson before I met Taylor."

Taylor flinched in surprise. "Really?"

"Ryker and Samson video call each other all the time," Huntley said like it was common knowledge.

"They do?" Taylor's voice hitched up on the last word.

"Ryker is the one Samson calls when he needs help with schoolwork," Huntley said.

Taylor shifted in her seat. "I guess that makes sense."

"Any way," Huntley said, "I've come to know Samson well. He's a great guy. I'm not sure what happened back there, but I know there has to be a reasonable explanation."

"I agree," Taylor said. "And I'm not saying that because he's my brother. You know how honest I am about them. Like when I told you Celeste and Neo would only last a couple of weeks. The guy doesn't like to settle down. He's a wanderer."

"But they looked so cozy," I said.

Daphne took a deep breath. "I can't believe I'm suggesting this since we all made fools out of ourselves, but I think we should go back. Give Samson a chance to explain himself. If it turns out he's a two-timing idiot, then Taylor can beat the crap out of him, and all will be well in the world again."

Taylor chuckled. "I like that idea."

Weston blew out a shaky breath. "Okay. Go back. I can do that. *We* can do that."

Daphne rubbed his back. "We'll survive the crowd together."

They all stared at my expectantly.

"Fine. Let's go find out if Samson is a jerk or not."

CHAPTER FORTY-FIVE

More confidence embraced our steps as we walked back to the party. Since we'd already done the walk before, we knew what to expect when we rounded the corner, climbed up the porch steps, and went into the house.

We'd left all our shields in the trunk for safety measures. We didn't need a repeat disaster.

"Hey, they're back!" A girl dressed as Maleficent held up a plastic cup in salute to us. "You guys are hilarious!"

"We are?" Daphne asked in a shocked tone.

A guy dressed as Eddie Munson from Stranger Things nodded. "That whole skit of superheroes getting stuck and then clumsily freeing themselves was absolute perfection. My followers are eating up the video I posted."

Huntley grinned. "We love to please."

A few of the people in the entryway clapped.

Eddie Munson held up his pointer finger and pinky. "Rock on." He walked away with some others, going back to whatever conversation they were having before we came in.

Daphne sunk into me. I had to put an arm around her to keep her steady.

"They thought it was a joke," she mumbled. "We stressed out over nothing."

Huntley draped an arm around Taylor. "Maybe it was Taylor's bow that did the trick."

Weston rubbed his hands together. "Okay. We're here on a mission. Let's do it, and then go get some pancakes from IHOP. Maybe Ryker will meet us there."

"Shouldn't we get shawarma or something?" Huntley asked with a grin.

Daphne glared at him. "No, Huntley, we should not. That sounds absolutely disgusting."

"Do you even know what shawarma is?" Taylor asked.

"No, Taylor, I do not." Daphne looked around the room. "Where is he?"

"Maybe we should split up and ..." Huntley trailed off when he saw all the looks on our faces. "Yeah, we should stick together."

I drummed up some courage and worked my way through the crowd and into the front room. Everyone else trailed behind me, creating a train as we all held hands.

Samson wasn't where he previously was with Lois Lane. Maybe they were somewhere in a room together.

Nope. Not going there. Positive thoughts.

We went down a long hallway and checked in some rooms, but Samson was nowhere to be found.

My phone rang from inside a secret pocket Daphne had sewn into the underside of my skirt. I fished it out and answered, not bothering to check the caller I.D. "Hello?" I pressed a finger to my ear, hoping to hear the caller. It was still super loud in the hallway.

"Veronica?" Samson asked.

A smile broke out on my face at the sound of his voice. "Where are you?"

"Where are *you?*" Samson's voice was a lot calmer, like he was somewhere much quieter.

"At the party," I yelled over the noise.

"I was wondering when you'd get here," Samson said. "I'm out back in the yard. It's not as loud here."

"We'll meet you back there." I ended the call and slipped my phone back into the pocket. I looked at the train of people. "He's outside!"

Huntley, who was at the end of the train, turned around and guided us back through the hall, into the kitchen, and onto the back patio.

There were several people hanging around and talking outside, but it wasn't nearly as loud as it was inside.

A bunch of portable lamps lined the yard, casting some light over the area. I spotted Samson standing near Lois Lane and my throat tightened.

I wouldn't get upset or hurt. Not until I knew what was happening.

Samson's gaze found mine and his eyes bulged. He stood there, frozen.

"What's wrong with Samson?" Weston asked.

Daphne snickered like she knew something the rest of us didn't.

"What?" Weston asked.

Daphne leaned in and whispered something into his ear.

Weston's eyes lit up. "Oh, okay. That makes sense."

I wanted to ask her what she was smiling about, but I wanted to talk to Samson more. Holding onto the rail, I descended the porch steps until I was on the concrete slab below.

Samson hadn't moved from his spot. His eyes were fixated on me.

I smoothed out my skirt, hoping I looked okay. I hadn't checked in the mirror, which I should have since I had cried a little. I quickly wiped at my cheeks and then stopped myself, worried I'd wipe off my concealer and reveal the ugly truth beneath.

Lois Lane suddenly stepped in front of me, a wide smile on her face. "I *love love love* your costume. Where did you get it?"

"Huh?" I licked my lips, trying to register her words. Then I pointed at Daphne, who stood right behind me. "Uh, she made it."

Lois' jaw dropped. She walked in a circle around me, shaking her head the whole time. Then she pointed at Daphne. "You're brilliant." She cupped her hands over her mouth. "Someone get this lady a crown!"

Daphne's head shook furiously. "No. No crown needed. I mean, it would totally ruin the Captain America vibe."

A girl who had been standing near us sauntered forward and pulled the Red Queen crown from on top of her head. "Girl, you need the crown."

The Red Queen tried to place it on Daphne's head, but Daphne slinked away. "As much as I'd love to wear your crown, you need it to complete your outfit."

The Red Queen tilted her head. With a small red heart in the middle of her lips, painted white face, and drastic blue eyeshadow, she was quite the sight.

"And I'd probably end up losing it or breaking it," Daphne quickly went on.

The Red Queen finally nodded and gently placed the crown back on her head.

The whole thing had distracted me from Samson. I turned around to find him still staring at me. "Uh, hi?"

Samson swallowed, his large Adam's apple moving with the motion. "Hi."

"Are you okay?" I asked.

I couldn't get a read on him. A ton of shock danced in his eyes, but something else I couldn't pin down.

Samson took a shaky step forward. "You look ..." He blew out a deep breath. "Wow."

"A good wow or bad wow?" I asked.

"Definitely a go—" Samson started.

Lois Lane drifted over and linked arms with Samson. "Is this Veronica?"

Samson nodded, swallowing yet again.

"I'm so glad you came." Lois patted Samson's arm. "He won't stop talking about you."

He was talking about me? But he was cozied up with Lois Lane. I was beyond confused.

Daphne awkwardly leaned forward. "Sorry to interrupt, but do you by chance have a name? Or should I keep referring to you as Lois in my head?"

I smiled, wondering the same thing.

Lois laughed. "Lois is fine, but my real name is Jules."

"Cool." Daphne turned to the Red Queen. "Should I call you, Your Majesty?"

The Red Queen laughed, high-pitched and weird as she tried to stay in character. "You can call me that any day. But my name is Monique."

Monique motioned for Daphne and the others to step off to the side, an obvious gesture to get Samson and me alone. "I want to hear *all* about these outfits."

I was hoping Jules would get the hint as well, but she stayed put, arm still linked with Samson.

I swept a finger back and forth at them. "And how do you two know each other?"

"Oh!" Jules lightly laughed, the sound so sweet and charming. She patted Samson's arm. "We met freshman year at a church activity. Turns out, we're majoring in the same thing, so we had a ton to talk about."

"How ... neat." Neat? It wouldn't normally be my first choice of words, yet here we were. I held in a sigh.

"We hit it right off the bat," Jules went on.

Well, that didn't sound good. Had Samson been seeing Jules all this time? But why would he never mention her?

"Been friends ever since." The words flew out of Samson's mouth in a panic.

Jules looked surprised before understanding passed over her eyes. "Right. Yeah, we're friends. Just friends."

That didn't sound the least bit convincing.

Samson's eyes suddenly widened as he looked behind me.

I turned around to see a super freaky clown stomping toward us with fake blood spattered all over its costume. They even had specks of it in their bright red wig. Their face was painted like a clown from a horror movie, overly excited to the point it would make someone pee their pants.

Oh, no. Where was Daphne? She *hated* clowns. I found her still talking with Mo and the others, completely oblivious to what was going on. I needed to somehow keep it that way.

My focus went back to the clown. Their head tilted to the side, their red eyes on me. They had to have been wearing colored contacts. They raised their arm, pointing what looked to be a water gun at me, their gloved finger on the trigger.

A loud roar filled the backyard before Daphne sprinted

into view. With a battle cry, she flew at the clown, tackling them to the ground. Then she stood, placing her booted foot on his chest. She lifted her chin and set a hand on her hip, looking tough in her Captain America costume. "Not today, Satan!"

CHAPTER FORTY-SIX

A collective gasp filled the air as everyone watched Daphne tackle the clown and pin them to the ground with her foot. The clown released some of the content from the water gun in the process of flying, sending a spray of red paint into the air. It rained down on some people at the party, causing them to scream and scramble to get out of the way.

The clown groaned on the ground, clearly in pain.

A bunch of other clowns ran over to help the fallen clown.

Daphne's eyes bulged out of her sockets as she took in all the creepy clowns before her. Her head bobbled in a weird shake as she backed away. "Nope. Nope. And nope." She looked at me. "You're on your own." She ran away screaming, "I'll love you forever!"

Weston smiled sheepishly at me and then ran after Daphne.

"They'd seriously be the worst Captain America's ever," Huntley muttered as he watched them cower on the porch with their hands gripping the rods of the banister tight.

My attention went back to the groaning clown. His clown friends helped him stand. He ripped off his red wig to reveal closed cropped black hair.

I took a step toward him. "DeShawn?"

He doubled over, holding onto his stomach. Daphne had knocked the wind from the guy. More proof that the guy was a terrible football player.

"What are you doing here?" I couldn't hide the embarrassment from my tone. Had he followed me here? How creepy was that?

Another clown looked at me, a frown forming on his face which contrasted from the smile painted on. "What are *you* doing here?" It was Christian.

Samson wrapped an arm around my shoulders. "She was invited. Were you?"

DeShawn coughed and stood up straight. He turned to me as he rubbed the back of his neck. "A friend of mine invited me."

"But, seriously," Christian said with shock in his tone. "Why *is* Veronica here? She's like the biggest loser."

Samson lowered his arm and moved toward Christian.

Taylor yelled, "Sneak attack!" before she slammed her brother to the ground, stopping him from pummeling Christian.

I rolled my eyes at Christian. "Are you ever going to quit acting like you're five? Or is it a permanent thing?"

A chorus of, "Oh!" rang through the air, a lot of them coming from Christian's friends.

Taylor helped Samson to his feet. He lunged toward Christian again with so much anger on his face. Taylor intervened, placing her hand on Samson's chest and pushing him back.

"You don't want to go there," Taylor said to him. "These guys are clowns. Literally and figuratively."

I smiled. "They pretty much hit the nail on the head with their costume choice." I took in DeShawn's costume again. It wasn't what he'd been talking about at school. "Where's Autumn? I thought she was your date?"

DeShawn rubbed the back of his head, a telltale sign that he was lying. "Uh, plans changed." She was probably never going with him in the first place. He wanted to make me jealous and didn't think I'd be at the party to call him out.

I glared at DeShawn. "I thought we were done with this? You acting like an immature middle schooler and trying to bully me?"

"Trying?" Christian scoffed. "I'd say the guy succeeded."

"To my dismay," I said, "he did at first. But then I realized what a waste of time you all are. You're the ones with absolutely no lives. All you do is walk around, trying to act cool, while treating other people like trash. I'm honestly embarrassed for *you*."

"To tell you the truth," DeShawn said. "I saw Samson and realized who he was. I thought it would be funny to spray him down with some fake blood. I didn't notice Veronica at first." He sighed. "She's right, though. This is stupid. We should go."

"You're seriously going to agree with that pig?" Christian asked.

This time, it was me who ran at Christian, but DeShawn got to him first, punching him right in the face.

Christian yelled out and clamped a hand over his nose that bled profusely.

DeShawn shook out his hand. "Man, I should have

done that forever ago. You're a racist, egotistical loser who happens to probably be one of the worst wide receivers I've ever met. We're done." He turned to me. "Sorry. I thought the blood would be a funny prank. That was it."

Samson relaxed his shoulders. "As long as that's all it was, we're good."

DeShawn nodded his head toward me. "Take it easy, Veronica." He turned to his friends. "Let's go."

Christian watched them go. "What about me?" His voice came out muffled since he still had his hand over his probably broken nose.

"You can leave," Monique said, stepping forward and placing a hand on her hip. "You are never welcomed here again. If I so much as see your ugly face near my property, I will call the cops."

"Wait, this is your place?" Taylor asked.

Monique nodded. "Bought this beauty about a year ago after my clothing stores took off."

"What stores?" I asked.

"Adelmotique. We have a few in Orange and LA Counties."

"You're Adella's co-owner?" I couldn't hide the awe in my voice. "That's like my favorite clothing store, ever."

Monique took a step back. "Wait. Are you the one who bought the *stunning* red dress from the shop in Yorba Linda?"

I pulled out my phone and scrolled through it until I found the picture. I showed it to Monique.

She gasped. "Shanice wasn't kidding when she said this dress was designed for you. You're going to be the best dressed as the event."

"Don't tell my mom that." I slipped my phone back into its secret pocket. I looked up to find Samson staring at me again like he had when I first walked into the backyard.

"Isn't anyone going to help me?" Christian wailed. "I think my nose is broken."

Monique sauntered over to a couple of the guests. "Will you two mind escorting the racist pig off of my property? I'm sick of his squealing."

They both smiled, went to Christian, each grabbed an arm, and dragged him out of sight.

Monique lifted her chin high in the air, really selling the Red Queen. "Now that that's over, can we please go back to the party?"

As everyone walked away, going back to having fun, I turned my focus back on Samson.

"We're going to check on Daphne and Weston." Taylor took Huntley's hand, so Samson and I were alone.

"Who is Jules?" I asked.

Samson furrowed his eyebrows. "You just met her."

"I know, but who is she to *you*."

"We're just friends, like we said." His tone told me he was beyond confused.

I folded my arms. "I saw her kiss you, Samson. I saw all the flirting and touchy-feely going on. If you're a couple, say it. I deserve the truth."

Samson cracked a smile, but it quickly went away when he saw my glare. "We thought it was crazy that we showed up as Clark Kent and Lois Lane. We didn't plan it. And we didn't come here together." When I stared expectantly, he went on. "Her kissing me on the cheek was one-hundred-percent friendly. I promise. Jules like girls."

His words slowly sunk in. "She's gay?"

He nodded. "Yes. As much as we get along, I'm very

much *not* her type. And I've never looked at her that way. Not the way I look at you."

"You've been looking at me super weird tonight, so that's not really helpful."

Samson stepped close and placed a warm hand on my hip, making my breath hitch. "I've been staring at you like you're the most gorgeous girl I've ever seen. Do you know how hot you look in this costume?" He ran his fingers through his hair, messing up the perfect curl that had been on his forehead. "Then you lift your skirt to get your phone? You literally took my breath away, Veronica."

I had no idea what to say. He thought I was gorgeous. Samson Thomas thought *I* was gorgeous.

He set his hand on my cheek. "Listen, I know I said I'd wait and to take all the time you need, but I can't wait any longer. I love you and want to be with you. So, tell me how to make that happen and I'll do it."

I strained my neck to meet his eyes, and I so didn't care. "Did you say you love me?"

"I've been in love with you for over a year. I never did anything because you were my sister's friend." He sighed. "Then you were with not-worth-it for forever. I was waiting for you to be ready."

"What if I didn't feel the same way?" My voice shook, giving away my nerves. "What if your wait was for nothing?"

He suddenly reached around me, set his hands on the back of my legs, and lifted me into the air so easily. I wrapped my legs around his waist, holding on tight.

"Tell me it was for nothing." His nose touched mine, and a heatwave traveled through my body. "Tell me you don't feel the same way, and I'll let you go."

He was so calm. So sure. He didn't so much as teeter holding my weight.

Then he lightly brushed his lips over mine, teasing me.

I completely lost it. I wrapped my hand around his neck and closed the distance between our lips, melding them together.

I kissed him with everything I had in me. I kissed him in a way that I hoped screamed, "I love you, too," because I truly did.

Samson was *my person*. Knowing was one thing. Accepting it was another.

I suddenly pulled back and gasped.

"What?" Samson asked.

I tried not to smile at my lipstick smeared all over and around his lips. Then I remembered why I gasped. "You haven't seen me without my makeup."

Samson shrugged, and I moved with the motion since he somehow hadn't put me down. "So?"

"*No one* has seen me without my makeup, Samson. Not even Daphne and Taylor."

He flinched in surprise. "Not even your family? Do you wear makeup twenty-four-seven?"

I shook my head. "My family has. My immediate family. But trust me, Samson, I look like a completely different person."

He kissed my cheeks and then my chin. "Trust me when I say you're beautiful no matter what."

"You don't know that! I could scare you away."

He laughed but then stopped when he saw I was serious. "Veronica, there's no way you could scare me away."

"DeShawn stopped liking me when I got fat," I said. "So, it's totally plausible for you to stop liking me when you see me in all my glory." I blushed. "And by that, I mean without makeup! That's it!"

With a sigh, Samson set me down. He backed away, putting his hands on his hips. "First of all, we don't use not-worth-its name. Because he's not worth it. Also, I think it's been scientifically proven that he's a moron. It's also been scientifically proven that I'm attracted to you no matter what you are or are not wearing."

When I placed my hands on my hot neck, trying to shut down all the blushing I was doing, he smiled.

His typical all-is-right-in-the-world smile.

This was Samson Thomas. The guy spoke exactly what was on his mind. He wasn't one to pretend or sugarcoat anything. He knew what it was like to be stabbed in the back, so he'd never do it to someone.

He loved me. Exactly how I was.

Did I love me? That was the more important question. I glanced down at myself. I'd been of the belief that fat equaled ugly, and that couldn't have been farther than the truth. It was our personality and our confidence that made us who we are.

I, Veronica Rodriguez, was beautiful and worthy of love.

I snatched his tie and yanked him down toward me. "Well, I decided that if you aren't attracted to me after you see me makeup-less, tough luck, buddy. I love you and I want you in my life for as long as I can. This girl isn't going anywhere."

Samson grinned ear-to-ear. "There she is."

"Who?"

"The confident, doesn't take crap from anyone, Veronica I fell in love with." He wrapped his arms around my back. "She's the sexiest girl I've ever seen."

I kissed him slower this time, knowing there would be many more kisses to come.

Then a smile broke out on my face, and I couldn't hold it back.

Samson's lips left mine. "What?"

I ran my finger along his clean-shaven jaw. "I've found my Michael."

"He dies and she ends up with someone else."

"Don't ruin this for me." I pulled back. "Wait. How do you know that?" We were only starting season two.

He smiled sheepishly. "I may have looked up how it ended."

"Samson!" I took a deep breath, getting ready to tell him all the reasons that was *so* wrong, but he pressed his lips against mine and it suddenly didn't matter anymore.

CHAPTER FORTY-SEVEN

My whole family stood under an oversized archway my dad's younger brother Felípé had hand-carved from wood.

Mom wore her white dress with flowers made of rhinestones. Dad's eyes filled with tears as he gazed at her.

Dad wore a white suit with a red tie and pocket square. He had his hair nicely gelled, and his face cleanly shaven.

Javier stood on the other side of dad in an entirely red suit, with a skinny white tie and a white rose pinned to his blazer. He'd gelled his hair into one piece instead of his usual two devil horns. There had been a little argument about it, but Mom won in the end, like she always did.

Luciana had requested flowers to be woven through a braid in her hair. Celeste had done an amazing job, making Luci beam as we stood near our mom. She'd also found a pair of red heels in her size, amping up her sassy attitude.

Once I stepped under the archway with my family, I felt sort of ridiculous with my humongous dress. I worried it would demand any and all attention.

But as I looked out at the crowd sitting in the white chairs with a red ribbon tied around them, I couldn't help but notice that most of them had their eyes on my mom and dad.

Mom and Dad. They grinned at each other like they were newlyweds about to start a new life together. I guess in a way, they were. Our whole family was starting over. I crossed my fingers that we would build something with the firmest foundation possible. We couldn't handle it if it crumbled again.

My bisabuelo Marco officiated. He was my mom's abuelo and still acting like he was in his seventies, not his nineties, even though he was in a wheelchair.

My mom's brother, Alfredo, had wheeled my bisabuelo up to the front, and then had taken a seat up front near mom's side of the family.

Taylor had hired a string quartet to provide the music before and after the ceremony. She had gone above and beyond to make my parent's day special. Everything had the perfect touch on it.

The quartet finished their song, and all eyes went up front.

Bisabuelo lightly smiled. "I'm so very grateful we can all gather on this lovely fall day to celebrate the never-ending love of Matías and Kemena Rodriguez, and the beautiful family they have created."

Luciana smiled up at me, clutching her bouquet of white roses in excitement. I winked at her as I held my own bouquet.

My bisabuelo went on, his soft voice soothing. "Life throws us all sorts of challenges. It tests our strength, our faith, and our commitment to one another." He paused, smiling at my parents. "True love is rare to find. It's all consuming and quite irrational."

A small chuckle drifted over the crowd.

"Matías. Kemena. You two have an obligation to one another and to your children. You must stay by each other's sides through the good and the bad."

Tears flowed down Dad's cheeks. Mom never wavered or gave up on him. The fact that Dad had tried to walk away probably weighed heavy on his heart.

"You must stand up for each other," my bisabuelo said. "You must be an example of unwavering love unto your children. You must be patient and kind, understanding and supportive." His gaze wandered to Javier, then Luciana, and finally landed on me. "You children also have an obligation to your parents. A marriage is between the spouses and God."

Javier and I shared an embarrassed look.

"But the family includes all of you. Your parents need your love and your support. They will need your help on their bad days. So be a light in the darkness. Help them find their way back to each other."

Tears filled my eyes, and I tried to blink them away, but they trickled down my cheeks. Javier cried as well. Luciana, well, she grinned ear to ear because she was so happy to have our family back together.

"Matías and Kemena. I believe you each have something to say."

I wiped at my tears with a handkerchief attached to my bouquet. Taylor had made sure everyone had one, including those in the crowd. As I looked out, I noticed most were using them.

My mom reached out and took my dad's hand. "Matías,

the day I met you changed my life forever. I knew in my heart that we were going to have something bigger than life itself. I know we can't always see the good in ourselves, but I see you Matías. I see your love and wisdom. Your good heart and giving spirit. I see that you put your family first, though others may not see it that way. Your number one priority has always been me and these beautiful children up here with us. You may think retreating equals protecting but, mi amor, that couldn't be farther than the truth. We are your way to make it through the difficult times. You will always have my full heart."

Dad pressed his tissue to his mouth and took a few shaky breaths. I'd never seen the man cry so much.

He finally lowered his hand. "Kemena, you and the kids are my entire world. I promise you that I will never abandon you again. I will stay by your side until the day we die." He looked at Javier, Luciana, and me. "I love you kids with all my heart. I know you have every reason to have wavering faith in me, but I'm asking you to give me another chance. I will prove to you that I will support you through all your choices and challenges. I vow to never leave you again." He looked me straight in the eye. "Ever."

I mouthed, '*I love you*' before he turned his focus back to Mom.

"You are the strongest person I have ever met. You make me want to be a better person. You have my heart and my soul. You always have."

So many sniffles filled the air. I wasn't sure if there was a dry eye in the place.

I watched my parents gaze adoringly at each other and saw their love, and I knew in that instant what true love really was.

My eyes wandered the crowd until they settled on

Samson sitting near the back with his family. When we locked eyes, he smiled. Not his typical all-is-well-in-the-world smile. It was a smile that said he found me the most beautiful girl in the world, and I'd captured his heart.

I smiled back, wanting him to know he'd captured mine.

CHAPTER FORTY-EIGHT

Partway during the after-party, Taylor, Daphne, and I snuck off to get changed. Daphne had said she'd put our outfits together, but I wasn't expecting the matching dresses she brought out.

They were white fifties-style dresses with cherries on them. A red belt wrapped around the middle.

Taylor held hers up. "When did you have time to make these?"

Daphne unzipped the dress she was wearing. "I made these a few months ago."

We stared at her in shock.

"You did?" I asked.

"Yep." Daphne hung up her red dress she wore to the ceremony and stepped into the white dress. "I have a whole bunch of matching outfits for us for all different occasions." She zipped up the side of her dress, one of the features she always insisted on. She hated zippers being in the back.

"Uh, why?" Taylor asked, sharing a confused look with me.

Daphne put on her belt. "You gotta be prepared for

anything life throws at you, Tay. There may come a day when we need to perform in front of people. I've got dresses in blue, yellow, pink, red, purple, and green. Also got some really nice black ones for a funeral."

Taylor chuckled as she slipped into her dress and zipped it up. It fit perfectly.

I stared at mine. It looked like it would fit. But Daphne said she'd made it a few months ago before she knew my exact measurements.

Daphne came to my side. "Have faith in me, V. It'll fit."

Both Taylor and Daphne had to help me out of my dress. It wasn't until I stood in my bra and underwear that I realized I'd let them see my body. I watched their reactions but neither of them flinched or gawked. Taylor went about hanging up my ceremony dress and Daphne unzipped the side of the dress she made for me and held it up.

"Ready to blow your entire family away with your supreme awesomeness?" Daphne shook the dress at me and wiggled her eyebrows.

With a smile, I took the dress from her, slipped it on, and zipped up the side. Sure enough, it fit like a glove.

"How do you do it?" I asked in awe as I stared at myself in the mirror.

"Magic." Daphne shimmied over to a bag and pulled out three pairs of red wedges with ankle straps. "Also got us these bad girls. We're going to rock it."

After we dressed, I snapped a picture and uploaded it to my private social media account. For a split second, I thought about switching my account to public but then realized the whole world didn't need to know my life. Some things were best saved for friends and family.

Taylor had let the band know what we were going to do.

The three of us snuck to the side of the stage and waited for them to announce us.

When the song ended, the lead singer addressed the crowd. "We have a special surprise for you tonight."

I scanned the crowd until I saw my parents. They exchanged an excited smile. I really hoped they enjoyed the performance.

Then my eyes went to Samson. He looked around the crowd, his eyes confused. Huntley and Weston stood by his side, equally confused. We'd slipped out without telling them.

Daphne and Taylor took my hands.

"Ready, girls?" Taylor asked.

Daphne blew a loud raspberry. "Maybe this was a horrible idea, and we should go hide inside and never come out again."

I squeezed her hand. "Daphne, you've got this. We're right here with you. And if your nerves get the better of you, keep your eyes trained on Weston or your mom. They'll keep you calm."

She licked her lips. "Yeah. Okay. We can do this. I can do this. We're going to rock this. We're going to blow every-one's minds."

I leaned over and kissed her on the cheek, making her grin.

The lead singer grinned at the crowd. "Apparently, a member of the Rodriguez family has a talent they've been keeping a secret. But they're about to give you the perfor-mance of a lifetime. Please put your hands together for Veronica, Daphne, and Taylor!"

I watched as Samson, Weston, and Huntley all looked at the stage in shock.

The three of us stepped onto the stage and took our

spots in the front. I stood in the middle with Daphne and Taylor flanking my sides. We each had our own microphone attached to a stand.

I nodded at the guitarist and the band began to play "Made You Look" by Meghan Trainor.

It was my first time singing in public. It was terrifying at first, but then I took a glance at Taylor and Daphne and they both gave me encouraging smiles.

I remembered what all my friends and family had kept saying. They missed the old Veronica. The one who didn't care what anyone thought and was comfortable in her own skin.

It didn't take long for me to get into the performance and really let loose. The crowd went wild, helping my confidence.

My eyes settled on Samson, who was looking at me with the smile he had just for me. He mouthed, '*I love you,*' which I returned with a wink.

Then I sought out my family. My parents looked so incredibly proud. Javier had his hands cupped over his mouth, cheering me on. Luciana jumped up and down, squealing. Then she turned to the person next to her and I could clearly read her lips when she said, "That's my sister!"

When the song ended and we stepped off stage, we were practically mauled by my entire family. All my aunts, uncles, cousins, and grandparents hugged and kissed us.

I watched Daphne as she took it all in stride, wearing a nervous smile. I knew how hard it was for her to get up in front of people, and even more difficult to have all the attention.

When we cleared my family, she came to my side. "I love you, but we're never doing that again."

I laughed. "You say that now, but we'll get you back on stage."

Samson suddenly wrapped his arms around me, lifted me off the ground, and rested his forehead against mine.

"Are you ever going to cease to amaze me?" Samson asked. "Or are you going to keep throwing surprises my way for the rest of our lives?"

"Guess you'll have to wait and see."

He set me down, dipped me back, and pressed our noses together. "I'm looking forward to it."

He kissed me, steady and sure. I placed my hand on his warm cheek, wishing I could pause the moment forever. It was weird to think that *my person* had been in my life all along, but I wasn't paying close enough attention. Looking back, the subtle hints became more obvious, like how I hated any girl he dated. Not because they weren't worthy of him, but because they weren't me.

It didn't take long for my entire family to whistle and holler, causing Samson to lift me back up and smile at the crowd that had gathered around us.

I patted his chest. "You better get used to them, too. It's an entire package."

"It's more than worth it." Samson kissed my cheek and then pulled me out onto the dance floor.

My family didn't get home until almost one in the morning. We were all so exhausted, yet full of a buzzing energy. It was a brand-new beginning for us full of hope and laughter.

I hugged my dad. "I love you, Pops."

"I love you, too, my sweet girl." He kissed the top of my head. "I promise I'll never leave you again."

I let go and backed toward the stairs. "You better not, because I know a guy who has a house *full* of every insect and reptile imaginable."

Mom tsked. "Veronica!"

But Dad laughed, making her do the same.

Mom's eyes lit up like she suddenly remembered something. "I got you something, Veronica. I meant to give it to you before the ceremony."

She hustled into the office and then came back with a small red box and handed it to me. She watched with excited eyes as I opened the box.

Inside, a small red and yellow marigold pendant hung from a gold chain. "It's beautiful, Ma."

She clasped it around my neck for me. "I'm so glad you like it."

Luciana squeezed between Mom and me. "Where's mine?"

Mom ran a hand down Luciana's hair. "You'll get yours when you find *your person.*" She winked at me.

Luciana scrunched her nose. "My what?"

My eyes narrowed at Mom. "What does that mean?"

Mom nonchalantly shrugged. "I want you to remember to keep all your pretty petals intact anytime you're alone with Samson."

Javier grimaced. "Oh, gross, Ma."

With a grunt, I moved toward the stairs. "Way to ruin the moment."

Mom put a hand on her hip. "It's a good reminder!"

Dad chuckled as Javier and I ran up the stairs, eager to be away from them.

When I got to my bedroom and closed the door, I

changed into my pajamas. I sat down at my vanity, taking in my makeup-smothered face. One day I'd have to let people see me without makeup. I couldn't hide forever.

I glanced down at my phone sitting on the vanity. Guess there was no time like the present.

I set my phone upright against the mirror, found the Meghan Trainor song "Don't I Make It Easy," and pulled up my TikTok.

I recorded myself singing along as I took off my layers of makeup until the real Veronica Rodriguez confidently smiled at me through the mirror.

A calm swept over me as I uploaded the video and let the world in on the truth.

I was beautiful exactly the way I was.

ACKNOWLEDGMENTS

A huge shout-out to Amy Michelle at Monster Ivy for her unwavering support of The Spunky Girl's Guide to Dating series. Your faith in my writing and knowing the importance of my stories means the world to me.

Cammie, once again, your cover design is brilliant. Finding you and Mary has been one of the best things to ever happen to me, and I'll forever be grateful for you both.

Meghan Trainor, thanks for creating such fun, relatable, and important songs. Your album Takin' It Back was a HUGE inspiration for this book. The world needs the messages you share. You're an inspiration to everyone and I hope one day I can give you a big, squishy hug.

Chad, thanks for helping me through my recent bout of anxiety/depression. You keep me afloat and help me find myself once again. You're the love of my life, and I'm excited to spend eternity with you.

To all my readers, thanks for your continued support. I would have given up long ago if it weren't for you.

ABOUT THE AUTHOR

Sara Jo Cluff grew up in Yorba Linda, California, right next to the Happiest Place on Earth (aka her second home). Now, she resides in Utah with her husband, Chad, and crazy cats.

She loves creating stories from scratch and seeing where the characters take her. When she's not writing, she's hanging out with her husband, watching Netflix, reading, or doing jigsaw puzzles.

She's a proud #PepperPack #Ambassador for the Most Delicious Beverage on Earth: Dr Pepper.

Visit her author website, www.sarajocluff.com, and for merchandise, visit shop.spreadshirt.com/awkwardpepper.

I needed a license plate frame that said, "I'd rather be kissing." Because, honestly, if I could be doing anything right now, it would be kissing.

Which was why I pressed my freshly glossed lips against my boyfriend's somewhat dry lips. They wouldn't be dry when I was done with him. Dylan didn't hesitate—he pulled me into his lean chest, and our lips moved in perfect harmony like Pentatonix. After being together for over a year, it all came naturally.

We were on the leather couch in the front room of my house, me in his lap, his firm arms wrapped tightly around me, holding my body close, and his warm hand cradling the back of my neck. His long fingers drummed like they wanted to move, but he knew better than to let his hands wander. He'd get a solid smack across the cheek, like every time he'd ever tried.

I drew the line at kissing. A dark, thick line that wouldn't be going away any time soon, no matter how big of an eraser Dylan tried to use.

"Break it up." At Dad's deep voice, Dylan picked me up off his lap and set me down next to him.

Dad had one of those voices that no matter what he said, he came across serious, and slightly life-threatening. Add in his short-cropped military hair and huge muscles, and a lot of people stayed clear of him.

Dad didn't really care that much about us kissing. As long as we weren't alone in my bedroom, he was okay with it. But, obviously, it wasn't his favorite thing to watch.

"Hey, Mr. Collins," Dylan said, showing his dazzling white teeth and using his charming tone that made every adult smile. Except my dad.

Dad was in his 'at ease' stance, feet shoulder width apart, arms folded, and chin tilted up. He had on his hardly worn button-down shirt and slacks. The blue paisley tie was tied like it had been an afterthought. Mom would fix it when she got the chance.

Dad exhaled loudly through his nose—his calming technique—then turned his attention to me. "Camille, your mom and I need you to watch Seth tonight."

As if on cue, my little brother bounded into the room and put his hands on his hips. "Dad, I'm ten. I can take care of myself." He had his blond hair in a short mohawk and wore his favorite Minecraft shirt that was developing a few holes since he wore it so often.

Dad broke out in a fit of laughter, the rumbly sound making Dylan and me laugh as well. With his habit of opening the door for anyone, Seth couldn't stay home by himself, but Dad loved how grown up he tried to be.

"You all suck." Seth glared, his blue eyes too adorable to take seriously.

Dad's laughter cut off, and he slapped Seth upside the head. "Language."

Seth rubbed the back of his head, the glare intensifying. "Camille says it all the time."

I leaned my arms on the back of the couch and kneeled on the cushion, my bare knees sliding on the leather so I could face them. "That's because I'm seventeen. I can get away with almost anything."

Mom rounded the corner of the hall, dressed in her typical form-fitting black dress, her blue eyes intently on her smart phone, her manicured thumb moving across it at lightning speed. She put my friends and me to shame when it came to how often she used her phone and how fast she could go. She was a teenage girl in an adult's body.

"Not true." Mom didn't take her eyes off the phone as she went into the kitchen and opened the fridge. She had a new case at her law firm that was occupying most of her time.

I held up a finger. "I said *almost.*"

Dad snatched the phone from Mom's hand. She threw out her hands to retrieve it, but he just turned his back on her, a sly grin sliding onto his face. He loved to see Mom squirm.

"I was using that," Mom said with the same tone she used on Seth when he was misbehaving.

"I know," Dad said, dropping the phone into his jeans pocket. "But your clients will live until tomorrow. I promise."

Mom dropped her hands with a sigh. She opened her mouth, her eyes ready to challenge him, but instead, she grabbed a lime Diet Coke from the fridge, popped it open, and downed it.

"That's so impressive," Dylan whispered next to me.

I elbowed him, and he grunted, rubbing his stomach

where I hit him. Mom didn't like anyone commenting on her "drinking problem," as Dad called it.

Dad pointed his thick finger at us. "Dylan can't be here."

I rolled my eyes. "Yeah, I know."

He told us that every time he and Mom left me in charge. He didn't like the thought of Dylan and me being alone in the house without them there. I once tried to argue that we weren't alone since Seth would be home. The intense glare that followed, with Dad's jaw pulled tight, and veins popping out basically everywhere, forced me to never bring that up again.

Dylan kissed my cheek, leaving behind some of my lip gloss I'd given him earlier. "I gotta get home anyway. Have fun tonight, Mr. and Mrs. Collins." He jogged over to Seth and held his hand high in the air. Seth jumped up, slapping his hand against Dylan's, smiling brightly the whole time.

Normally, I hated seeing him go, and I'd beg him to stay just a little while longer. But as I watched his backside as he left the house, nothing flitted inside me—good or bad. I shook the random thought from my head. I was probably just tired.

Dad took the opportunity to come up behind me and slap the back of my head—his favorite thing to do.

"Not in my house," he mumbled.

"What? Looking at my boyfriend?"

He rubbed the top of my hair until it became a tangled mess. "Lusting after him."

I threw my head back and laughed so hard, I snorted. It took me a few seconds to calm enough that I could talk. "*Lusting?* Seriously, Dad? Gah. Will you please not use that word around me?"

Dad folded his arms, emphasizing his muscles. "If you stop lusting, then I'll have no reason to use it."

Seth had his small fingers in his ears and his eyes closed as he hummed the Star Wars theme song.

"Maybe we could grab an early dinner as a family before Dad and I leave for the party," Mom said, tossing her empty can in the recycle bin. She brushed back the blonde curls blocking part of her eye.

"Who has a party on a Thursday night anyway?" I asked.

Dad pointed his thumb at Mom. "Her weird clients."

Mom slapped his arm, and he huffed, smiling the whole time. A smile finally broke out on her face as well. Until she noticed Dad's tie, huffed, and stepped in to fix it.

When she finished, she went to Seth—still humming and plugging his ears—wrapped her arms around him, squeezed him tight, and pressed her lips close to his ear. "Food."

Seth took his fingers out of his ears, but couldn't lower his arms since Mom still had him in her grasp. He smiled wide, showing off his crooked front teeth. "Can we go to McDonald's?"

Dad scrunched his face, disgust filling every wrinkle. "No."

"You never let us go there," Seth said, flapping his hands awkwardly. Mom wouldn't release him, but he wasn't trying to get away.

"Because I'm being a responsible parent," Dad said. "I love you kids and care about your wellbeing."

I hopped over the couch, landing on the tile, shuffling closer to them and swaying my hips like a little girl. "Is that why you're going to take us to Chick-fil-A?"

Dad wiggled his eyebrows, his smile splitting wide. "You know it."

"What's the difference?" Seth asked, holding his palms up. "They both have chicken nuggets that are delicious."

"Oh, Seth." I squeezed his cheeks since Mom held him in place and he couldn't do anything about it. "One day your taste buds will develop, and you'll know the difference between gross and delicious."

Mom kissed the side of Seth's head, avoiding his Mohawk. "I personally love McDonald's chicken nuggets. Maybe we could go there, and your father and sister can go to Chick-fil-A."

Dad held up a hand. "We eat as a family." When Seth pouted, Dad sighed. "They're right next to each other. You two can bring your food over and eat with us."

Seth tried to pump his fist, but couldn't move. He grunted. "Mom, you're making it hard for me to do anything."

"I know," she said, rocking him left and right.

Dad caught my eye, and I nodded. Seth saw our interaction and squealed, trying to wiggle away from Mom. "Stay away!"

With wicked grins, Dad and I swarmed in on Seth and tickled him while Mom held him in place. Seth squirmed and giggled, his eyes closing tight.

"Stop!"

We kept on tickling, getting his sides, armpits, and stomach. When I ventured down to his feet, he kicked out his legs, smacking his foot into my cheek. It hurt a little, but it was all too funny for me to care.

"Stop!" He laughed. "I'm going to pee my pants!"

Dad immediately stepped back and threw up his hands. "I don't want to clean that up."

Seth danced where he stood, so Mom let him go and pushed him toward the hall. He took off running, his socks sliding on the tile as he neared the bathroom. He already had his pants unzipped.

I leaned over laughing, clapping my hands. Tears pricked at the corner of my eyes. It didn't take long until Mom and Dad were laughing uncontrollably like me. Seth came out of the bathroom glaring, but couldn't help laughing when he got a good look at us.

He threw his arms wide. "Glad I can entertain you guys. Can we go now? I'm starving, and those chicken nuggets aren't going to eat themselves."

Dad patted Seth's shoulder and turned him toward the front door, but then spotted Mom on her phone, probably emailing a client. He glanced at his jeans pocket, looking both annoyed and impressed that Mom had somehow wrangled it free. He opened the door, and they were about to step outside before I spoke up.

"I'm thinking Seth should probably put some shoes on," I said, pointing at his socked feet. What would they do without me?

Dad looked down at them. "Huh." He rubbed Seth's shoulders. "Hurry before I beat you to the car."

Seth plopped down in the entryway and scrambled to get his shoes on. Dad kept jerking like he was going to take off toward the car, causing Seth to whine. When he finished with the laces, Seth flew to his feet, past Dad, and out the door. Dad had to sprint to keep up.

"Mom, can I go to a concert with Dylan next weekend?" I asked. The best time to ask her for things was when she was preoccupied. Which was actually most of the time.

"Uh huh," Mom said, her eyes glued to her phone. We

walked out the front door, and I locked it since that would be another thing they'd forget to do.

I could tell her anything, and it wouldn't register. "It's one of those wild ones. Lots of drugs, clothes coming off and such."

"That sounds fun." Mom opened the passenger door of the car, her thumb moving across the screen of her phone.

"Also, I'm an assassin."

Mom pressed *send* on her phone and smiled up at me. "That's nice, dear." She got into the car and closed the door.

With a sigh, I joined my crazy family in the car and wished for once that Mom would pay attention to us during dinner. But I never liked to get my hopes up.